I0566420

THE CYBORG

At the end of *The Cyborg and the Sorcerers*, Sam Turner was making a life for himself on the planet Dest. He thought he had left the long-lost interstellar war between Earth and its rebellious colonies behind him forever.

"Forever" turned out to be eleven years. That was how long it took for another Independent Reconnaissance Unit to respond to the distress call his ship had sent before it was destroyed.

And *this* one made his own berserk killer computer look sane.

WAR SURPLUS, VOLUME 2

THE WIZARD AND THE WAR MACHINE

LAWRENCE WATT-EVANS

WILDSIDE PRESS

Dedicated to
Lester del Rey

THE WIZARD AND THE WAR MACHINE

ONE

Bright daylight spilled through the chunks of colored glass set into the windows, striping the fur carpets with bands of red and green and blue. The children were using the slowly-shifting streaks of colored light in a complicated game of their own devising; Sam Turner watched for a moment, standing in the kitchen doorway, but could make no sense of it. The only rule he could see was that when the daylight's movement caused any particular stripe to touch a new rug, everybody screamed with excitement and ran about wildly.

Perhaps, he thought with a smile, that was really the only rule there was.

Back on Old Earth or Mars the sun's movement would have been too slow to use in a children's game; even here on Dest, in the deep of winter when the elongated stripes made its motion more obvious, he was surprised to see it involved.

"Daddy!" little Zhrellia called, "Daddy, Daddy, you play!"

He shook his head. "No, I don't know how. Besides, I should get to the market before all the good stuff is gone." He gestured at the folded linen sack he had tucked under one arm.

All three children expressed polite dismay, Zhrellia pouting, Debovar downcast, and Ket impassive; Ket added, "Will you bring us some honey? It was all gone at breakfast."

"I'll see." He smiled fondly. "You just go on with your game. If you need anything, shout; your mother will hear you."

He was lucky, he told himself as he crossed the room, to have three such children, all healthy, without a visible mutation amongst them. He was lucky to have the wife he did, and his position in the community. Most of all, he was lucky to be alive, after what he had been through in his younger days. Back then, when he was traveling through space with a bomb in his head, fighting under the direction of an irrational computer a war that was long over, he would never have believed he would someday have children and a comfortable home.

He paused at the threshold to wave a farewell, then stepped through the door to the little platform beyond, leaving the luxuries of his family's apartments behind.

Around him were four bare wooden walls, and two floors above him was a patchwork of metal, wood, and concrete that served as a ceiling. The wooden platform on which he stood was secured to only two of the walls, forming a triangle across one corner of the chamber. Other doors opened onto similar platforms from other walls and on other levels, but most of the area that should have been floor was simply open space over a hundred-meter drop.

He glanced over the edge, gathered his concentration, and stepped off.

At first he hung suspended in mid-air, but then he allowed himself to sink slowly but steadily downward.

He looked about casually, watching the walls slide up past him; the rusty, blast-twisted steel frame of the ancient skyscraper showed plainly through the cobbled-on walls of glass and wood. When he had first settled in Praunce, eleven years earlier, he had worried that the damaged metal structure might not be sound, that his cozy new home might someday fall, brought down by high winds or ground tremors, killing him in its collapse.

He smiled to himself at the memory.

Later, as an apprentice wizard, he had also been frightened by the necessity of levitating himself up and down the central shaft. His master, however, had insisted. Wizards lived in the towers; that was the way it was done in Praunce. It always had been the way, ever since the first wizard arrived there not long after the Bad Times, and it presumably always would be. As an apprentice, Turner had lived in his master Arrelis' tower, and he had levitated up and down the central shaft. Since by then he had already survived any number of things that should have killed him, he had ignored his nervousness.

Now a master wizard himself, albeit not a particularly good one, Turner knew that his fears for the building's safety had been groundless; he could perceive the strengths and weaknesses of the structure, could feel the stress upon it, and knew that despite rust, despite the damage done by the nuclear blast that had destroyed the city on whose ruins Praunce had been built, despite everything, the tower could easily stand for another century or two.

The drop down the shaft, however, still worried him on occasion, and when his children had been younger the thought that one of them might somehow open a wrong door and fall off the platform had terrified him. Even now, at times, he still worried about Zhrellia, despite locks and warnings. Like any two-year-old, she had more curiosity than caution.

He smiled anew when he thought of her.

He looked down; he had made more than half the descent. He could see clearly, despite the dim light and drifting dust, the stacked sacks of grain that covered the floor to a depth of a dozen meters or so. The piles had been shrinking since the onset of winter, but they were still substantial. The city was well-supplied this year, as it usually was.

He sneezed, and fell a meter or so before he caught himself. The dust had tickled his nose. The hollow centers of the towers were always drab and dirty, because nobody could be bothered to clean them; the stored grain inevitably left behind dust and grit that drifted about and slowly encrusted every surface, including, whenever he passed through, his skin and the inside of his nose.

At least, he thought, it was reasonably warm in here. He could have gone out a window and down the outside of the building, but the outside air was freezing cold, and as a wizard he was expected to generate his own heat-field rather than wear a coat — it helped maintain the impression that wizards were not subject to the weaknesses that troubled lesser breeds of humanity.

Generating heat could get tiring, though; better to put up with a little dirt than to exhaust himself for no reason, he told himself as he settled onto the trap door that led into the tower's eight lowest floors. Ordinary men and women lived in the base of the tower — along with a good many mutants, sports, and other non-ordinary men and women, most of them the result of the lingering radiation and chemical contamination in the area.

No wizards lived below him, though. Wizards, and only wizards and their families, lived in the tops of the towers. The rest of the populace stayed close to the ground. Even after eleven years, Turner had not quite decided whether he approved of this division between the city's elite and the common masses. It was certainly undemocratic, and Turner's parents had brought him up as a believer in democracy, but on the other hand, wizards really *were* different from other people, and to pretend otherwise would be hypocritical.

Besides, the wizardly elite was by no means a closed society. Anyone could apply for an apprenticeship and stand a reasonable chance of being accepted, virtually every apprentice became a wizard, and all wizards were accepted as equals, regardless of whether they had been born to princes, peasants, or even other wizards. Minor distinctions might be made on the basis of seniority or ability, but never on the basis of birth. Turner himself, after all, had been as complete an outsider as anyone might imagine, and yet he had been fully accepted.

Few people did apply for apprenticeships, though, which puzzled him. He preferred to attribute it to a combination of laziness and mistrust. Wizardry was mysterious, Turner thought, and probably looked a good bit harder than it actually was.

Still, he reluctantly admitted to himself that the wizards did discourage would-be apprentices. Apprentices meant work and responsibility, and more wizards meant a wider distribution of the powers and privileges they enjoyed.

But anyone *could* apply. Turner soothed his egalitarian instincts with that reminder.

He opened the trap door without touching it, lifting himself up out of the way as it swung back. When it had fallen back as far as the hinges would allow he let himself sink slowly downward through the opening.

He paused a few centimeters off the floor of the corridor below the trap, aware of an odd, unfamiliar sensation, the sort of sensation that he would once have described as "feeling as if he were being watched." Oddly, the phrase came to him in his native tongue, rather than the Prauncer dialect of Anglo-Spanish that he had spoken and thought in for the past decade.

Nobody, though, should be able to watch an alert wizard without the wizard knowing it. Turner had accepted that as fact for several years now. He rotated slowly in mid-air, looking with both his eyes and his psychic senses, but could neither see nor feel anyone paying any attention to him. A few people were in the rooms along the corridor, behind their closed doors, but none showed any sign that they were aware of his presence. He sensed their auras as calm and blue.

With the mental equivalent of a shrug he dropped to the floor and began walking toward the stairs. He was imagining things, he told himself; either that, or some of the circuitry in his body was acting up. Perhaps some obscure component, a chip or a bit of wiring somewhere inside him, was reacting to static electricity built up in the cold air, or to sunspots — or starspots, if that was the word, since Dest's primary was not Old Earth's sun. Perhaps, he theorized, some mechanism in his body was breaking down from age and lack of maintenance, and was disturbing the equilibrium of his senses.

The latter was not a particularly pleasant possibility to dwell on, with all it implied for future breakdowns. He pushed it aside.

He was halfway down the second flight when he again thought he sensed something; this time it seemed to be a sound he didn't quite hear. He slowed his pace, then paused at the bottom of the staircase, listening intently.

His ears caught nothing but the distant sounds of the city going about its business. His psychic senses detected nothing but casual disinterest. Nonetheless, he was uneasily certain that he *did* hear something — he *knew* he did. He tried to remember how to listen to the electronics wired into his nervous system, but it had been so long that he struggled for several seconds before he again picked up a faint tremor of something.

He concentrated, willed himself to hear it, and began to pick up something, too faint to be considered a sound, but with a distinct rhythm. He recognized it as speech, but the rhythm did not fit any dialect he had heard on Dest.

It did, however, fit Old Earth's polyglot common language, the language used in government, trade, and the military, the language he had, as the child of a bureaucrat and a corporate executive in urban North America, spoken as his own until reaching Praunce. The mysterious speech fit the rhythms of polyglot, and it was growing steadily louder and clearer.

"Oh, my God," he said aloud in his childhood tongue, the years of practice in using Prauncer terms, swearing by the three Prauncer gods, forgotten for the moment. He could make out the words now. He stood motionless in the corridor at the foot of the stairs, staring at nothing and listening to the barely audible voice in his head endlessly repeating in his native language, in a distant monotone, "...Anyone loyal to Old Earth, please respond. Anyone loyal to Old Earth, please respond. Anyone loyal to Old Earth, please respond..."

"I'm here!" he shouted silently, reacting automatically, without any thought of what it might mean, "I'm here!"

TWO

For eleven local years the communications equipment that had been built into his skull back at the training base on Mars had not been used, simply because he had had no one in Dest's entire star system to talk to with it. For eleven years he had done nothing to maintain any of the artificial systems in his body and had not been bothered on occasions when a psionic self-inspection revealed that some minor device had failed. He had had little use for any of his internal technology, and his computer, which the system designers had made responsible for checking and maintaining both his natural and his cyborg parts, had been shut down permanently shortly after his arrival on the planet. Before that arrival he and his computer had been gradually deteriorating together for fourteen terrestrial years of subjective time as they wandered aimlessly through interstellar space.

It was therefore almost as surprising that his transceiver could still receive, he decided after the initial shock and confusion wore off, as it was that there was something for it *to* receive.

As the message "...Anyone loyal to Old Earth, please respond..." continued to repeat, for long minutes after his unthinking mental shout, Turner realized that his response had not reached whoever was transmitting. The transmitter in his skull, powered by his own body's electricity, had a useful range of no more than a light-minute or two, and while the sender of the message might not have a ready answer, he or she — or it — would surely have stopped the endless repetition immediately upon getting a response.

Turner had no way of knowing whether something was wrong with his transmitter, or with the other party's receiver, or whether the distance was simply too great. He guessed the last was most likely, but knew neither of the other possibilities should surprise him.

Whatever the reason, the transmission droned on endlessly, "...Anyone loyal to Old Earth, please respond..."

And whatever the reason, he told himself, it was probably a very good thing indeed that his answer had not been heard. He did not know who or what was out there, or whether it had any direct connection with his own presence on Dest. He could only guess what other natives of Old Earth might still be wandering among the stars.

He sat down on the dusty floor of the corridor to think, trying to ignore the constant faint repetition of "...Anyone loyal to Old Earth, please respond..." that muttered in the back of his head.

He had been on Dest for eleven years of local time — that would be, he estimated, a little over ten years on Old Earth, since the shorter days on Dest more than made up for the four hundred and two of them in a year. That meant he had left Mars three hundred and fourteen years ago by Old Earth time, three hundred and thirty-eight years ago by Dest time, ignoring, as he always did, the fact that it was virtually meaningless to speak of simultaneity on two planets so far apart in a relativistic universe.

Of course, in his own subjective time, it was twenty-five personal years, fourteen measured by shipboard clocks and eleven by Dest's seasons. He had never worked out the conversion necessary to express it entirely in terms of one planet or the other; he had had no reason to.

At first thought it seemed that after three centuries there could be no more survivors of the war he had fought in, the war the people of Dest called "The Bad Times," still roaming around out there, but after an instant's consideration he knew that was wrong. After all, he himself had wandered through space for over three hundred years; what was another ten or eleven on top of that? Relativistic time dilation effects on near-light-speed space travel had a way of making "common sense" not work. He had never worried about why that should be, never tried to understand the nature of relativity; he had simply accepted it as fact, as he had accepted so many things throughout his life. Now, again, he accepted it, and knew that the new arrival could have left Old Earth at almost any time since the development of interstellar travel, two centuries before he himself had been born.

"...Anyone loyal to Old Earth, please respond..." the voice repeated, each repetition almost imperceptibly louder and clearer than the one before.

Whatever was transmitting the signal could easily be a surviving unit of Old Earth's military, just as he was himself. Depending on its flight path it could be anywhere from a decade to a few centuries out from base, by shipboard time. The crew aboard, if any were still alive, surely knew that the war was long since lost and both Old Earth and Mars blasted by the enemy's D-series. The news had been broadcast throughout known space.

"...Anyone loyal to Old Earth, please respond..." What, he asked himself bitterly, was left for anyone to be loyal to?

Of course, if the transmitter was military, knowledge of Old Earth's destruction didn't necessarily mean that the signaller or signallers would be ready to surrender peacefully. For himself, he had certainly been eager enough to give up his mission once he knew he had nothing left to fight for, but he guessed that not everyone would have felt that way.

Some people, he supposed, would seek revenge for Old Earth's obliteration. Some would carry on out of a sense of duty, even when that duty was obviously meaningless — or perhaps not a sense of duty, but simply a lack of anything better to do.

"...Anyone loyal to Old Earth, please respond..." repeated endlessly, mechanically in his head.

And, of course, some survivors would be forced by their machines to carry on, as he had been.

The very thought of that still induced an almost physical pain; the memories of those wasted years still hurt. He had signed up to fight when he was eighteen, and studying art in college, with no clear idea of what he wanted from life, no real conception of what he was getting into. Volunteering for the military had seemed brave and patriotic and no worse, no more frightening, than any other available course of action. To the young man he had once been, the prospect of flying off into space to fight had seemed no more terrifying, and a good bit more romantic, than going out to find a job and support himself.

And in a way he had made the right choice. He was still alive, at a physiological age of forty-three, or forty-four, or whatever it was, while if he had stayed on Old Earth he would probably have died a good bit younger, when the D-series hit.

He certainly would have been dead by now, three centuries later.

When he had been wandering through space after the war ended he had often thought he would have preferred death.

He stared at the blank wall of the corridor as he remembered, absently adjusting the cyborged lenses of his eyes, zooming in and then back as he studied the grain of the wood. At any rate, he told himself with mild satisfaction, that particular modification to his body had not yet deteriorated. His eyesight was quite literally superhuman. He could also shift to sensing with his psychic abilities, the psionic "magic" that made him a wizard, the underlying energies of the wood; viewed that way, the wall was overlaid with a delicate tracery of golden light that showed him every point where the material was stressed, every place that still held traces of sap, and a mosaic of other information. As he stared at the wood without really seeing it, the soundless voice in his head spoke its message over and over.

He had always been a loner when he was young — quiet, self-contained, with no strong interests, no great passions, no close relationships, not given much to either introspection or interaction with others. That, it turned out, was a personality type that the military needed very badly for one of their programs. After signing up to fight he had volunteered once again, though they probably would have taken him in any case, and he had been shipped to Mars, where he was systematically rebuilt, physically and mentally, until he was no longer Samuel Turner, a nondescript art student who had grown up in a dozen cities scattered all over eastern North America, but Independent Reconnaissance Unit Cyborg 205, code-named Slant, with superhuman speed and strength, with innumerable devices built into his body, including an elaborate communications system in his skull that linked him tightly to his one-man starship's computer.

His memories of the period following his arrival on Mars were oddly fractured, because one part of his reconditioning had been the artificial division of his mind into eighteen separate personalities, each specialized in various ways. Some had been trained and conditioned for specific functions, such as combat or piloting, with all irrelevant knowledge and emotion suppressed; others had given the outward appearance of normality and were intended to serve as cover identities, should he ever undertake any active spying or sabotage. His superiors had also suppressed his civilian identity and all its memories, lest some childhood trauma or personal idealism somehow interfere with his duties, so in a way he had not even existed during his body's service as an IRU cyborg. He tended to identify himself most strongly with the default personality, the passive, generalized individual that dominated when no particular talent or identity was called for. The default identity had been made up of what was left of his personality after the other seventeen were formed and his memories suppressed, so it had been the most similar to his original self in many ways, but all eighteen personalities had really been parts of himself. When he had finally been reintegrated into the original Samuel Turner, he had kept the memories of all eighteen — not really as a continuous whole, but as a sort of mental patchwork, eighteen separate pieces tied loosely together by a shared chronology. He could remember times when he had been the default personality one second and his ruthlessly efficient warrior self the next, and he knew, intellectually, that the change had been virtually instantaneous, but the two personalities had been so different that the gap seemed years long, as wide as the disparity between his naive trust and innocence at the age of four and the core of insecurity he had disguised with carefully contrived cynicism at the age of fourteen.

The gap actually seemed even wider than that, for when he tried he could remember the intermediate stages between being a child of four and being a lad of fourteen, but no intermediate stages had ever existed between his default personality and his combat self.

The sort of induced insanity he had lived with as an IRU cyborg was very effective for military purposes over the short run, allowing a single cyborg to serve an assortment of functions and to travel interstellar distances alone without breaking down mentally or emotionally. It had never been intended to last indefinitely.

When his conditioning, mental and physical, was complete, they had given him his ship — it had had no special name, but was just called IRU Vessel 205. It was controlled by Computer Control Complex IRU 205 and equipped with a wide variety of weapons and other equipment.

One of his personalities was programmed to pilot the ship as effectively as the computer could, just in case that should become necessary, but ordinarily running the ship was the computer's job. In theory, the computer was to serve almost as an extension of his own brain, but in practice it had never worked that way; the computer's programming was too different from any of his own personalities. Even when hardwired together, with the computer's control cable secured in its socket in the back of his neck, they had always remained separate and not particularly compatible intelligences.

It occurred to him to wonder, for the first time, whether that "control cable" had been intended to allow him to control the computer, or to help the computer to control him. The technicians had never specified, and his other superiors had never mentioned it at all.

He had been dominant in most matters, by virtue of being the more complex and creative of the pair, but the computer, CCC-IRU 205, had always held the trump cards of being able to override his control of all their equipment, including the modifications to his own body, and of having sole control of the thermite charge in the base of his skull that would blow his head off if he attempted to surrender or to otherwise seriously disobey the orders of the Command.

Removing that explosive charge had been an obsession for years.

He reached up and idly fingered the bent and corroded remains of the socket in his neck. His skin had grown in over most of the edges now, reducing the opening to perhaps half its original size. Even without that, though, the socket had long ago been ruined, twisted out of shape and unusable. The wizards of Praunce — his friends and teachers, and his compatriots now — had removed the thermite from his skull, but the computer had detonated it before it could be safely disposed of. The explosion had scorched and deformed the socket, as well as burning off hair and skin and giving him a concussion. He had been cut off from full contact with the computer after that, limited to reception over a simple verbal communication circuit. The computer had still been able to receive almost as much of his sensory input as did his own brain, but the two of them had never again been in full, direct communication.

Of course, they had not really communicated all that well to begin with, even with the control cable in place.

Back on Mars the Command had told him that his failure to meld properly with the computer would not matter. Like his own mental restructuring, his ship and its computer were designed and programmed with the idea that they would return within a few years of subjective time, before any subtle flaws that might exist could develop into anything serious. The two of them, he was told, should be able to get along well enough until the war ended.

Sure enough, the war had been over within six months of subjective time after his departure. Unfortunately, Old Earth lost, a possibility that had not been covered in his design. The rebellious colonies had somehow gotten their D-series weapons, whatever they were, through the defenses guarding Mars and Old Earth.

The computer that had controlled his ship and his life had not been programmed to acknowledge defeat or surrender; Slant and his machines were to conquer or die. At most, CCC-IRU 205 might tolerate a strategic retreat at times, but anything that might have meant a peaceful end to the mission was out of the question once Mars and Old Earth had been fried. IRU 205's assignment had been vague and open-ended, to be terminated by the transmission of Slant's release code or the ship's recall code, and his superiors on Mars had all died so quickly that they had never had a chance to send any release or recall codes even if they had wanted to — and Turner doubted very much that the hard-line military thinkers of the Command would have wanted to.

Without his release code he had been condemned to wander on through space, fighting a war that was already lost.

He had accepted that, thanks to the passivity of his splintered personality and to the thermite charge in his head. He had had no other choice he could think of but death, and whatever he might have done in other circumstances, in his fractured and heavily conditioned mental state suicide had not been possible. At least, it had not been possible for him; as the computer's programming deteriorated through the random loss of occasional bits to stray electromagnetic impulses or wear on overused memory systems, and as more and more negative data were compiled, the computer had gradually developed suicidal tendencies of its own. CCC-IRU 205 had wanted to fulfill its programming, and that programming had been designed to culminate in either a recall to base or the ship's destruction in action. Although it was not able to act appropriately on the information, the computer had known that it would never be recalled, which left its own termination as its only long-term goal. It had used that in making decisions; whenever it was offered a choice with no other reason to prefer one alternative over another, it chose the option most likely to result in its own eventual destruction. That had made Slant's life difficult, since he had not shared the computer's death wish.

Once Turner, as Slant, had known that the war was lost and that the damage he and his ship did to other people they encountered could do no one any good, he had always done what he could to keep the damage to a minimum. He had tried his best to keep the ship away from inhabited worlds entirely, since the computer had picked up and understood enough to assume that no place outside the solar system remained loyal to Old Earth after the D-series hit; humans, unlike computers, saw no point in remaining loyal to a burnt-out ruin.

At least, rational humans who knew what had happened, such as those who inhabited most colony planets, had seen no point in such loyalty. On Dest, no one had had any idea what was going on, so the question had never come up. Elsewhere, anyone who might still have possessed starships or any sort of long-range telecommunications surely knew that nothing was left on Old Earth to fight for.

Someone, though, was out there now, calling, "...Anyone loyal to Old Earth, please respond..."

He thrust that thought aside for the moment as he continued reviewing what he knew.

The computer had, despite Slant's best efforts, forced him to land on a few inhabited planets, and one of them, the last, had been Dest. The computer having detected anomalies in the planet's gravitational field, as if the natives here had invented anti-gravity, quite logically had interpreted this as enemy weapons research.

Turner shook his head. Even now he could not understand why the anomalies had shown up on the ship's sensors as anti-gravity. The actual cause had been the psionic abilities known to the natives as "wizardry" or "magic". These abilities had apparently originated as a chance mutation after an Old Earth fleet, for reasons Turner could only guess at, had been sent out here and had bombed Dest back to barbarism; the resulting radiation was still, centuries later, causing mutations, most of which were far less favorable. His computer had had records of the fleet being sent, but no records of *why* it had been sent, and so far as Turner knew, no one on Dest had even realized the fleet was human in origin. The ships had suddenly appeared above them, and their cities had vanished, and knowing nothing of the rebellion against Old Earth, most of them had naturally assumed the attackers to be hostile extraterrestrials. Some might have realized what was happening, but when Slant had arrived in Praunce, three hundred years after the attack, his statement that Old Earth had sent the fleet had come as a shock to the wizards there.

The Bad Times had destroyed Dest's old civilization pretty thoroughly, and only the fabulous good luck that wizardry had turned up in the aftermath had permitted the survivors to rebuild as well, and as quickly, as they had. However the talent had originated, it could be passed on, and not merely to the mutants' direct descendants — the psionic ability itself allowed one to telekinetically alter the neurons of the human brain so as to induce psionic abilities in others. Of course, these psionically created wizards did not breed true, since only the brain had been changed, and not the genes, but that was enough. In fact, the original mutant strain had died out, yet wizardry had survived and spread quickly, and had become a cornerstone of most postwar societies on Dest.

Wizards could levitate, either themselves, or others, or anything else in sight that was not too heavy, but Turner did not think it was actually anti-gravity that they used. For one thing, almost all wizardry, not just levitation but anything that required much energy, had registered as gravitational anomalies, and he simply didn't see how mind reading or the eerie psionic senses could involve anti-gravity. He had no idea what they were, but they seemed more likely to be electromagnetic in nature than anything else. At close range, even before he became a wizard himself, he had been able to sense when magic was in use because he felt a sort of electric tingle, like static in the air, which seemed to indicate an electromagnetic nature. Ordinary people felt no such sensation; it was his cyborg circuitry that registered it somehow. The computer had been unable to detect or explain the tingling. It had only been able to discern the "gravitational anomalies."

Even now, when he knew exactly what changes were necessary to make a human brain capable of wizardry, he had no idea how the phenomenon worked, any more than a caveman could have explained a radio after being taught to wire together the appropriate parts. He only knew that it worked.

His own theory of why wizardry registered as anti-gravity was that all psionic activity somehow created some sort of interference that had affected the ship's most delicate and sensitive equipment, its gravity sensors, without actually having any connection with gravity at all.

Even if they were not anti-gravity, however, the computer had found these mysterious talents quite dangerous enough, and it had insisted that Slant learn how this "magic" operated, so that the information could be taken back to Old Earth. Once the secrets were known as much of the planet's population as possible was to be destroyed, to eliminate any future threat to Old Earth's well-being.

It had taken everything he could do, as well as the efforts of a good many wizards and the manipulation of the computer's own desire for self-destruction, to shut down CCC-IRU 205 for good. He had unintentionally brought down his ship in the process, wrecking it beyond hope of repair.

Once that was done, leaving him permanently stranded on this curious planet, he had accepted an apprenticeship in this strange psionic wizardry, and thereafter had led the normal life of a wizard in Praunce. He had married, fathered three healthy children, served on the wizards' advisory council to Praunce's government, and done his bit in various ways to help the Prauncer efforts to unite the entire continent — the only one of Dest's four continents that was known to be inhabited — under a single government. He had never been all that enthusiastic about the form of that government, with its patchwork oligarchy, but at least a unified planetary government meant there would be no major wars, so he had always cooperated. With the passage of time and his acceptance into Prauncer society, he had almost forgotten that he was the only person on Dest not born there, a war-surplus cyborg centuries out of his own era.

"...Anyone loyal to Old Earth, please respond..." Well, he told himself, he wasn't loyal to Old Earth. He hadn't been since the war ended. He would not respond. Whoever or whatever was calling, Turner wasn't what he/she/it wanted.

He stretched out his legs, which had gotten slightly cramped, and then got slowly and carefully to his feet.

As he left the corridor and headed on down the next flight of stairs he promised himself that although he wouldn't answer, he would listen very closely to whatever he could pick up. If a ship from Old Earth was approaching Dest it might well be military, and could be just as hostile as his own had been. In that case, he was undoubtedly the single person on the planet best equipped to deal with such a menace.

THREE

The midwinter market was somewhat skimpy, without the variety or quality of produce to be found the rest of the year. Even so, Turner managed to fill his shopping bag to overflowing before he headed home. For the past several days he had been putting off buying a variety of foods; he disliked outdoor shopping in cold weather. Maintaining a heat-field took enough concentration that he carried his groceries in his ordinary linen bag tucked into the curve of his left arm, rather than levitating them, and the sack gave him a rather undignified, unwizardly air. Nobody commented on this minor breach of custom, though he was sure they noticed. One did not criticize a wizard to his face unless one was another wizard. Still, Turner felt very slightly embarrassed.

At least, he thought, he had not been forced to waste energy floating above mud or slush to keep his feet clean; the winter had been dry, with no trace of snow, and the ground had remained hard-packed dirt. He had been able to walk like any ordinary mortal without risking criticism.

Concentrating on restocking the cupboards had been an excellent distraction; rather than simply fretting about the mysterious messages, Turner had involved himself in picking out the best of the market's relatively meager pickings. Well before he left the square he had managed to more or less tune out the constant chant of "...Anyone loyal to Old Earth, please respond...", reducing it to mere mental background noise.

Nonetheless, to shorten the time before he was free to concentrate on the signal, when he reached his home tower he ignored the effort involved and lifted himself directly up the outside of the building instead of following the stairways and corridors up to the tower's hollow center.

A few people on the street below glanced up, but quickly ducked their heads back down into their collars to help keep out the cold winter air. Other than that, nobody paid any attention to Turner's ascent. The sight of a wizard going home by air was commonplace in central Praunce.

When he reached his home level, he held his grocery sack in both hands while he unlocked a window telekinetically. As he stepped in, allowing the bag of food to hang unsupported in the cold outside air for a moment while he slipped through the narrow casement, he pondered anew what the repeating message might signify.

He drifted into the room and settled to the floor, still lost in thought. His son Ket, eldest of his three offspring, had seen him coming and had rushed to the window to help him in; now the child pulled the sack inside and closed the window.

Turner thanked the boy absently and ambled toward the kitchen, the bag of produce floating along behind him, as he tried to decide whether there was anything he should do about the signal — anything beyond listening to it, which he could not avoid.

He did not notice Debovar and Zhrellia wrestling furiously and noisily on a nearby rug in a friendly but desperately uneven match, and did not hear when Ket, after latching the window, called after him, "Did you get any honey, Daddy?"

When Turner disappeared into the kitchen without replying, Ket stared after him, slightly puzzled. His father had not answered a simple question, had not yelled at his sisters to stop fighting, and had not given him the usual returning-home hug. This sort of neglect happened sometimes, when Daddy was thinking very hard about something especially important or difficult, but Ket was not aware of anything important or difficult that had come up lately, or anything that might have happened in the public market.

Well, whatever it was, he told himself, it was probably just boring grown-up stuff, like when the other wizards had asked Daddy to decide what to do with that man who had been caught hurting women. Daddy would be all right. If it were anything that concerned the rest of the family, Daddy would have said something. Ket dismissed the matter from his mind and went to pull Debovar off the shrieking Zhrellia; Debovar was not hurting Zhrellia, just tickling her, but the shrieking bothered his ears.

In the kitchen Turner began putting his purchases away in the appropriate bins and cupboards, automatically finding most of the correct places despite his preoccupation.

Weapons, he thought as he stacked jars of preserves on a high shelf. He should check out what weapons he had available. If the message came from an incoming ship, rather than a robot probe or some other possibility he had not yet thought of, he might need to fight whoever was aboard — if anyone was. A ship from Old Earth might well be hostile, and would surely have a full arsenal, with everything from tranquilizer darts to nuclear missiles.

Or would it? If it had fought enough before reaching Dest its armament might be depleted by use. If it took three hundred years to reach Dest, then it had presumably not come directly from pre-war Old Earth by straight-line course, so it might well have fired off a good bit of its original supply of ammunition at stops along the way, and so far as he knew, it would not have been able to re-arm anywhere.

He could not count on that, though. Until he learned otherwise, he would have to assume that the newcomer's firepower was virtually endless.

His own arsenal was limited. He had salvaged some weapons from his own ship after the crash, but had left behind all the heavier pieces — missiles, particle beams, and so forth. He had not seen any possible use for them. The nuclear warheads he would have disarmed or destroyed entirely, had he known how.

It occurred to him for the first time that a good wizard could *see* how to disarm the warheads, but he had not known that when he had done his salvage work, a few days after the crash. He was not entirely certain that he could do it safely himself, even now. Although he could and did handle all the simple, everyday magic, such as flight or the most obvious applications of wizard-sight, he had never become very expert at the more delicate and sensitive sorts of wizardry, a fact that had been a great disappointment to his master and his other teachers; he had the raw talent, and could draw on as much psionic energy as anyone when he forced himself to, but he had found himself lacking in the sort of tight concentration that the really good wizards could muster. He also kept overlooking possible ways to use his abilities. He attributed his failure of concentration to lingering psychic damage from his fourteen years of total isolation and the after-effects of induced multiple personality; for fourteen years of wandering through space he had tried very hard not to think, because it had only depressed him in his trapped state, and the specialization of his different selves had made concentration so automatic when he needed it that now that it was voluntary, he found it hard to contrive consciously. As for overlooking possibilities, he assumed that was simply because he had spent the first three-fourths of his life with no knowledge of psionics at all, and was too set in his ways to adjust completely to his new talents. The other wizards had all grown up knowing that wizardry existed, and roughly what it could do, so that as children they had all spent time imagining what they would do if they ever became wizards themselves. Now they *were* wizards, and could draw on those childhood imaginings. Turner had none to draw on. He suspected that if he had grown up on Dest he would be more creative in his magic.

If whatever was transmitting the repeating message did prove hostile, and Turner found himself forced to fight it, he would have wizardry on his side, and the weapons he had salvaged, but that would be all. After all this time he felt sure that anything left in his wrecked ship would almost certainly be useless. The hull had been breached in the crash, allowing everything from rats and rain to mold and mildew into the mechanisms. The nuclear warheads in their shielded casings could well be intact, but the missiles to deliver them would hardly be trustworthy — fuel lines might be chewed through, fuel contaminated, or control chips warped or cracked.

Even the energy weapons that he had salvaged, snarks and lasers and shockguns, would probably have lost their charges by now. He had not checked on them in years, and the charge tended to trickle away. Not that he could have done anything about it if he had checked on them; if they were drained, as he expected, he had no way of recharging them, since the ship's fusion plant had been ruined in the crash. They were almost certainly useless.

He had a variety of firearms, though, everything from easily concealed pocket pistols to high-powered machine guns and portable rocket launchers. He had kept them for his own use, rather than turning them over to the city government — now the imperial government — for reasons that he himself was not sure of. His experiences back on Old Earth and Mars had left him with a permanent mistrust of all governments, a mistrust more emotional in origin than rational, and the government on Old Earth had at least made a pretense of being representative, where the rulers of Praunce, both wizard and normal, held their posts by appointment of their fellows and predecessors, claiming to know better than their subjects what the city and empire needed.

Turner had to admit, despite his democratic predilections, that Praunce's government ran at least as well as Old Earth's had. That was still not very well, however, and he attributed the oligarchy's relative success to Praunce's smaller population and simpler way of life.

And, democratic or not, he had always had the nagging egotistical suspicion that he could do far better at running a nation than had any government he had ever encountered. With that in mind, he had kept his private arsenal private.

His selfishness and mistrust were just as well, he decided, since it meant that he still had guns and ammunition now, when he might need them.

He knew, though, that no small arms, not even his heaviest shoulder-launched rockets, would be much use against an armored starship. The only hand-held weapon he had that might be able to pierce a starship's hull would be a snark, and that would be possible only at extreme close range — assuming that any of his snarks still held a charge.

Against a warship he would be virtually helpless.

Was a warship coming? If it was, would he have to fight it?

He didn't know. He didn't know much of anything. The message might mean nothing, or it might herald an entire fleet about to come in shooting, like the one that had destroyed Dest's cities three centuries ago. He shelved the last of his purchases, a large crock of honey most of which was destined for Ket's breakfast cakes, then tucked the emptied market sack back in its corner and leaned against the table, weighing his options.

Should he check out his weapons, see how much firepower he actually had? Parrah would almost certainly notice; she would want to know why. Did he have a good enough reason to worry her, and probably incite her to alarm every wizard in Praunce?

The voice in his head had grown quite loud now, indicating that he probably needed to reach a decision quickly; the repeating message was becoming harder to ignore.

Then, abruptly, he no longer wanted to ignore it, as the droning chant broke.

"...Anyone loyal to Old Earth...told you, let me send my own message. Oh, I'm transmitting? I am? Well, good, damn it, it's about time. I don't see why we have to warn the bastards in the first place, but if you won't give me fire control without it, I'm not going to make an issue of it, I'll just do the damn warning myself. You'd screw it up somehow, you stupid machine. You don't know what you're doing half the time; I have to watch everything you do. So, if we're really transmitting, hello, down there, if anyone can hear me, which I doubt. This is Independent Reconnaissance Unit 247, responding to a total-shutdown distress signal from IRU 205. If there *is* anyone down there who can hear me, and knows a reason I shouldn't open fire, you had damn well better answer quickly. I'm entering orbit around the only inhabited planet I can find in this system, the one with those weird gravitational anomalies flickering all over it, and unless someone tells me otherwise in the next ten minutes I'm going to assume it's inhabited by murdering rebels, like any other planet, and I'm going to start nuking cities. Speak now or forever hold your peace. Over."

The transmission ended, and the sudden mental silence left Turner momentarily dazed.

When he could think again, and had recalled as best he could the technique of subvocalizing messages over his communications circuit, he wasted no time in calling out silently, "IRU 247, this is IRU 205 — don't shoot! The planet's friendly!" He hoped he was remembering how to transmit correctly, and he hoped that his transmitter still worked.

Although the hostile nature of the message shocked him, he was, in a way, grateful that it was another IRU arriving, and not a heavy warship or a fleet, not only because an IRU was much smaller, with less firepower and only a single person aboard for him to deal with, but because he was so intimately familiar with its capabilities; having been the human half of an IRU himself, he knew exactly what he was now facing. An IRU might be bad, but another sort of warship, or an entire fleet, would almost certainly have been worse.

Still, with that ten-minute deadline, this IRU 247 seemed frighteningly eager to attack. His own computer had been more interested in learning the nature of those "gravitational anomalies" than in indiscriminate destruction. IRU 247 seemed to be taking a different approach, presumably either because of different mission programming or because an IRU, his own, had already been lost on this planet, and it might not leave Turner any time at all to spare for details such as figuring out whether his transmitter was working properly.

He had to make a quick check, though, for his own peace of mind; there would be no point in calling if his transmitter was broken. He closed his eyes and tried to sense the inside of his skull, to trace the circuitry and check for flaws. Self- evaluation was difficult for any wizard, and he was especially bad at it, but everything seemed to be intact, as far as he could determine in a quick scan. He dared not take the time for a close inspection; he called again.

"IRU 247, I hear you," he thought as loudly as he could, his old familiarity with the method returning quickly despite a decade of disuse. "This is IRU 205 responding. Hold your fire! Hold your fire!"

After an instant's pause, he remembered a bit of ancient procedure and added, "Do you read me? Over."

He waited several long seconds, holding his breath, for a reply.

During those seconds he was able to marvel that this ship had come looking for *him*. He had never anticipated that.

If he could get a message through to it, he foresaw no real problem. He would assure it that Dest had always been friendly, that he was content to stay there, and the newcomer was free to stay or go, and all would be well.

That assumed, though, that his transmissions got through. If they did not, he and his family and friends, along with most of Dest's urban population, might have less than ten minutes to live.

"Well, I'll be damned!" he heard at last. "IRU 205? Is that really you? Hell, I figured you must have been dead for years!"

"Well, I'm not," Turner began, but before he could get any further another transmission reached him. It was not exactly another voice, since the internal communications circuit did not use sound or any direct analogue of sound, but something about it, the rhythm perhaps, told him that this was not the same entity speaking.

"Further identification is required."

That, Turner realized, almost certainly came from CCC-IRU 247. Naturally, it would not simply take his word without some sort of confirmation. "This is Cyborg Unit IRU 205, code designation Slant," he replied.

The computer accepted his code-name, and asked, "Query: Reason for failure of Computer Control Complex IRU 205 to respond."

Turner felt an odd chill at the computer's words; its phrasing was identical to what his own computer would have said. It was almost as if his long-defunct keeper and antagonist had been reincarnated. The question and that familiar wording also implied that he might have a slightly harder time than he had hoped convincing IRU 247 that nothing on Dest deserved destruction. He remembered innumerable arguments with his own computer, which had steadfastly maintained that Dest had to be enemy territory, or at best neutral and therefore a potential enemy, since Old Earth had sent a fleet to attack it, and besides, there was no record of anti-gravity research being done by anyone friendly.

He hoped that IRU 247 would be more reasonable, but the hope seemed pretty forlorn.

"CCC-IRU 205 was shut down ten years ago as dangerously dysfunctional, after it had received severe damage," he subvocalized. It was curious, he thought, how the military phrasing came back to him so readily after years of neglect, allowing him to say things like "dangerously dysfunctional" instead of "insane."

After only a very brief pause, CCC-IRU 247 asked, "Query: Status of IRU Vessel 205."

"It's a wreck, a total loss," Turner replied immediately. "The computer let it crash." IIe was unsure of the wisdom in admitting this, since it was consistent with his having been defeated and having surrendered after his ship's destruction, but he dared not hesitate long enough to think out the best possible answer; this pair of newcomers did not seem to trust him and was clearly not overly patient. He saw no obvious problem in telling the truth; it was by no means an actual admission of surrender.

"Query: Nature of damage to Computer Control Complex IRU 205 resulting in shutdown."

"Ah...I'm not really sure." On this point he was less ready to speak frankly, since he and other wizards, all of whom he wanted IRU 247 to accept as friendly, had been responsible for a good deal of the damage his computer had received before its final destruction. He remembered how his own computer had constantly doubted his loyalty and suspected him of wanting to surrender at every opportunity, and he realized that this was dangerous ground. He had to phrase his explanation carefully, so that IRU 247 would accept it without concluding that Turner had sided with Old Earth's enemies, but he still felt that he had to speak quickly, so that he would give no appearance of having to take time to devise lies.

He also wanted to stay as close to the truth as he could, just in case this newly arrived computer might have some means of judging his veracity. It surely knew exactly how his own computer had been constructed and programmed, far better than he did, and would catch any technical flaws in his explanation. It was also barely possible that it could read his internal systems well enough to use them as a lie detector, though he doubted that; his own computer had been unable to do so. But then, before his personalities were recombined he had had greater control over his modified body and had been able to regulate his pulse rate and other such functions to a greater degree than he could now.

He dared not say anything that would make Dest appear hostile, or himself disloyal. That would be an invitation to attack.

"It had been shut down temporarily by enemy action, after an extended period without maintenance," he said, "When it was brought back on line its behavior was dangerously erratic." He paused, then added, "That first shutdown was when the distress signal went out."

He had long since entirely forgotten about that distress signal, until IRU 247's call had reminded him; for one thing, he had never really believed it had been sent. Sending it had not been anything he himself had done. On one occasion before the final crash the ship had had its power drained by a cabal of wizards from the city-state of Awlmei, and the shutdown had activated an automatic system that had played a tape giving him his release code, accompanied by a short pep talk from the Command that included telling him that a distress call had been sent. He had never believed that any such call really *had* been sent, despite what the Command said — the ship's power had already been so low that it did not seem possible for it to have transmitted anything that could be picked up over interstellar distances. He had assumed that the Command had lied, in hopes of keeping him from helping the other side once the computer was no longer around to ensure his loyalty. His superiors had never been above using such deceptions.

It seemed he had been wrong. The distress signal had not only gone out, it had been answered, which was so unlikely as to be almost unbelievable. His ship must have had some sort of emergency power reserve he had not known about, he guessed, and this newcomer, IRU 247, must have been cruising nearby, as interstellar distances go, with receivers at extreme sensitivity.

Of course, he had known that his ship had had reserves. The wizards of Awlmei had been careless, and had left some of those reserves. One of the service robots, acting on an emergency program triggered by the ship's shutdown, had been able to restore itself to operation by tapping what little current remained in the batteries of the other robots. Once it was running it had brought the ship and computer back to life by charging the reserve batteries from photoelectric panels. Another reserve, sufficient to send the distress signal, had apparently existed as well.

Turner mentioned none of these details. He was not lying, but he was slanting the truth toward what he wanted both halves of IRU 247 to believe, and preferred to gloss over what had happened to his ship, as well as his own apathetic attitude toward the war once Old Earth had been flash-fried.

"Its behavior presented a danger to the local population, which had remained completely loyal to Old Earth," he continued.

That was very nearly the truth. Most of Dest's people had never even known the Rebellion had taken place, even when the fleet from Old Earth came and flattened their cities. Until Slant/Turner had arrived no one had bothered to tell them the truth. One way or another some of the planet's inhabitants surely knew what had really happened — Turner had told a few — but most of the population was still unaware that Dest was no longer a loyal colony of Old Earth.

Of course, no one on Dest much cared, since except for his own and this newcomer no starships had arrived, from Old Earth or anywhere else, since before the Bad Times. Dest had been cut off from whatever civilization might still exist elsewhere, and consequently from any concerns over interstellar politics or loyalties.

"Therefore," he concluded, "I used our release code, and once its mission programming was aborted, CCC-IRU 205 realized the extent of its own damage and shut itself down, permanently."

That was more or less what had happened; he saw no need to explain that the computer had suicided not because it knew it was damaged, but because it had *wanted* to, as much as a military computer could "want" anything.

It was the cyborg, not the computer, who replied to this explanation. "Your release code? How the hell did you get your release code?" Before he could even begin to answer, the cyborg went on, "No, it doesn't matter, don't tell me."

Turner was suddenly frightened. Except for the cyborg's initial threat, the conversation had seemed to be going well enough. But if this was indeed an IRU cyborg he was communicating with, how could he or she not be desperately interested in how another, similar cyborg had obtained his release code? The release code would free the cyborg from the computer's domination. Turner, when he had been Slant, had sometimes gone for weeks at a time thinking of almost nothing else.

How could this cyborg not care?

He wondered whether the IRU 247 cyborg might have just switched from one personality to another. Presumably he or she had eighteen available, just as Slant had. Surely, the default personality, the largest remnant of the original mind, would not dismiss a release code as unimportant!

The cyborg was still transmitting. "It doesn't matter, because you'll probably just lie about it. Friendly planet, like hell. There are no friendly planets. You're another traitor, Slant, just like so many of the others, aren't you? You shut down your computer so you could go over to the other side without getting your head blown off."

"No!" he protested, honestly shocked despite the truth of the accusation, forgetting about such details as which personality he might be dealing with. "How could I have done that? I couldn't!"

He suddenly felt sure that this cyborg was not going to meekly accept his explanations and leave Dest in peace.

FOUR

"No evidence has been presented to support a hypothesis of treason," the computer said. Turner calmed slightly. His own denial of the other cyborg's accusation had been an unthinking outburst, and even to himself the computer's calm statement seemed to carry more conviction. "Release code would not have been given to cyborg unit designated 'Slant' if evidence of disloyalty existed."

"He got it by some trick," the cyborg insisted, "So he could quit, so he could surrender without getting his head blown off."

"No, I didn't," Turner insisted with equal fervor. "I got it from a recorded message that played automatically when the distress signal was sent. I can tell you what yours probably is, if you like — not the code itself, but the form it takes."

That was a safe enough offer. His release code had been his civilian name, either transmitted on the command frequency or spoken aloud three times within hearing of the computer's shipboard audio system; undoubtedly the release code for *any* IRU would be the cyborg's name, spoken three times. The Command would have no reason to vary the pattern.

He knew that, as Slant, he would have accepted such an offer instantly.

Even though he had already had misgivings about this newcomer, he was still startled and disappointed when he or she barked back, "Don't bother lying anymore, Slant. It's a trick. It's got to be."

"Negative," the computer said. Since the two parts of IRU 247 did not truly have distinct voices, it sounded to Turner as if someone were arguing with himself. "Cyborg unit designated 'Slant' is correct. Emergency systems in IRU ships include audio recording of instructions and advice from Command, including release code."

"They do?" The cyborg was plainly astonished. Turner, too, was surprised — not by the existence of the recorded message, since he had known that for years, ever since he heard it play, but that CCC-IRU 247 was aware of it. His own computer had never shown any indication that it knew of any such thing.

But then, the subject had never come up, since Slant had not known his ship had any such emergency systems, and had therefore never asked about it.

There was a moment of dead air as all three parties considered the situation. The IRU 247 cyborg was the next to speak, but Turner missed the beginning of what was said as his wife stuck her head into the kitchen.

"Sam? Are you in here?" she asked before she saw him.

Startled, Turner turned to face her; her audible voice made a sharp contrast with the internal communications. Small and light as she was, she had approached the door without alerting him with her footsteps. "Oh, hello, Parrah," he said. "Ah...could you excuse me for a moment?" He tuned himself back in to his internal communicator, switching his thoughts back from the Prauncer Anglo-Spanish he had spoken aloud to his native tongue.

"...pick you up, blow a few cities away, and then get out of here," the cyborg was saying. "I still think you're probably a deserter, but that's the Command's problem — or it would be if they were still alive. I'm just supposed to pick you up and take you to the nearest friendly port or larger unit, according to standard orders. After that it's not my problem, if there *is* any 'after that.'"

"This *is* a friendly port," Turner argued. "You can leave me here."

"No, it isn't," the other cyborg retorted immediately. "There aren't any friendly ports. I figure you and I will be cruising the stars together for the rest of our lives, Slant, but that doesn't bother me. We'll get used to it."

"Well, it sure as hell bothers *me*," Turner replied. "I don't want to leave, and there's no reason to destroy any cities. The planet's friendly."

"That's crap. Nothing's friendly. Hey, computer, how do we know this is really Slant? From what he's been saying, this could be an enemy spy we've been talking to."

"Negative. Telemetry indicates subject is cyborg unit designated 'Slant'. Probability of counterfeit sufficiently exact to deceive telemetry is minimal. All available data confirm subject identity."

That, Turner thought, was at least mildly comforting. The computer accepted that he was who he said he was, and that was a step in the right direction.

"But damn it, he says the planet's friendly!" the cyborg insisted. "He's got to be lying!"

"Information insufficient," the computer replied.

"This planet," Turner said, forcing himself to be calm, "has remained steadfastly loyal to Old Earth for more than three hundred years. Ask anybody, anywhere on Dest."

"Sam, what are you doing?" Parrah's voice was puzzled.

Turner ignored her, concentrating instead on IRU 247.

"Oh, really?" Turner could sense the cyborg's sarcasm even through the tonelessness of the communication circuit. "Then how is it that on this *friendly* planet your ship was shut down by enemy action?"

"Sam?" The puzzlement had changed to worry, and Turner could feel the faint tingle that meant she was looking at him with more than just her big brown eyes.

"Just a minute," he insisted in Anglo-Spanish, before switching back to subvocal polyglot. "My ship was shut down by a party of rebels," he improvised quickly. "However, the rightful planetary government, which remains loyal, has stamped out the rebellion."

"Hligosh!" Parrah spat, as realization of what she must be perceiving dawned. "Your demon!"

"No, it's *not* my demon," Turner said, annoyed. "Could you just wait a minute, please, Parrah?"

"Gravitational anomaly occurring in immediate vicinity of cyborg unit designated 'Slant'," the computer informed him.

"I know that," Turner said. "It's not important."

"What's going on?" the other cyborg demanded. "Computer, let me see."

Before Turner could formulate a reply, the computer demanded, "Query: Identity of unidentified individual in immediate vicinity of cyborg unit designated 'Slant'."

"She's my..." he began aloud in Anglo-Spanish. Realizing he was using both the wrong language and the wrong medium, Turner stopped and continued silently, "I mean, she's my wife. Her name is Parrah."

"Ah, so that's it!" the other cyborg said, gloating. "No wonder you don't want to leave, you've gone native. See, computer? I told you he was another damn traitor. He's gone native!"

"Well, what the hell was I supposed to do?" Turner shouted aloud in his own language. "I've been stranded here for ten years!"

"Sam!" Terror distorted Parrah's face. "What are you saying?"

"Will you all wait a minute?" he shouted in Prauncer Anglo-Spanish, wanting simultaneously to comfort his wife and to ignore her while he argued with IRU 247.

"Message not understood," the computer replied. Parrah subsided into silence, but her fright and concern were still plain on her face. The other cyborg said nothing, and Turner had no way of guessing what he or she was thinking.

He paused to collect his thoughts. The computer, he realized with some surprise, did not understand the Prauncer dialect; that seemed mildly odd, since variations of Anglo-Spanish were prevalent on at least half the colony worlds. Perhaps the local version, which he was now so familiar with, was stranger than he had remembered. His own computer had been able to interpret the language immediately, but he had initially encountered the Teyzhan dialect, not the Prauncer one, and the difference, which seemed slight to him, might be crucial. Almost certainly, however, once it had heard more, CCC-IRU 247 would be able to translate Prauncer speech, unless by some fluke its language programming had seriously deteriorated with time or had been damaged somehow.

For the moment, though, he could speak privately. He seized the opportunity.

"Listen, Parrah," he said, grabbing her by the shoulder and speaking rapidly both to get the information across quickly and to make it harder for the computer to interpret, "It's not *my* demon; I'm safe enough, it won't control me or blow my head off. It's *another* demon, though, the same kind, with another man-machine like myself. They're in orbit right now, up above the sky. I need to talk to them and convince them that Dest is friendly, so they won't have any reason to attack. I know you never saw what my ship could do, but you must have heard about it, heard what it did to Teyzha, so you must know that this ship could probably destroy all of Praunce. You've seen the crater — it might be able to do that. Even if it can't, it could certainly kill both of *us*. It accepts me as a friend, though, so I can talk it out of attacking, if you stop interrupting. Please don't disturb me again until I'm through, because they could be very dangerous. I'm sorry if I worried you, but it's all right, really it is."

The terror faded to simple concern, and her soft brown eyes blinked twice. "Are you sure it's all right, Sam?" she asked uncertainly.

"I think so."

"Should I tell anyone?"

He hesitated, then admitted, "I don't know."

She looked at him a moment longer. "Call me as soon as you can," she said, and turned and stepped back out into the living area.

Turner watched her go, relieved by her acceptance of his statements and decisions.

"What did you tell her?" the cyborg demanded. "Computer, watch for a trick of some kind — are you sure there aren't any planetary defenses?"

"No evidence of planetary defense systems has been detected unless gravitational anomalies reported previously represent unknown defense systems," the computer said, answering the second question before Turner could reply to the first.

"Yes, well, all the same, to think that a disarmed enemy can't kill you is to think a spark can't start a fire," the cyborg said. "What did you tell her, Slant?"

"I told her the truth," he replied. "She knows who I am; after all, the war is over, and Dest is loyal and at peace, and I decommissioned myself eleven years ago, local time. I told her that another IRU was arriving. I think she wants to arrange a big welcome."

That was followed by a long moment of dead air, and Turner inwardly cursed himself for that last, stupid lie; to his surprise, it was the computer who spoke first, asking, "Query: Advisability of course of action described by cyborg unit designated 'Slant'."

Before Turner could reply, the other cyborg said, "I told you, he's a traitor. Computer, to hell with picking him up, and to hell with those gravitational anomalies; I say we nuke the place *now*, before he can do anything more to screw us up."

FIVE

It was time, Turner decided after a moment of stark terror as he anticipated an immediate nuclear attack, to take the offensive. After all, what could he lose? The newcomer seemed determined not to believe him about Dest's allegiance, and so determined to destroy Dest's cities that Turner could not imagine how he could make matters much worse. The computer, at any rate, seemed willing to listen, and despite the cyborg's insistence it had not yet agreed to launch any missiles. Turner thought he might be able to keep the two divided. He did his best to force down his own confusion and uncertainty, and to focus instead on his anger.

"Oh, yeah?" he demanded, "Just who in hell do you think you are? If you're IRU 247 — and *if* you are, just what is your damn code name, anyway? If you *are* IRU 247, which I'm beginning to doubt, then *I* am the senior officer here, since 205 just happens to come before 247, and *I* give the orders. You hear me?"

"The hell you say!" the cyborg spat back immediately. "You're a stinking rebel traitor, and I'll die before I take orders from you! I don't take orders from *anyone*!"

"And I repeat, who are *you* to say that?"

Turner knew it was his imagination, but it almost seemed that he could feel the other's wordless fury in the second or so of dead air that followed.

It was the computer that replied, "This is Independent Reconnaissance Unit 247. Query: Information required by cyborg unit designated 'Slant' for satisfactory confirmation of identity of this unit." Turner felt a slight easing of tension. The computer, at least, was still ready to talk, and for the moment it was following his lead.

He had to maintain that lead. "First off," he demanded, "What's the cyborg unit's code name? I like to know who I'm talking to."

"Cyborg unit, Independent Reconnaissance Unit 247, is designated 'Flame'," the computer said.

"Flame. Good. And where are you now?"

"In synchronous orbit over planetary equator."

That explained why the signal strength had stabilized. Turner remembered that his own ship had had a habit of using low orbits that kept it below the horizon, and out of contact, much of the time. Dest had no relay satellites or Heaviside layer, so any sort of broadcast communication was limited to line of sight. He wondered why the two computers differed on that. Was it related to CCC-IRU 205's suicidal tendencies? Did it mean that CCC-IRU 247 was *not* suicidal?

Or did CCC-IRU 247 have its own aberrations?

A low orbit made quick landings or attacks easy, but made communication difficult. A synchronous orbit made communication easy, but landings or attacks would take longer, since the ship had much farther to descend.

IRU 247's synchronous orbit implied that, at least so far, the computer was more interested in communication than combat, regardless of what its cyborg might think.

"Good," Turner said. He tried to think of another demand or question, but nothing came readily to mind. "Stay there for now," he finished at last, rather lamely.

"Why should we?" the Flame cyborg demanded.

"Because I'm senior and I told you to, damn it!" Turner shot back, annoyed.

"But you're decommissioned," Flame said, gloating. "You said so yourself. You're not senior to anybody anymore, you lousy deserter!"

Turner realized he had slipped up. He had, indeed, said that he had decommissioned himself; he could not deny that now. Even if the computer might somehow come to accept his version of reality over its own cyborg's beliefs, which seemed unlikely, it could scarcely do so if he were to prove himself a liar.

"You're right," he admitted. "I forgot."

The computer would be programmed to accept human failings, within reason, particularly from civilians — and by his own admission, he was a civilian. Flame, he guessed, would know that he was using any argument he could in order to save his own life, but the computer would be more trusting. It had identified him as an IRU cyborg, which meant he was an ally, to be given the benefit of the doubt.

And in the long run he figured that it didn't much matter what Flame thought. The computer controlled the ship and its armament.

"All right," he said, "I'm not the senior officer anymore, you're right. I made an honest human mistake about that. I'm a loyal citizen though, and a veteran, even if I am a civilian, and you still owe me a little respect. I've been here eleven years; I know this planet, and you don't. Dest is completely loyal to Old Earth, and destroying its cities *would* be treason, far worse than mere desertion or surrender or whatever you've been accusing me of. It would be actively aiding and abetting the enemy."

"That's stupid," Flame retorted immediately. "There *are* no loyal planets! Old Earth was destroyed; how can anyone be loyal to a cinder?"

Turner did not allow himself to relax sufficiently to gloat, but the other cyborg had made a mistake. "If a planet's population can't be loyal, then how can *you* be loyal?" he replied.

There was a pause of almost five seconds before the Flame cyborg replied, "All right, you bastard! So you think you can out-talk me. I don't care. I *know* this planet's just as foul as all the rest, and I'm going to see it burn; you can't talk your way out of *that*. If it's so loyal, why didn't anyone else answer our call? Why aren't there any Terran ships around?"

Turner responded immediately, "Because the civilization here hasn't got space travel or electronic communications! It's been cut off for centuries, idiot!"

"Don't you call me an idiot, traitor!"

Although the signal did not convey tone or reflect actual spoken volume, it did somehow convey emphasis, and from the emphasis on Flame's words Turner was sure he or she was screaming aloud. "I..."

The transmission was cut off abruptly, and for several seconds Turner was on the verge of panic, wondering what was happening thirty-some thousand kilometers over his head. Was the computer launching its missiles? Was the Flame cyborg arguing with the computer? Would the city of Praunce vanish in a nuclear fireball at any moment?

The computer spoke at last. "Cyborg unit designated Flame has manifested signs of unreasonable agitation, and tranquilizers have been administered. Communication was interrupted by inadvertent removal of control cable from cyborg unit. Internal discussion of situation in progress. Stand by."

Turner breathed a little more easily; the computer seemed to have accepted that Dest was friendly, if it was discussing the situation instead of launching the missiles Flame was surely demanding. That mention of tranquilizers was also encouraging; the computer must know that its cyborg was not rational.

And Flame had apparently jerked about violently enough to pull the plug from the neck socket. That would take some doing.

Flame struck Turner as paranoid, convinced that the universe was hostile and refusing to accept any evidence to the contrary. He supposed that the long isolation aboard ship was responsible.

He also thought that he and Flame seemed to irritate each other more than they should, even in their present inimical situation. He was unsure whether it was simply a personality clash, or something else, something more significant. Whatever it was, it wouldn't make it any easier to keep the peace.

"Whatever you say," he said. "Let me know if I can help."

"Oh, you can help all right!" The Flame cyborg was back on line. "You can explain to us how a planet too primitive even for radio can have those anti-gravity flares, whatever they are. This place isn't primitive.

You're all just hiding everything. All the machines must be underground or something, all the communications by wire or fiber or tightbeam."

Turner had forgotten, for the moment, that the ship's sensors reacted to every use of wizardry on the entire planet.

"No, really," he hastened to explain. "There are no machines. That's not really anti-gravity. It's a misreading; my ship picked it up coming in, too. That's why we landed. But it's not anti-gravity, it's of biological origin — a mutation indigenous to Dest."

"Oh, sure!"

Before either Flame or Turner could say anything more, the computer interrupted.

"Query: Nature of mutation."

"That's hard to explain." He had no intention of actually explaining. Wizardry might be useful as an unsuspected ace in the hole later on, and if he explained it now the computer might decide it sounded too dangerous. And Flame probably would not believe him in any case; quite aside from her demonstrated skepticism, psionic wizardry was pretty incredible. He hesitated. "If you land I might be able to show you."

Sooner or later, he realized, he was going to have to deal more directly with this ship and its cyborg pilot, one way or another. They were obviously not going to simply take his word and leave peacefully. He might be able to talk the ship out of attacking, but unfortunately he had no authority to order it to leave — no one on the planet possessed any authority it would recognize — and it was plain that Flame was not going to let it leave Dest until matters had been settled permanently, and probably fatally for one side or the other.

Flame's personality worried him considerably; the cyborg was clearly somewhat paranoid. That did not bode well. If it came down to the worst case, to kill or be killed, a starship would be an easier target on the ground, much easier — especially if he could somehow separate the cyborg and the ship. The cyborg, superhuman as he or she was, could carry only so much weaponry, inflict only so much damage, and the ship, without the cyborg to advise it, would be stupid. Even the best military computers, when it came down to it, were stupid.

This one was no exception. It mulled over Turner's suggestion for so long that the cyborg replied first.

"You want us to land?" Flame asked suspiciously.

"I don't really care," Turner replied, assuming a false nonchalance. Anger and attempts at command had gotten him nowhere with Flame; he hoped that apparent unconcern would serve him better. "Just so long as you don't start killing innocent people without even taking a look at them. You came here to help me, but I don't need help, so you don't have any business here. As far as I'm concerned, you can just turn around and go back out of the system. If you want, I'm pretty sure I can figure out your release code and you can go home."

As soon as he framed that final word he knew he had slipped up, but it was too late to recall it.

"Oh, right!" Flame's derision needed no tone to be plain. "Home where? I have no home. You know as well as I do that everything I ever knew is gone. Even if Old Earth were still there, which it isn't, it's been about three hundred years, hasn't it?"

"More than three hundred," Turner admitted. "You're right. Well, that doesn't matter; you're here, so you might as well land and stay for a while. You can settle here the way I did; it's not a bad world. A little primitive, maybe, but not bad."

"I don't intend to settle anywhere! I'm going to keep going until I've killed off every damn rebel I can find."

"Until you've exterminated the human race, you mean?" Turner retorted, "You seem to think everyone's a rebel!"

Flame ignored his sarcasm. "Yes, damn you, I'd kill them all if I could! They put me up here with no one but this infernal idiot machine, and *left* me here, and I'll kill every last one of you! I'll blast this planet clean as soon as I can get this stinking computer to obey me!"

Turner was taken aback by the cyborg's vehemence. He wondered how sane Flame actually was, whether this hostility and irrationality were simply a reaction to long confinement, or the manifestation of a real and permanent psychosis. Flame had surely been alone in space for a very long time, nurturing an intense hatred, building up anger and looking for someone to vent it on, and the result might be genuine, lasting insanity. Flame felt betrayed, Turner realized, betrayed that his or her world had been destroyed, leaving him or her alone and stranded.

Turner could think of no reply, and Flame seemed content not to follow up this outburst, so it was the computer that was the next to transmit.

"Unable to determine acceptability of proposed course of action," the computer said.

"What course of action?" Turner asked.

"Destruction of cities on planet, as recommended by cyborg unit designated 'Flame'."

"It's *not* acceptable! Dest is loyal!"

"Unable to determine accuracy of statement by cyborg unit designated 'Slant'."

"Why?"

"Restate question."

"Why are you unable to determine my accuracy?"

"Information insufficient."

Turner shifted his weight, realizing for the first time that he had been leaning heavily against the kitchen table for so long that the back of his left thigh was numb. He was uncertain whether the computer meant that it had insufficient information to determine whether Dest was loyal, or that it had insufficient information to know whether Turner was lying.

The distinction didn't matter, he decided, and instead of worrying the matter further he said, "Well, you aren't going to get any more useful information from up there, are you? You'll have to land and gather it on the surface."

"Query: Nature of phenomenon registered as gravitational anomalies."

"I told you, I can't tell you that."

"Query: Reason for impossibility of describing phenomenon registered as gravitational anomalies."

"You don't have the necessary technical vocabulary. I'd need to show you everything."

"Demonstrations may be performed while vessel is in orbit. All optical data received by cyborg unit designated 'Slant' are included in cyborg telemetry."

Turner had forgotten that, or perhaps had not fully realized that this computer had complete access to all the information that his own computer could have received from his implanted equipment. Anything he saw, the computer could see.

"Well, there's another reason too," he said, playing for time.

"Query: Additional reason."

"Well, as I told you, it's a mutation."

"Affirmative."

"But it might have possible military uses, so it's been classified as secret. By the local government, I mean, which is loyal to Old Earth, so that in effect it's been classified by the government of Old Earth."

The computer hesitated for an instant before replying, "Acknowledged. IRU 247 carries Level Four clearance."

"Ah!" Turner said, getting into the spirit of his yarn. "But you don't have the necessary 'need to know'. And besides, we don't want to transmit any data off-planet without the proper encryption, and we have no encrypting equipment on this planet. If we tell you about it, the transmission will drift on out and might be intercepted by the enemy, eventually. If you land and observe on the surface there won't have to be any questionable transmission."

After a brief pause, the computer acknowledged, "Affirmative."

"What a lot of crap!" Flame said, clearly and emphatically. He or she immediately added, "But it's fine with me, traitor, if you want me to land. I'll land, and maybe I'll get to kill you myself, with my own hands. We'll find those anti-gravity gadgets, whatever they are, and whatever else you're hiding down there, and then we'll blow it all to bits." A broken, staticky noise came over the mental circuit that Turner identified only with difficulty as laughter.

"Fine with me, too," he said, ignoring the threats. "Tell me when and where you'll be landing, and I'll try to meet you."

"You do that, Slant," Flame replied, "You just do that. We'll let you know. IRU 247, over and out."

Sudden internal silence fell. Turner stood, flexed his left leg to help restore the circulation, then, ignoring the twinges, limped out of the kitchen looking for Parrah.

He hurried. Wherever IRU 247 landed, he wanted to be there to meet it. He was very much afraid that if he were not, Flame would find an excuse to start killing people.

SIX

In the control cabin of her starship, thirty-six thousand kilometers above Dest's equator, Flame stared belligerently at the plastic holographic poster clipped to the forward bulkhead. She had not yet completely lost touch with reality, and still knew that the sneering, black-haired man in the picture was only a long-dead video idol of her teen years, that he was not real, not connected to the computer, but she found it easier to talk to him, to argue with him, than with the disembodied voice in her head or with the blank beige-carpeted walls. She knew where the computer really was — she had crawled into the access shaft that led into its core many times — but she had never really been able to accept the ceramic sheets of circuitry as the source of the mental voice that was her only companion.

"Slant can't hear us anymore, can he?" she asked the poster.

"Negative," the computer replied.

She nodded. "Good. Now what?" she demanded aloud.

The video star's expression did not change, but Flame twisted her head almost imperceptibly, unconscious of her own action, so that his thin lips shifted slightly as the computer said, "Landing may be made at discretion of cyborg unit." The motion added to the illusion that she was speaking to the poster, and not to the ship. She had been doing this for almost a decade and had completely forgotten that she did it at all.

"Do we really want to land?" she asked, with mixed apprehension and wistfulness. "We could just drop our last few warheads and then get out of here."

"Negative. No action may be taken against this planet until affiliation is determined. Planet may be friendly."

The flat, silent words did not fit the arrogant face before her; she had not consciously recognized the incongruity for years, but now it suddenly struck her anew.

"Oh, screw that," she said tiredly. "No place is friendly. What missiles have we got left?" The poster's eyes, once intensely blue but now somewhat faded, stared blindly back at her, and she looked away.

Sometimes, she thought, she hated not just the enemy, but everything, including the ship and even herself. The man in the poster had been dead for centuries, and she despised and envied him for it.

"Remaining shipboard armament includes two units ordnance model MTN-two, serial numbers zero-three-zero-nine-four-three and zero-three-zero-nine-four-four, nuclear warhead, tactical, two hundred kiloton yield, fully optional detonation systems; one unit ordnance model

MTN-four, serial number nine-five-five-one-zero-one, nuclear warhead, tactical, eighty kiloton yield, pressure fuse; six units ordnance..."

"Speed it up, stupid," she said, her moment of weakness past. The tranquilizers were wearing off. "Three tactical nukes; any other big stuff left?"

"Restate question."

"Any other nuclear warheads?" Her eyes had wandered across the carpeted ceiling and extruded white plastic lightbars, but now her gaze returned to the poster for lack of anywhere better to focus. The man's black jumpsuit and black hair stood out sharply against the poster's yellow background and the beige of the bulkhead.

"Negative," the computer said. "All other nuclear armaments have been expended."

"That's what I thought. So we could take out three small cities — which isn't too bad, since this planet only has one really big one, and that's already radioactive enough that even one of those little jobs should be enough to push it over the edge and make it uninhabitable. We couldn't wipe out everything, though, could we?"

"Shipboard armaments insufficient to destroy all inhabitants of subject planet. No action may be taken against this planet until affiliation is determined. Planet may be friendly."

Flame ignored the computer's insistence on the possibility of not attacking; she stared calculatingly at the blue eyes and crooked mouth. "Any way we could winter them?" she asked, "Screw up their climate somehow? Drop an asteroid on them or something?"

"Negative. Ship's present firepower insufficient to trigger nuclear winter. System is extremely low in celestial debris. Ship systems insufficient for adequate utilization of available resources. No action may be taken against this planet until affiliation is determined. Planet may be friendly."

"How do you suppose that big city got so radioactive, if the planet's friendly?" she demanded, tired of the computer's repetition.

"Information insufficient. Evidence of extensive use of nuclear weapons exists."

"And you don't think it was the Command that sent those weapons?"

"Information insufficient. Possibility of assault by either friendly, enemy, or neutral forces exists. Recorded cultural and technological level of this system at time of initiation of hostilities between Old Earth and rebel worlds does not preclude possibility of indigenous dispute using high-yield nuclear warheads delivered within planetary atmosphere, and no proof of assault from above atmosphere has been found. Recorded political and economic situation of this system at time of initiation of hostilities between Old Earth and rebel worlds does not preclude possibility of assault by rebel fleet."

"That's crap. It was Old Earth that blasted them, I'm sure of it, and it's our duty to finish the job."

"Evidence insufficient to confirm or deny cyborg unit's hypothesis."

She studied the poster for a moment longer, watching the narrow, high-cheekboned face and lank black hair; the man in the poster did not move, but stared back with calm self-assurance. She lay back on the acceleration couch and stared at the curved, blank ceiling instead. "I could insist, you know," she said. "I could give you a choice of nuking this planet or being eaten alive." She wondered what Slant, so proud of obtaining his release code, would have thought of a certain little arrangement of hers. She had not been willing to go on indefinitely as her computer's slave, any more than he had, but she hadn't settled for just finding a way out from under. She hadn't betrayed the Command and Old Earth and herself. She had taken control herself. If she died, the computer went with her. If she lived, she could destroy the computer any time she wanted badly enough to destroy it.

Her doomsday device was a by-product of the attack on the second planet IRU 247 had obliterated. That had taken place several years ago — several years of shipboard time, and over a century of planetary time.

It had been a lovely attack. That planet's inhabitants had been few, huddled in a handful of cities, and the cities had all vanished in nuclear firestorms.

Despite their low population they had maintained an impressive level of technology. One of their suborbital fighters had managed a lucky shot before IRU 247 blew it into fragments, and had landed a breeder lamprey missile on the hull of Flame's ship.

The lamprey missile's tiny cybernetic offspring had tunneled their way into the ship in a dozen places before the breeder machine could be removed, and Flame had had to hunt them down one by one and destroy them with a hand-held snark.

The computer's programming had been seriously damaged. More than one of the electronic termites had been systematically destroying computer memory when Flame located them, and not all of the lost material could be replaced from the surviving back-ups.

The computer had not judged the damage to be critical, and had carried on.

Flame, also unaware of the actual extent of the damage, had watched the computer a little more carefully after that, but had never noticed anything seriously wrong. The machine had seemed stupider than before, but it had always seemed stupid, and a little more did not seem to matter.

Of course, she knew that she was not really the best judge of the computer's fitness; she was no technician. Two of her alternate personalities were, but she had no intention of committing suicide even temporarily by allowing any of them to take over. She didn't really believe that, once freed, another personality would ever allow her back into control. Her other selves were alien, and therefore had to be presumed hostile. She would have to deal with the possibility that the computer was seriously damaged on her own, without the aid of anything the Command had buried in her brain.

She had taken precautions, in case the damage was worse than she knew. When she had located the last of the electronic termites she had not turned the snark on it, but had instead trapped it in an equipment case. Later, after she had watched the spreading smoke clouds that would bring on a nuclear winter, after she had seen the glowing radioactive craters where the cities had stood, after she had sent her ship out of orbit and back out into interstellar space, she had carefully studied the termite.

It was a simple machine, really; it had, after all, been manufactured by a mere missile. Even with her limited technical skills, she had easily located its power supply and cut the main lead.

That had deactivated the device. She had then patched a spare timer into the power line, set so that if the timer ever registered zero the circuit would be completed and the termite reactivated.

The computer had watched all this without comment, accepting her explanation that she was studying the enemy's technology. Only when she then slipped the termite into the computer's central core and coded the access hatch to open only to her own thumbprint, and not to computer commands or service equipment, did the computer object.

By then it was too late.

"It's just a precaution," she had explained. "You might have been damaged more than we think. I'll just reset the timer every so often, and it'll be fine. It will only count down to zero if I get killed, and I'll only get killed if you screw up. It will keep the enemy from capturing you intact if I die."

The computer had objected, but had been unable to do anything. The service robots could not get through the coded access hatch. The termite had stayed in place, and, as she had promised, every so often Flame reset it to its maximum of ninety-nine hours, fifty-nine minutes, and fifty-nine seconds.

As she saw it, it simply kept things in balance. The computer had always been able to kill her by means of the thermite charge in the base of her skull; now she could kill the computer just by doing nothing. If she died, the computer and ship went with her. That seemed only fair.

Slant might have gotten his release code somewhere, but using it had robbed him of his ship and his conditioning. That left him alive, but virtually powerless. Such a bargain did not appeal to her. She was happy with her own little device.

The computer occasionally complained that the termite's presence created programming conflicts, but she had never let that concern her.

The computer had always been stupid, as far as she was concerned. It still was. How could it argue so much, when she held the upper hand as she did? She reminded it every so often of the termite's presence, but it did not seem very concerned.

"Acknowledged," was all it said, as usual.

She sighed. The computer's reaction was scarcely satisfying. She was not yet ready to press the issue to its ultimate conclusion, however; if she destroyed the computer she would be dooming herself, as well, and she was not ready to commit suicide just yet. Not quite yet, and not without taking as much as she could with her. She had been conditioned strongly against suicide, and that conditioning still lingered.

"Do you believe Slant's story?" she asked the computer. "It seems to me he should be helping us, not arguing and giving us that crap about friendly natives." She felt a new twinge of anger and pain at the thought of this latest betrayal. When she had first heard the distress call she had told herself that Slant was certainly long dead, that it meant nothing beyond choosing her next target for her, but she had secretly cherished a hope that she might have found a companion, a fellow in misery. When Slant had turned up alive her hopes had soared, but then he had revealed himself to be another traitor, like so many others, and she had plunged back into her morass of hatred, anger, and self-pity.

"Term 'believe' not applicable," the computer told her.

"No, you stupid machine, I guess it's not. You don't believe in anything, you just do what the Command told you, whether it makes sense or not." She lay silently thinking for a moment, then asked, "Do you think he was telling the truth about what happened to his ship?"

"Insufficient evidence."

"Could the ship be down there somewhere, hidden?" His ship might somehow provide sufficient evidence of Slant's treason to convince even a computer.

"Wreckage of IRU-class starship has been located approximately one hundred twenty kilometers to planetary west of largest known metropolitan area."

She sat up, startled. "It has? Damn it, you stupid machine, why didn't you tell me earlier?"

"Cyborg unit did not previously request information."

She snorted derisively, at both herself and the computer. "Do you think it's Slant's ship?" she asked.

"Affirmative."

"You said it was wreckage; how bad is it? Does anything look salvageable?"

"Information insufficient."

That was annoyingly unhelpful. Obviously, the wreck had not provided any clear evidence of treason, or the computer would have noticed and mentioned it. There might be subtle proof, of course, something not visible from orbit — a recording, perhaps.

The ship's presence suggested other possibilities as well, though, and a new enthusiasm fired her.

"Do you think we could get it off the ground? Maybe it still has a few unfired missiles of its own!" The prospect of greater numbers of deaths excited her.

"Negative. Evidence indicates destroyed IRU-class starship is beyond repair capacity of this ship."

"What about missiles?" she persisted, "Think it has any? And if it does, is there any way we could use them?"

"Information insufficient."

She sighed. "Damn, you're stupid. Damn, damn, *damn*. Ever since that lamprey missile got us, you've been a complete idiot. Not that you were brilliant before that. It's a good thing I rigged that termite the way I did, or I wouldn't be able to trust you at *all*."

She pressed her hands together, thinking. "All right, I guess we land as close to the wreck as we can and look it over, right? If the missiles are there, we can have the service robots load them aboard, and maybe we can take out the whole planet after all." She smiled at the thought of another barrage, of watching the mushroom clouds boil up, of knowing that she had destroyed more of her enemies, and swept another world clean of the infection called humanity. It was the only pleasure she had left.

Of course, afterward she would be depressed for weeks. She knew that from previous experience. It was worth it, though, particularly since the computer would treat her depression with the ship's dwindling stock of euphorics, to which she was not permitted access otherwise. During the worst spells the computer would sedate her, which was, in a way, even better. The machines kept her alive, whether she wanted to live or not, but they did not always insist on keeping her conscious.

And the initial thrill of watching the atomic fires was worth the depression that followed.

"No action may be taken against this planet until affiliation is determined. Planet may be friendly," the computer insisted.

"Yeah, sure." She knew better. All of humanity was her enemy, for allowing her to remain an IRU cyborg for so long. "Look, I want to land as close to the wreck as we can. And you can call Slant back, tell him we've picked a landing site, and he can meet us there." She smiled again. If Slant had any guilty secrets, his ship would be the place to look for them, certainly. She would find some way to avenge herself on that lying, self- righteous bastard before she blew the cities away. How could he refuse to join her? How could he leave her alone aboard her ship?

It would serve him right if she killed him with one of the missiles from his own ship.

"Affirmative," the computer said. She sensed, very faintly, a slight alteration of some indescribable sort that she realized was the computer opening the internal communication circuit to broadcast. She had never noticed the difference before; it would have been very easy to miss if she had not been alertly expecting it.

"Landing site has been chosen," the computer said, and she knew that it was speaking to Slant, not to herself.

A moment later the voice in her head asked, "Where are you landing, then?"

For an instant the similarity of Slant's mental "voice" to the computer's sent a shiver of uncertainty through her. Was all this really happening? Had she really found another IRU cyborg, or was she just imagining it? Was the computer playing games with her? Had she gone mad? Had one of her other personalities somehow escaped, without her knowledge and against her will, and programmed this whole series of events into the computer as some sort of obscure joke?

She had no contact with anything outside the ship, anything at all, except through the computer. There were no portholes, no displays not run by the computer. She had no way of knowing that she was really orbiting a new planet. She had no way of knowing, really, that she had ever left Mars. The images she saw in her head looked unimaginably real, more real than anything she could remember, more real than the interior of the ship, somehow, but she knew that that could all be trickery, could be special effects, or recorded images. She could not *know* that those stars were real, that the blue-white planet below her was real, that she had really gone anywhere. She had watched the destruction of all human life on two inhabited planets, destruction she had ordered, but had it been real? Had those impossibly bright flashes, the glowing clouds that rose, darkened, and slowly dissipated, been real?

Were there really any inhabited planets out there, anywhere?

Maybe this was all still part of her training, the endless years in her ship all a hypnotic suggestion. The whole horrible thing could just be a test of her loyalty, to see whether she would yield under extreme circumstances.

Maybe she had imagined *everything*, her entire life, and the reality was that the universe consisted of nothing but herself and her ship, no stars, no planets, no Command, no other life at all.

She, herself, might not really exist. She thought, but did that really mean she was real?

No, she told herself firmly, such thoughts were all just daydreams and wish- fulfillment. She had been through all these fantasies before, many times, but they weren't real, and she knew she must not allow herself to believe them, even for a moment. She could go mad if she believed them, she knew that. Mars and Old Earth were real, and dead, and she was alone in the void with her ship and her computer. She knew that those two planets she had attacked had been real, because one of them had sent the lamprey missile, and she had seen the missile's termites with her own eyes, had captured and rewired one with her own hands. That had been real and solid.

Of course, that had been aboard the ship, and could have been part of some test.

She knew it wasn't, though. The outside universe was real, it had to be. And in any case it did not really matter. Whatever the truth was, she had to go on as she always had. She had nothing else. The war machines would not let her die, would not let her surrender, and she had to prove herself. She was loyal, the only loyal one left, and she would fight on against the bastards who had destroyed her life and trapped her here — the rebels, and the traitors who had allowed the rebels to win.

Then she realized abruptly that perhaps she need not be trapped much longer. If she landed, she could leave the ship. She had never done that before. The other two planets she had attacked from orbit, without landing, since they had admitted outright to being disloyal. The computer had monitored their communications, had asked data banks which side the planets had taken in the Rebellion, and had been told, and the people of those two worlds had died, had all died with Flame watching, picking the targets and launching the missiles. She had never left the ship, never landed.

She had never left the ship before, not once since she first boarded it back on Mars.

On this planet, though, she could leave the ship, breathe fresh air, see the sky.

A thrill of mixed anticipation and terror ran through her at the thought. She knew then that whatever she eventually did to the planet, she *had* to land first and leave the ship. She could not bear to miss this chance, could not bear to fire her missiles and turn back into space again without landing, even had the computer allowed it.

She would be able to see for herself that the outside universe still actually existed. She would feel the wind on her skin, smell the trees and the earth, see the veins of leaves and the clouds overhead. If she wanted to she could let her termite booby trap destroy the computer, without necessarily leaving herself to die alone in interstellar space.

A ferocious longing excitement grew quickly within her, piling upon itself like a building thunderstorm.

"All right, Slant," she said, keeping her mouth tightly closed as if to hold her excitement inside, "We've decided to check out the wreckage of your ship. We'll be there as soon as we can get down. See you there!"

For an instant there was no reply, but then Turner protested, "That's two days' ride from here!"

"Is it?" She smiled to herself. "That's fine, then. Two days should give me a chance to look around a little before you get there and start arguing." She giggled nervously, then burst out laughing, though she was unsure what had amused her. She would be leaving the ship soon, but that was not funny. Terrifying, and exciting, yes, but not funny. "Computer," she said, still smiling and ignoring Turner's continuing protests, "shut that idiot off and take us down."

SEVEN

"Talk to Arzadel first, Sam," Parrah said.

Though she was forcing herself to appear calm, her voice trembled, and she rubbed her hands nervously against her hips. They had both remained standing despite the presence of chairs on either side of the small decorative table Turner had used to sort his supplies.

"You talk to him," Turner replied, not looking at her. "I haven't got time. They'll be landing out by my ship any minute now, and I need to get there fast. I don't want them to see me flying, since they already think that something strange is going on, so I need to get there by horse. As it is, they'll be down long before I arrive, maybe *days* before, and I just hope they don't talk to some wandering half-wit or mutant who'll say the wrong thing before I get there." Turner sighted down the barrel of the rapid-fire rocket rifle he had selected, decided it would do, and slung the weapon on his shoulder, the strap snug against the heavy winter coat he had dug out of mothballs. Where he was going nobody would care whether he used a coat or a heat-field, and a coat took much less effort. He had also exchanged his wizard's robe for a woolen tunic and leather pants, and had unearthed his sturdiest pair of boots and a pair of thin leather gloves. He had been unable to locate a decent hat or scarf. His long hair and beard would have to do to keep his head and face warm.

He thought of the extensive wardrobe he had once had aboard his starship, and puzzled for a moment over what had become of the cold-weather gear it had included. The sheepskin and leather coat he now wore was Prauncer-made, not something he had brought with him, and he could not recall what he had done, if anything, with the various garments from the ship. One of the lightweight impermeable-polymer parkas or body-suits would have been welcome, but so far as he could remember he had foolishly left them in the wreckage.

He marveled at his own stupidity, glancing derisively at his image in a nearby mirror. He looked positively medieval in the knee-length, high-collared coat, and the sleek, flat finish of the rocket rifle was startlingly incongruous.

"I don't like this," Parrah said, eyeing the rifle nervously. "I don't like anything about it."

"I don't like it either," Turner agreed. "But it's happening, and I've got to do what I can to keep that lunatic from blowing us all into radioactive dust."

"You really don't want me to come with you?" Her voice was wistful, not pleading; she already knew what he would say.

He looked across the little table at her. Her narrow face seemed even longer than usual, thanks to her worried expression. Her straight black hair was in disarray from helping him burrow through their storeroom. He leaned over and kissed her lightly. "No, I don't," he said. "At least, not right now. Someone's got to look after the kids, and tell the other wizards where I've gone and what's happening. I can make better time alone, and besides, I don't think this Flame person would like it if I brought anyone else along. I'm the only one who knows anything much about IRUs or Old Earth, so it has to be me who goes. I'm not happy about that, but it's the truth. Is that horse I asked for ready?"

"It should be; I mind-spoke to Haiger ten minutes ago, and I think I was clear enough. It should be waiting on the street."

"Good." Telepathy was one of the wizardly arts he had never really gotten the hang of; his own mental aura was so distorted by his cyborg parts that he had far more difficulty in matching it to other brains than did any of the wizards native to Dest. He had always let Parrah handle all the long-range communication for the family — or at least, all the long-range *magical* communication. She was good at it, very good indeed; telepathy was her personal specialty. She could communicate over almost five kilometers, under ideal conditions, which was really exceptional.

As far as his own telepathic sensitivity went, he was lucky if he could tell lies from truth when speaking face to face.

He ran a final check on his hastily gathered supplies. The rifle rested comfortably on his shoulder, a knife and laser — its charge of 20 percent the best he could find out of all his energy weapons — hung on his belt, under the coat. He had a good supply of food, most of it dried fruit and dried, salted meat, tucked away in the various large pockets that adorned the coat, both inside and out. A small black plastic pack on his back, salvaged from his ship, held a high-tensile line, two hundred rounds of ammunition, and a few other items. Satisfied, he stepped over and opened a window. Cold air blew in on his face; he paused.

"Good-bye," he called back over his shoulder, "I love you."

"Be careful," Parrah called in reply.

"I will," he answered, then stepped out over the sill into space.

Parrah watched silently as he hovered for an instant, then plummeted out of sight.

He let himself fall almost half the height of the tower before he slowed his descent, and even then he sank more quickly than usual, hitting the cobbled pavement with an ankle-jarring bump.

He had half expected the computer to notice his use of magic, to point out the gravitational anomaly; he was ready to argue about it. Using magic was the only way to get down from his tower.

The computer said nothing. Perhaps, he thought, it had not noticed. It might have been somewhere in its approach path where it could not keep a close watch on him.

In any case, he was down safely. He looked around at the nearly deserted street. The cold had driven most people inside. The chill was harsh on his face, and he threw up a small, mild heat-field.

The horse he had asked for was there, and Haiger stood beside it. Tall and gangling, looking bony even in his flowing black wizard's robe, he was holding the animal's bridle and looking very worried.

"Sam, are you all right?" Haiger asked, staring at the rifle muzzle projecting above Turner's shoulder.

"I'm fine," Turner replied sharply.

"You came down awfully fast," Haiger suggested tentatively.

"I'm in a hurry." He took the reins and lifted his foot into the stirrup.

"Is there anything I can do to help? Parrah didn't tell me what you're doing, but she was worried —"

"I *know* she's worried!" Turner interrupted, suddenly annoyed. As he swung himself into the saddle he said, "Do you think I don't know my own wife? *I'm* worried. She'll tell you all about it, but I just don't have any time." He turned the horse's head toward the city's western gate.

Haiger was still stubbornly holding the bridle. Turner sighed, and forced himself to calm down. "Listen, Haiger," he said. "This is really urgent; let go of the horse. I don't have time to explain. Go home and give Ahnao my best — or if you have to, go talk to Parrah, and she'll tell you all about it. But whatever you do, for now, just let go, will you?"

Reluctantly, Haiger released his hold, and Turner spurred the horse forward.

Haiger watched him go.

Before Turner was out of sight, Haiger felt a gentle psychic pressure. He let himself slip into the partial trance necessary for long-range mind-speech.

"*Is he gone?*" Parrah's voice asked silently in his head.

Haiger gave a wordless, affirmative response.

"Are you busy? Or Ahnao?"

"*No,*" Haiger replied, "*Not particularly. Why?*"

"*I need someone to look after the children; could you and Ahnao handle them for a few days?*"

"*You're going after him?*"

"*Of course!*"

Haiger sighed. He doubted that Sam had wanted Parrah to follow. He still didn't know what was happening, but if Sam had wanted Parrah along, he would have taken her with him, Haiger was sure.

That was typical of Parrah. He was inexpressibly glad that his own wife, Ahnao, had more sense and would not go running off hither and yon when told not to. Ahnao was Awlmeian, and believed women should be submissive and concern themselves primarily with family and children — though she was still a wizard in her own right, and still had the spirit to speak her mind when she felt strongly about something.

Parrah was from Praunce, where the sexes were more nearly equal, especially among the wizards, but she carried her independence to extremes that her origin could not justify. No one else in Praunce carried equality of the sexes as far as Parrah and Sam did; women were allowed their opportunities, certainly, but everyone — except Sam and Parrah — knew that men, being bigger and stronger and less susceptible to emotional upset, were still in charge. Nor was her independence Parrah's only quirk. Haiger sometimes suspected that nobody but Sam, with his alien and radical ideas on a variety of subjects, would ever have married her. Certainly Haiger himself never would have.

She and Sam got along well, though, which puzzled Haiger; despite their preachments, how could they manage without one or the other being in charge? It simply didn't seem practical. If they voted on everything, how could they break the inevitable frequent ties?

Somebody had to be in charge. It didn't much matter who, but Haiger knew the only alternative to authority to be chaos. Praunce's empire was founded on that belief.

Well, it was not his problem. Right now, the prospect of adding Parrah's three children to his own two was his problem.

Ahnao would not mind, he knew. She loved kids. *"All right,"* he mind-spoke resignedly. *"We'll babysit for you."* He paused, then added as an afterthought, *"But check with Arzadel first, all right?"*

"Thank you," she said. *"I will. I was planning to in any case — I'll probably want to talk to the whole Council. I wanted to ask you about taking care of the children first, though. Please come up as soon as you can; you can watch them while I look for Arzadel."*

Haiger nodded, though he knew she could not see him.

He was halfway up the side of the tower when something flashed through the corner of his field of vision; he turned in midair to see a narrow line of vivid orange cutting rapidly across the sky, its head wider, brighter, and yellower, the tail trailing away gradually and fading at last into invisibility.

This vision was so sudden, so silent, and gone so quickly that Haiger was almost convinced that he had imagined it when the thunderclap and shockwave rocked him back, almost flinging him against the side of the tower.

"Hligosh!" he said, "What was that?"

He was alone in mid-air; no one answered. He continued his ascent, more worried than ever.

EIGHT

Turner was not yet out of the city when he saw the streak of fire across the southwestern sky, its appearance followed a moment later by a bone-jarring sonic boom. He turned and stared, shocked. IRU 247 was obviously not concerned with stealth. His own initial landing, as Slant, had been a good deal quieter — he had come in in a relatively slow glide, not at supersonic speed with heatshields blazing. Flame and CCC- IRU 247 were a good bit more reckless. Didn't such a flamboyant landing violate some part of the computer's programming? They were simply asking to be shot at, had Dest had any planetary defenses at all. Whatever Flame might have claimed, he or she was acting as if she or he believed no such defenses existed.

But then, why had the cyborg argued when Turner had said the planet was technologically backward, if he or she accepted the absence of ground defenses?

Perhaps Flame accepted nothing of the kind; perhaps IRU 247 *wanted* to encounter ground fire, a fight of some sort, an excuse to attack the planet, whatever the consequences.

A chill slipped through Turner's coat and heat-field, or perhaps arose somewhere within. He spurred the horse to greater speed, telekinetically boosting it forward and shoving aside the pedestrians in his path in extravagant waste of his magical energies. If IRU 247 was watching now, he would explain the gravitational anomalies later.

He doubted that he would need to. IRU 247 was down by now, he was sure, landed somewhere in the forests to the west of Praunce, and it could not freely scan the planet's gravity field from the surface. At most, it could watch for anomalies in the area immediately surrounding itself; further away the surrounding trees and hills would block its sensors. It could still monitor his cyborg systems, of course; it could see what he saw, hear what he heard, and feel what he felt, if he was above its broadcast horizon, so that he dared not fly. Flight was obvious, though, while other wizardry generally was not. His internal equipment had once included gravity sensors of some sort, sensitive enough to detect magic in use, but they had been delicate, and he was fairly certain they had failed long ago, perhaps damaged by the explosion that had ruined his cable socket. He had never been entirely sure just which instrument was which, but he did not believe that his telemetry still included anything that worked on gravitational fields. He himself could still feel the presence of psionic magic as an electric tingling, but for some unknown reason that did not transmit — or at least, it had not transmitted to his own computer.

The ship was down. That meant it could not rain missiles freely across the planet, or strafe towns and cities, but while the ship's destructive capabilities were limited as long as it was on the ground, the cyborg was now free to roam, to gather evidence that Dest was a rebel world.

He knew that Dest had never actually been a part of the rebellion against Old Earth's rule, but neither had it fought against the rebels. Evidence could be largely a matter of interpretation. Flame might be able to convince her computer that the most innocent things were proof of the planet's hostility.

The ignorance of most of the people on Dest that the rebellion had ever taken place at all might be damning; IRU 247 might interpret that as willful deception.

Fortunately, his ship had crashed in a largely deserted area, a broad expanse of uninhabited forest. Flame might not encounter anyone until after he arrived.

Was there any possible evidence in his own wrecked ship? He was not at all sure, one way or the other. Might not the fact that the ship was wrecked be sufficient evidence? What but rebel action could have destroyed it?

No, that was no problem; rebel action had *not* destroyed it. For all intents and purposes, the ship had crashed itself. The computer had committed suicide. The ship was no problem, or at any rate, *should* be no problem.

He was nearing the city wall, the great black stone barrier that encircled Praunce's urban area. Three sides of it had been erected magically from rubble; the fourth, southern side was the northern rim of the crater where Dest's pre-war capital city had stood. Praunce, now the greatest city on the planet, had been merely the northern corner of that metropolis until Old Earth's forces decided to remove Dest as a potential threat.

Assuming, of course, that that had been the justification for the attack; he could only guess why Old Earth had sent the fleet.

Flame and her computer had just passed over the crater; would they consider the crater itself to be evidence to be added to the case against Dest? After all, what but the military might of Old Earth could have created such destruction? And if Old Earth had attacked Dest, then Dest must have been an enemy — so the faulty, simplified logic of the military mind might say. He had told the computer that Dest had *always* been loyal; that was true, the attack had been unjustified, but would IRU 247 believe such a story? No, given Flame's obvious hatred and the computer's programmed belief in the rightness of everything the Command did, they would brand Turner a liar and a traitor, and that would be the end of everything.

Flame would not have seen the crater for more than an instant, though, and then only if he or she happened to be watching the ship's descent. The computer might well fail to draw any conclusions from it. After all, they had surely been able to see the crater from orbit, yet had not mentioned it.

Perhaps they had taken it for something natural, an impact crater or something volcanic in origin. Any close inspection would reveal otherwise, of course.

At least, so far as he knew there were no other craters as large and obvious as Praunce's. Whatever weapons the fleet had used, Praunce's predecessor had received special attention.

Even if the two halves of IRU 247 paid no attention to the crater, though, they might yet find people out there in the forest, wanderers, villagers, and others. They might ask them if they were loyal citizens of Old Earth's empire. He kept coming back to that thought; it was the most worrisome prospect.

Most people would simply be confused by such a question. Some might say yes, out of respect for ancient history. Others might say no, out of respect for their current allegiance to Praunce's own growing empire. That could be disastrous.

Of course, so far, the computer and Flame seemed unable to interpret Prauncer Anglo-Spanish, and his ship's wreckage lay well within Praunce's territory, both politically and linguistically. IRU 247 might not be able to ask intelligible questions or understand their answers.

He could not rely on that, though. The language was simple enough, really.

Whatever the truth, whatever they did or did not notice, Turner was sure Flame would find evidence to support his or her position. People were good at that. People, Turner knew, would always believe what they wanted to believe, playing up any supporting evidence and ignoring or discounting anything to the contrary, and Flame was obviously no exception. The poor computer would be no match for human ingenuity, he was sure; without his own arguments to counterbalance Flame's prejudice, CCC-IRU 247 would, sooner or later, be forced to whatever conclusion Flame wanted.

And Flame, he knew, wanted Dest to be hostile.

He had to reach them before the computer was brought around to that conclusion.

"IRU 247," he called. "Come in, IRU 247, this is Slant of IRU 205."

No one answered. He guessed that the fused stone of the city wall was blocking his signal, or perhaps the ship, now landed, was below the horizon.

He galloped down through the western gates, out of the city and through the frozen mud streets of the slums that huddled around the walls of the capital. As the kilometers sped past the huts thinned on either side, the street beneath the horse's hooves narrowed, and before Dest's primary had dropped out of sight he was on the highway through the surrounding farmlands.

At this time of year the fields were empty and desolate. The weather had been unusually dry ever since the first frost; not a flake of snow had fallen, and nothing hid the dead brown grass and weeds or the bare gray soil of the furrows. The farmers themselves had mostly retreated into the city for the winter, abandoning their lands to the cold and the wind until spring returned.

Dest's star-sun rode the skyline in the southwest, ahead and to the left; as he drove westward the line of low hills before him was black with shadow. He glanced back at the city, but found little comfort in the sight. The tops of the towers were glittering golden in the afternoon's last light, but most of the city stood in a far more ominous shadow than any the forest might create. The lengthening shadow of the crater wall lay across it like the black on charred wood. The sight disturbed him; he was chilled anew as he looked back at it, knowing that new craters might soon replace Dest's cities. He could feel his heat-field fading as worry and fatigue ate away at his concentration. The weight of the rocket rifle dug into his shoulder a bit more with each beat of the horse's hooves.

That crater wall was no eroded ring of debris from some ancient meteor strike, worn down to a comfortable ridge; it was glazed black radioactive stone, fresh, harsh, sharp-edged and raw. Whatever hellish weapon had vaporized most of the old capital city had reduced the underlying bedrock, along with some of the more durable sands and building materials, to liquid, liquid that had been thrown up in a great splash and had somehow frozen in mid-leap, leaving a gigantic coronet of jagged stone and glass. Three centuries had done little to weather it. The crater wall was still the blackened image of the blast, stone thrown up by human violence. There could be no mistaking it for anything else.

The explosion had been off center, and a freak upthrust of molten rock had protected a northern corner of the city from the worst of the subsequent shockwave and firestorm. That corner had been rebuilt after the holocaust as the new city of Praunce.

Praunce had always stood in the crater's shadow, and over the years Turner had become accustomed to that looming black barrier, hanging over the city's southern side like a wave about to crash down upon the buildings beneath. Now, though, seeing it from this distance and knowing that it might be an omen of the future as well as a reminder of the past, he was struck all over again by the horror of it, and he spurred his horse on.

He remembered also that despite the farms, this was not healthy country he was traversing. In Praunce itself radioactivity had dropped to acceptable levels, partly because of the shelter from the initial blast and subsequent fallout that the crater wall itself had provided, and partly through the concerted efforts of the city's wizards over the past few decades. Outside the city, however, even this far from the crater, many highly radioactive spots still lingered, places where gobbets of molten debris had spattered across the landscape, or where the survivors had dumped contaminated materials, or where natural agents such as flowing groundwater or leaching plant life had accumulated odd pockets of radiation.

Slant ignored that. He trusted his wizardry and internal modifications to deal with any radiation hazards he might encounter, should he live long enough for them to matter. His bone marrow was sheathed in protective metal and plastic, and his psychic senses could tell him of any damage — he had lived with radiation for years now. He attributed his production of three healthy children, with only four miscarriages, to his special status as both cyborg and wizard. Most would-be parents in Praunce did far worse.

The daylight had faded to a pale glimmer in the west by the time he reached the first of the villages along the way, but he rode on into the darkness, keeping to the road as much by his wizard-sight as by the faint, cold starlight that spilled down between the scattered clouds.

"IRU 247," he called again, "IRU 247, this is Slant of IRU 205, come in, please."

Again, he received no answer. The ship was probably still below his broadcast horizon.

His horse slowed suddenly; he glanced down at the animal and realized that he had been driving it mercilessly for over an hour — closer to two, surely. The beast could not survive such treatment indefinitely; it had lasted this long only because he had been driving it on psionically, lending it energy and, without consciously meaning to, pushing at its emotions. Now, though, both his fatigue and the horse's own were taking a toll. He made no effort to force the animal back into a gallop; instead he let it slow to a weary amble.

He had, he saw, been treating the poor beast like a machine. Talking to Flame had brought back old habits, and he had behaved as if he were driving a groundcar rather than a horse. He realized for the first time that he had not even noted whether he was astride a mare, a stallion, or a gelding. This particular beast was not one he knew; he wondered where Haiger had gotten it.

It was a sturdy mount, but he had driven it to the limits of its strength. He was also, he knew, nearing the limits of his own strength. Reluctantly, he reached out with his senses, seeking someplace to rest for the remainder of the night.

No trees grew here; the forests were still several kilometers away. Around him were only a few sickly grasses, colorless and dead in the darkness and cold, and expanses of bare dirt. He could detect no shelter, and no fodder fit for his horse to eat.

He could feel his reserves failing him, though, and at last, reluctantly, he drew rein and slid from the saddle, willing to make do with a few hours huddled on a barren hillside.

The horse was almost instantly asleep once he allowed it to stop. His own eyes remained open a moment longer as he chewed a handful of figs and made one more unsuccessful attempt to contact Flame's ship.

His penultimate waking thought was that at least he had ridden far enough that if Praunce was bombed, he would survive the blast. That was followed immediately and finally by a burst of revulsion at his selfishness. Parrah and his children were still in the city, along with almost a million other unsuspecting citizens.

He fell asleep with the mingled images of his wife and a nuclear fireball tangled in his mind. His dreams were uneasy.

He awoke at first light, made a hasty breakfast, and then swung himself back into the saddle, urging his still-tired horse — a fine chestnut stallion, he noticed — onward, toward the forests that lined the western horizon.

NINE

Parrah looked fiercely across the table at the other wizards, her eyes blazing. "I don't know the details," she said. "I guess Sam didn't have time to explain them."

"Well, what *did* he say?" old Shopaur asked calmly.

"He said the demon-ship would be landing right away," Parrah answered, "and that he had to go and meet it to keep the demon from running amok. He knows more about the old machines and demons from the Bad Times than anyone else, so he was the right one to go on ahead." She paused for effect, then slammed her fist on the table and shouted, "But that doesn't mean no one else should go! This thing could kill us all — it *wants* to kill us all — and I don't want my husband facing it alone!"

The sound of her fist on the table was not as impressive as she might have hoped, a mere thump instead of a boom, since it was a very heavy table and she was a small woman, but she could see that she had gotten her point across. Several members of the Council shifted uneasily on their cushions.

"Nobody said he should face it alone," Arzadel answered her calmly. "However, it would be preferable if we did not all rush out unprepared, hurrying off without any sort of plan or organization."

"And we can't *all* go, in any case," Shopaur added, smoothing his golden robe. "Even if we wanted to, some of us aren't up to the journey. We'll need to decide who goes, if anyone, and who stays."

"Yes," young Wirozhess said, "*Someone* has to stay in Praunce to keep the city running — and the empire, for that matter. We can't just trust it to the ordinary people, can we?"

Several heads nodded in agreement.

"It seems to me," Arzadel said, "That where these demons and their ships are concerned, we really don't know what we're doing, and Sam does. We might do considerable harm if we go barging in with a small army just when he's in the middle of some delicate negotiation with the demon."

"He can't *negotiate* with demons!" Parrah replied disgustedly.

"You only show your own ignorance by that statement, Parrah," Arzadel replied sharply. "Your husband knows better. As I understand it, from the conversations I've had with Sam over the years, demons have their own laws, their own goals, and they often are willing to negotiate. The fact that we're all still alive right now indicates that this demon is willing to negotiate; if it weren't, it would surely have attacked the city directly by now."

"But we can't trust it!" Parrah insisted, "It might kill him!"

"It might well kill us all," Arzadel reminded her. "You weren't involved with Sam's own demon at all, Parrah, but I was. I never spoke to it directly, but I saw a little of what that ship could do before it was wrecked. It could have destroyed all of this city, I'm certain, even if it didn't carry whatever weapon made that crater." He gestured toward the room's southern windows, and the looming shadow of the crater wall. Several heads turned involuntarily, and Parrah, telepathically sensitive even through her own distress, felt a psychic shiver go through the chamber, a subtle discomfort that was not hampered by the rich furs and fine fabrics that surrounded the councillors with luxury. Everyone present had looked into that crater, knowing that it had once held a city. Everyone present knew that a single weapon had turned the city into the crater. They all knew what a starship's weapons could do.

"And this new demon might be even more powerful than Sam's ever was," Arzadel continued. "Sam's ship was only a one-man scouting vessel, after all, and we don't know what this new one is."

"If it could destroy us all so easily," Wirozhess asked Arzadel skeptically, "then why hasn't it?"

"I don't know," Arzadel answered frankly. "That's why I prefer that we not all go running off to confront it; we might antagonize it." He paused, then added thoughtfully, "It occurs to me that I would greatly prefer to have something like this demon-ship on *our* side. Aside from the military possibilities — and we hardly need any more military power at this point — I think perhaps it's time that Dest resumed its contacts with other worlds. This ship from the stars could do that for us, if it weren't for the demon controlling it." He turned to Parrah. "Are you sure Sam didn't tell you anything more? He didn't say anything about what we should do? I don't want any of us to rush in blindly with so much at stake. Did he make any suggestions, or have you thought of what we could do to help?"

Parrah hesitated, then collapsed onto her cushion.

"No," she said. "I haven't thought of anything. You're right, we shouldn't rush in blindly, but I was panicking." She shook her head. "I just wanted to protect Sam, to hurry off to help him, and I haven't been thinking. I don't have any idea what to do." She smiled weakly. "I told Sam to talk to you before he left, Arzadel, but I'm the one who really needed to talk to you."

"I'm flattered," Arzadel answered, dipping his chin in acknowledgement of the compliment. "Just what *did* Sam tell you?"

"Well, as I told you, there's a demon that calls itself Flame that has just arrived from the stars, and it's landing its ship out near the wreckage of Sam's old ship. Sam said — let me see — he said that he didn't want them to see him flying. I don't know why he said 'them;' he seemed to think there were two demons, not just one, but he only mentioned the one by name. He said, 'They already think that something strange is going on,' and that he was afraid they would talk to the wrong person before he got there, and that that person might say the wrong thing. I don't know what he meant, but you must be right, rushing us all out there could be exactly the wrong thing." She sighed. "But I can't stay here and do *nothing*."

Shopaur and Arzadel smiled sympathetically; Wirozhess snorted, while the other councillors remained unexpressive.

"I think you're right," Arzadel said. "Sam knows more about demons than any of us, and he fought his own successfully, but that doesn't mean he can't use a little help. We helped him against his own, as much as we could." He paused, thinking, and then continued, "It sounds to me as if he's been trying to convince the demon that we're all its friends — after all, since he was once possessed by a demon himself, and still carries all that machinery inside him, this new demon may accept him as an ally. That could be a very good thing indeed, if he can convince this demon that we're all its friends. As I said, I would like to have the demon, or at least its ship, on our side. If we all barge in on his negotiating — whatever it may be that he is, in fact, negotiating — the demon may take that as a sign of bad faith. The rest of us simply don't know anything about what the demon might be looking for."

Several wizards nodded, and Parrah slumped dejectedly.

"On the other hand," Arzadel said, "something as potentially valuable as this should probably not be left in the hands of a single individual. We all have an interest in what happens to this ship; when Sam's own ship was wrecked, eleven years ago, a great opportunity was missed. At the time, public opinion might not have favored the capture and use of such a ship. The border wars were still being fought, and the possibility of bringing in the weapons of the Bad Times would have terrified everyone so much as to blind them to the possibilities of the old technologies. None of us wanted to risk the sort of trouble that could bring." He waved that aside. "Times have changed, now. The government of Praunce is undisputed master of most of the continent, and at peace with the rest. Ideas have changed. I think that the rulers of Praunce would welcome a chance to contact other worlds, to recover some of the knowledge our ancestors lost in the Bad Times. We've built a new civilization through wizardry, but we may have taken wizardry as far as it can go; I think it's time to take a look at other ways. This ship can give us that. I, for one, would prefer that we not miss this opportunity as we missed the one eleven years ago. I say we should do everything we can to capture this new ship intact."

The other councillors stared at him for a hushed moment.

"Are you serious?" Shopaur asked at last. "This is a demon's ship we're discussing!"

"Of course he's serious!" Wirozhess answered. "He's right, too. Sam disposed of his own demon, didn't he? The ship only crashed because it was flying when the demon died. If Sam had killed it while the ship was on the ground we'd have it today! Think what we could have done with a ship like that in our war with Harthin!"

"No," Arzadel said, "That's a bad way to look at it. Using the demon's ship for war would be an incredible waste. It can take us to other stars! That's far more important than risking it in battle."

This was greeted with general approval, and Wirozhess reluctantly conceded the point.

"Still," he said, "I think we can all agree that the demon's ship would be invaluable to the empire of Praunce."

The other councillors nodded, eagerly or reluctantly or with calm acceptance. No one spoke up to dispute Wirozhess's statement.

"In that case," Shopaur said, "The next question is, How do we capture this ship?"

Wirozhess shrugged, and turned to Arzadel.

"I don't know," Arzadel admitted. "I know very little about demons. Sam has gone to ensure that the demon will not try to kill us all, and I'm sure that, if anyone can do that, he can. I would suppose that he will either kill the demon, as he did his own, or will somehow convince it that we are its friends. The question then becomes, What will Sam do once the demon has been handled? Parrah?"

"I don't know," she said. "Sam can be unpredictable."

"Perhaps, then," Arzadel said, "We should send a deputation to represent Praunce's interests in the matter. A small one. Whatever the demon's beliefs and desires, a small party of friends come to make sure that nothing has gone amiss should not be too upsetting, and Sam may need our aid. I think that a few of us should, indeed, follow him. These people, whoever they may be, will judge the situation carefully before they do anything, and must defer to Sam's judgment throughout, since he, and he alone, is knowledgeable about these demons, but insofar as circumstances allow, they must make every effort to see that the ship is captured intact, either with or without the demon. It could be a great asset to Praunce and to Dest, and I am not sure that Sam, personally involved as he is, will have properly considered this. Left to his own devices he might simply destroy the ship in order to save time and trouble."

"Then you *will* send someone?" Parrah demanded. "I don't care about the ship, I care about Sam, but you're saying we'll send a party?"

"I think so. Sam did not actually tell you that we shouldn't, did he?"

"No," she said eagerly. "He said that he had to go immediately, and that I couldn't accompany him because I was to inform you all of the situation and see that the children would be cared for, but he never said that I mustn't follow, or that other people shouldn't come as well."

"You're absolutely sure he didn't advise against it?" Shopaur asked uneasily.

"I'm sure," Parrah said firmly.

"In that case," Wirozhess said, "I think Arzadel is quite correct. The ship would be of incalculable value, and we can't afford not to do our best to acquire it. If there is no further disagreement on that point, it becomes merely a matter of deciding who is to go in this little party."

No one voiced any disagreement. Instead, after only a moment's hesitation, Parrah said, "Well, I'm going, of course."

Shopaur nodded, and no one else spoke for a moment.

"I think that Arzadel should go, as well," Shopaur said, breaking a growing silence. "He has had the experience of helping Sam against demons once before, when Sam first came to us. He is perhaps Sam's best friend, if I am not mistaken, and has, in addition, just demonstrated once again that he is no fool, nor is he foolhardy."

"Not to mention," Dekert commented, "that it was his idea to capture the thing, and he's probably the most powerful wizard we have."

Shopaur nodded, acknowledging Dekert's rather tactless comment. Comparisons of wizardly talent were generally considered in poor taste, since the members of the Council were sworn to cooperation, rather than competition, and as councillors were all theoretically equal.

"That's two," Wirozhess said. "Any more, or is that it?"

"I would prefer to have a third," Arzadel said, "For a variety of reasons."

"I wouldn't mind," Wirozhess said, assuming a falsely casual air.

"No," Parrah said, emphatically. "Sam and I hardly know you."

Stung, Wirozhess shrugged and sat back, saying no more.

"What of Haiger, or Ahnao? Aren't they Sam's good friends?" Pleido asked, speaking for the first time.

Parrah shook her head. "They're our friends, yes," she said, "but they'll be taking care of the children, and besides, Sam has never really trusted either of them with anything important. That might not be fair, but he hasn't, and I won't ask him to now." She glanced around the table. "Dekert, what about you? You helped out against the first demon, didn't you?"

"Yes," Dekert said, "I did. If you want me, I'll be glad to come."

"That makes three of us," Arzadel said. "I think that should do. We'll need to pack a few things; I suggest we leave in the morning."

Parrah glanced out the window at the fading daylight, and fought down an urge to demand that they leave immediately.

"All right," she said, "At dawn, then."

Arzadel smiled. "At dawn."

"Then I think that's everything," Shopaur said. "You will stay in touch, of course."

"Of course," Parrah said, rising.

TEN

Turner studied the two starships cautiously from the shelter of the surrounding forest, keeping one hand on the strap of his rocket rifle.

The ships presented a curious spectacle together. IRU 247 had of necessity landed directly in the wake of IRU 205, along the gash in the forest that Slant's fiery crash had made ten terrestrial years before. To either side towered mature, sturdy trees that would have been difficult, if not impossible, to clear completely out of the way, trees very much like the ones that had ripped open the hull of Slant's ship and torn one wing entirely off. Along that one narrow path, however, nothing older than a decade stood, and the incoming ship had been able to cut itself a landing strip with its lasers.

That had meant coming in from the west, although its original approach had been from the east, and then stopping mere meters short of the wreckage of IRU 205. Turner was now approaching from the east — slightly south of due east, since he had lost his way once or twice — so that Flame's vessel seemed to be rearing up from behind the mound of wreckage, like a predator frozen in the act of bursting from hiding for its final deadly pounce.

The newly landed ship was clearly visible from a distance of several hundred meters, despite the surrounding forest. It stood up sleek and bright, gleaming silver in the cloud-filtered daylight. Flame and her computer had not bothered with any sort of camouflage, which seemed odd.

Slant's ruined ship, by contrast, was almost invisible even close up, little more than a smooth hump in the dark undergrowth. The wreckage was green and brown with moss and creepers and dead leaves; the gray stalks of winter-killed weeds rattled against it in the faint breeze. The few spots where metal still showed were a dull gray from corrosion and weathering. Because of its tilt, and the wing lost in the crash, the body of the shipwreck was asymmetrical, making it seem even more a part of the natural landscape.

Turner saw no sign of motion. He allowed the horse to slow to a walk, both to rest the beast and to avoid alarming either Flame or CCC-IRU 247, but he did not stop. He continued riding directly toward the grounded vessels.

He had called IRU 247 repeatedly over the past day and a half, but had begun receiving answers only that morning, as he finished an unsatisfactory breakfast. Even then, the computer had not been willing to discuss events since the landing, but had only offered guidance in reaching the site of the wreck.

Of course, that guidance had been very welcome. The years that had intervened since his last visit had faded his memory of the route, and allowed the forest to grow and change so completely as to eliminate any landmarks he might recall.

Flame had refused to speak to him at all, at any time throughout his wild ride from Praunce to this place. That worried him.

Now, though, after two nights and half a day more, he had reached the rendezvous, and Flame would have to speak to him, so that they could settle the all-important questions of Dest's loyalties and future.

He had never really given Dest's future much thought until Flame had come along to threaten it.

"What's happening?" he called silently as he approached.

"Restate question," the computer replied.

"What's the current situation?"

"Ship is functioning normally. Cyborg unit designated 'Flame' is on extended reconnaissance on foot."

"He is?" That was not good. He had feared that the cyborg might go exploring, but he had not actually expected it, and had not prepared any plans for such a circumstance. He was out of practice at anticipating and countering the movements of an antagonist. He had not thought the situation through, but had simply charged onward, and despite his worrying he had still somehow expected to find Flame quietly waiting for him. His only concerns had been reaching the ships, and that Flame's ship had stayed grounded and launched no missiles.

He had come prepared to accept whatever he found, and that had been a mistake.

"Affirmative," the computer said.

"Let me speak to Flame," Turner said. He hoped he might be able to convince the cyborg to return before he or she did any damage. Flame would probably not have gone far, in unfamiliar territory like this forest — though that "extended reconnaissance" did sound like something more than a stroll around the immediate area.

"Negative," the computer replied.

Startled, he demanded, "Why not?"

"Cyborg unit designated 'Flame' maintains that contact with cyborg unit designated 'Slant' may facilitate deception by enemy insurgents of cyborg unit designated 'Flame'. Insufficient evidence exists to allow complete analysis of this hypothesis; therefore, cyborg unit has full discretion."

"I thought I was supposed to meet him here and talk to him!"

"Affirmative. Discussion of situation is to take place upon return of cyborg unit designated 'Flame' from extended reconnaissance."

"Damn," he said aloud. Flame had gotten away from him, at least for the moment. A killer cyborg was loose somewhere on Dest, probably heavily armed and looking for the slightest excuse to cut loose with all available weapons.

But had he or she gotten away cleanly?

"Where is Flame, then?" he asked.

"That information may not be provided to cyborg unit designated 'Slant'."

"Then how am I supposed to know when Flame will be back? Keeping me waiting here indefinitely is wasteful." Turner thought he was being clever, taking this approach; he allowed himself to relax slightly in the saddle.

There was a pause before the computer replied, and when the reply came, Turner's self-satisfaction evaporated.

"Cyborg unit designated 'Flame' maintains that no information regarding her location may be given to cyborg unit designated 'Slant'. She will return shortly."

That was something, anyway. "What does she mean by 'shortly?'" he asked.

"Information insufficient."

"Damn!" he said again. Flame had eluded him. It seemed as if her computer was cooperating with her more closely than his own had ever cooperated with him, in allowing her to cut herself off as she had. He wondered how she maintained so much control.

He realized he had learned one detail from the computer's phrasing. Flame was female. Not that that made any difference.

He was very close to both ships now; while he had conversed over the internal communications circuit he had covered most of the intervening distance. He stopped his horse and dismounted a few meters away from his own ruined ship, then wrapped the reins around a leafless bush and strode toward the overgrown heap, planning to go around it and board Flame's ship. His breath puffed out in a thin fog, and he could feel the warmth of the horse's body quickly fading from his thighs in the cold. Vague thoughts of sabotage were gathering in his mind. After all, Flame might be dangerous, but she was not carrying nuclear weapons about with her on her "extended reconnnaissance". If he could somehow cripple her ship any threat to his adopted world would be reduced by several orders of magnitude.

"Request permission to come aboard," he called.

"Permission denied."

He halted, the hem of his coat brushing against a hump of moss-covered debris. "Why?" he demanded silently.

"Loyalty of cyborg unit designated 'Slant' has not been established sufficiently to allow cyborg unit designated 'Slant' into high-security areas."

Another idea gone, then, he thought. The computer was stupid, but its programmers had not been. It could not think, but it could follow rules perfectly.

"All right," he said, resigned to the failure of another scheme. He stood silently for a moment, thinking.

The intense chill of the winter air seeped through his coat. He had dropped his heat-field before approaching the ship, lest CCC- IRU 247 take alarm upon detecting "anti-gravity" in use, and the moisture in his breath was turning to frost in his beard.

"I hope you don't mind if I take a look at my own ship," he said at last. He was grasping at straws now, looking for any advantage, however slight, that might enable him to defeat IRU 247 if it tried to destroy Dest. He hoped to find somewhere in the wreckage some weapon he could turn against Flame or her ship. Perhaps he could somehow restore power to one of the lasers in the fusion chamber and turn it against the newcomer's hull.

Another, more desperate thought came to him uninvited. If worse came to worst, and he could bring himself to do it, perhaps he could trigger one of his own nuclear warheads. That would almost certainly obliterate both ships and Flame as well, if she was anywhere in the area, without doing much harm to Dest beyond possibly wiping out a few isolated villages and raising somewhat the already high level of background radiation.

The drawback, of course, was that he, too, would fry. He did not want to die, and sincerely hoped that it would not be necessary, but if it came to a choice between dying with IRU 247 or dying with the entire population of Dest, he preferred taking IRU 247 with him. At least it would be quick; if Dest were to be nuked he might find himself dying of radiation poisoning, or from starvation during a nuclear winter, or in any number of other slow, unpleasant ways.

He wondered whether detonating one warhead would set off all of them. He had no idea, really, whether it would. He tried to remember how many nuclear warheads, and of what yield, he had had left when the ship crashed. The initial complement had been thirty-six, and, thinking back, he could remember using only two, both long before he reached Dest.

The computer did not answer his statement; presumably it did not consider an answer necessary.

He remembered that the hull had been breached on the southern side, and that the airlock on that side had been jammed open. He headed around toward the area of the gray-green mound where the airlock should be, then stopped.

He sensed something wrong. He looked, and saw tracks on the ground before him. The grass had been trampled down and ground into the mud. The mud was frozen hard now, but something had recently churned it up.

That made no sense. Certainly, Flame would have investigated the wreck, but she should have left no trail that would last more than a few hours, if that. Instead, he saw a beaten path, almost a road, leading from the break in the wall of his ship over to a belly hatch in her ship. An earthen ramp had been built up to the opening in the hull; an extruded metal ramp, now withdrawn, had presumably served at the other end.

Most of the tracks, he saw, had been left not by boots, or by any other sort of human footwear, but by caterpillar treads. That meant machines — probably service robots.

"What the hell have you been doing with my ship?" he demanded, even as he reached out psionically to feel for himself.

"Equipment and ordnance have been salvaged."

"*What* equipment and ordnance? What weapons? Start with those." Even as he asked, he guessed what they must have been; a sick, empty feeling spread through him as he reached out with his wizard-sight to sense the ship's structure and energy fields.

His own vessel was completely inert, simply a mass of metal and plastic. Nowhere in it could he sense any radiation.

He turned his attention to Flame's ship, even as the computer informed him, "Thirty-one missiles equipped with nuclear warheads were salvaged. Six missiles appear functional and tested positive. Propellant systems were removed from twenty- five missiles remaining and were disposed of, and warheads were inspected separately. Twenty-two warheads appear functional. Three are presently dysfunctional but may be reparable. Fissionable material from three destroyed warheads was also recovered for possible later use. Four missiles with high-explosive warheads were..."

"Never mind about the rest. What do you need with all those nukes? Haven't you got your own? And by what authority did you take those, anyway?" He tried to sound authoritative, but failed; he was terrified by the ship's actions. Did it mean to wipe out not just Dest, but other worlds as well? Dest's civilization could be effectively destroyed with a dozen high-yield missiles. Was the ship just providing a little overkill?

Or had its own missiles all been used up previously? Had the threats from orbit all been a bluff? If so, he had made a disastrous mistake in revealing his presence on Dest. If he had kept silent, Flame and her computer would probably never have bothered to explore his wrecked ship, and would never have found the warheads.

He was looking at Flame's ship with his every sense stretched to its utmost even as he asked his questions. Its hull was a graceful mass of shadows and gleaming metal by visible light, but now that he had tuned in psychically, he could sense the electrical networks within as webs of energy, webs he interpreted as violet and blue and gold even though he knew that he was not seeing actual colors at all. It was easier to think of them as colors than to try and develop an entire new vocabulary; most wizards spoke of the "colors" of fields and auras, though the purists among them denounced such misleading terminology.

Yes, he could see the faint radiation of the warheads. He struggled to count them. Maintaining the necessary concentration required a ferocious effort. The emptiness in his belly and the weight of the rocket rifle on his shoulder dragged on that effort.

"Salvage of materials from downed or abandoned military vessels, either friendly or enemy, is standard procedure, and fully covered by programming and military regulations. No further authority was required."

"But it was *my ship!*" Turner protested, as he continued his count.

"Negative," the computer replied. "IRU 205 was decommissioned. Vessel was abandoned."

He detected thirty-four warheads, plus the container holding the remains of three more. That made thirty-seven. Flame's armament had been low, but not gone. She could have destroyed three fair-sized cities. Her threats had not been mere bluffing.

That was, in a curious way, a relief. Although IRU 247 was now far more heavily armed, he had probably saved Praunce and two other cities from destruction, at least temporarily, by intervening.

Now, was there any way he could end the threat completely?

The wizards of Awlmei had drained the power of his own ship, eleven local years earlier. They had shut down the fusion drive and bled the reserve energy cells down to uselessness by tapping the power flow to one of the drive lasers. They had missed the emergency back-up batteries in the repair robots, true, but they had shut the ship down temporarily, at any rate. Could he do anything similar?

He reached out, and tried to sense details of the interior of Flame's vessel, but quickly gave up. A blaze of bright "yellow" just astern of the ship's center was surely the fusion drive, but he could "see" nothing of its structure — the fierce outpouring of energy hid all details. He could not sense anything in the starship but the parts that gave off energy — the various powered systems, the radiation of the nuclear weapons, and a faint "greenishness" in the wings that he realized must be the algae that supplied air and food. He could make out nothing of the ship's frame or the shapes of the interior spaces. He could not tell one system from another.

Could he interfere with the computer or the ship's power supply? He shook his head reluctantly. He did not dare. It had taken the seven best wizards on the Awlmeian Council to pull the stunt off on his own ship, and even that had been possible only because the computer had been devoting almost its entire capacity to a complex analysis at the time. CCC-IRU 247 was more or less idling; it would be running random system checks just to keep its circuits busy, and would spot a power drain much too quickly for such a drain to do any good. The Awlmeian wizards had tapped a power feed to one of the lasers heating the fusion chamber; Turner could not even distinguish the lasers themselves from the surrounding glow, let alone locate a power feed.

If he could arrange a distraction and get some of his comrades over from Praunce, wizards more sensitive than himself, a power drain might be worth trying.

Could he, as a last resort, trigger one of the nuclear warheads?

No, he decided, he could not. He could sense the faint radiation from the fissionable material, but the triggering mechanisms were inert and invisible to him, and he could not muster sufficient telekinetic force to pry the fissionables from their mountings and slap them together in hopes of creating a critical mass.

Even if he could, he was not sure it would work. He had never studied exactly how nuclear weapons functioned, but he had an impression that the masses had to be brought together very precisely to create an explosion.

Was there anything else he might do? He studied the intricate webs of energy.

No, he admitted reluctantly, he simply did not know enough. He had no way of knowing what he was seeing. If he tampered blindly with the computer he might disable the ship, or convince it to side with him, but he might equally well throw it into an all-out attack. If he interfered with anything other than the computer, the computer would spot the malfunction and take action to repair it and prevent a recurrence.

He couldn't even be sure which energy flows were parts of the computer, and which were autonomous systems, let alone how to safely manipulate any of them.

He had once, in its final moments before crashing, piloted his own ship by wizardry, but he had done that through the direct-control cable, using wizardry only to bridge the gap between the plug and the broken socket in his neck. If he could locate the plug in this ship he thought he might be able to do the same, despite the greater distance — but that would do no good, since the computer could simply override his input.

Besides, he could not even locate the plug.

He suddenly regretted rushing off alone, the lone hero on his way to save the world; Arzadel and the other wizards would have been a great help at this point.

They were not there, though, and he could not contact them over so great a distance. He was on his own, unless and until someone came after him — alone against a starship.

A moment earlier, several kilometers away, Flame had been resting quietly, sitting huddled on the hard ground in her jumpsuit with her back to the bole of a fair-sized oak. She was intently watching a squirrel as, sluggish with the cold, it explored the ground nearby for anything edible. Her reverie was been interrupted by the computer's announcement, "Gravitational anomaly occurring in immediate vicinity of ship of intensity sufficient to register against planetary background, centered on cyborg unit designated 'Slant'. Please advise."

Flame stirred very slightly, and asked, "Slant's there?" She spoke silently so as not to disturb the squirrel.

"Affirmative."

"And there's anti-gravity activity around him?"

"Affirmative."

"Do you think he's causing it?"

"Information insufficient."

"Did you tell him you'd detected it?"

"Negative, in accordance with previous order of cyborg unit designated 'Flame'."

She tightened her lips, rather than nodding. At least the idiot machine had gotten that much right. "Did he say anything about it?" she asked.

"Negative."

"He must be causing it somehow, I'm sure of it. There's no one else around?"

"Negative."

"Then it must be him. You see, I told you he was a traitor. I don't know what he's doing, or how he's doing it, but it's probably dangerous. You get the hell out of there before he can do anything to you. Get back into a synchronous orbit and wait there." She did not mention that what most worried her was the possibility that Slant would talk his way aboard and then remove the termite from the computer core, allowing the computer to side with him against her.

"Affirmative," the computer replied.

The ship stopped transmitting. Moodily, deliberately, Flame slipped a snark from her pocket and shot the squirrel.

Its left haunch disappeared in a swirl of dust, along with a small area of the surrounding ground and dead leaves. Blood sprayed briefly, and the little animal let out a single piercing squeal and thrashed once before it died.

"Serves you right, you little monster," she hissed hoarsely. "Living here peacefully all this time while I was out there rotting in space. This is *my* planet now, you understand that? It may be cold and uncomfortable as hell, but it's mine, and I'm going to kill everyone on it to prove that, to pay them all back for what they did to me!" She spat at the little corpse, then sank back against the oak again. The bark scraped her back uncomfortably, even through her jumpsuit.

Leaving the ship had been a mistake, she decided. This planet was cold and harsh and hostile. The freezing air stung her skin, and the dampness of the ground where she sat, once the heat of her body had melted the frost, made her skin crawl. The surrounding trees were either dark and ugly, covered with sharp, menacing needles, or else bare and threatening, like great brittle hands reaching for her from every side. The sky above the scratching branches was terrifying in its huge gray emptiness. The entire outside world was strange and frightening. She had become accustomed to her ship.

She would have preferred, however, not to have known that. She hated having her nose rubbed in the fact that she had been aboard the little vessel so long that she was no longer comfortable anywhere else.

What made it worse was that she was never really comfortable aboard the ship, either. She did not really trust the computer, despite its programming, despite her little timer gadget that would destroy the computer if she failed to reset it every hundred hours or so. She had its enforced loyalty, but she was not comfortable with it. She no longer fit in anywhere at all.

Maybe, she told herself, she would have been all right on Old Earth. Maybe it was just this planet that was wrong, with its dark sky and reddish sun.

All the more reason, then, to wipe it clean. In the interests of traveling light and not frightening away the natives she had not brought any large, obvious weapons, but she had three fully-charged snarks — less the charge used to kill the squirrel — and her own superhuman speed and strength.

She would be able to do some damage, whatever happened. Even if Slant somehow destroyed her ship, or caused her to destroy it, his planet would not be left unscathed.

She smiled at the thought.

Flame's conversations, with her ship and with the squirrel and with herself, took the same time as Turner's psionic study of the ship. As Turner decided that he was on his own in dealing with the starship, the vessel's forward lifters suddenly roared, breaking into his thoughts. His horse whinnied uneasily.

"Clear area for lift-off!" a toneless mechanical voice called loudly.

"Hligosh!" Turner said, backing away as a wave of heat reached him. "Computer, what do you think you're doing?"

"Cyborg unit designated 'Flame' has ordered immediate departure. Stand clear."

Turner needed no second warning; the heat of the ship's main drive could fry him instantly. He turned and ran at superhuman speed for the doubtful cover of the surrounding forest, forcing himself not to fly for still greater speed. He had no time to reach his mount, but he did reach out telekinetically to push at it, freeing the reins from the bush he had tied them to. That done, he erected a psionic barrier behind him, to provide what protection he could, an instant before the ship's main drive fired.

The ground shook beneath him and the roar blasted his ears; heat swept over him in a thick wave. He sensed, but could not hear, that the horse was screaming in panic.

Then the ground was still, and the sound and heat were fading. He turned and looked back, to see the ship already shrunk to a fiery spot of light rising into the sky, golden-white against the grey overcast, then gone as it pierced the clouds.

Far away, Flame glimpsed a flicker of light in the sky. A long moment later she heard a faint rumble.

"You made it, then," she said.

"Affirmative. Query: Advisability of landing to recover cyborg unit."

"No, don't do that — at least, not yet. I'm fine." Ugly and uncomfortable as the forest was, she was not yet ready to leave it. It was *different*, at any rate, and that was something she valued.

"Warning: Cyborg unit must allow for acceptable margin of error on timed destructive device."

"Don't worry about that. We still have time. You know that; you watched me reset it, just before I left the ship."

"Affirmative. Eighty-three hours, forty-six minutes, ten seconds remaining."

"You see? We have plenty of time, and I want to scout around some more," she said. "We still don't know what's going on on this planet, or what that anti-gravity stuff really is. Whatever it is, it must be portable if Slant had it there with him."

"Affirmative."

"Did you see any equipment on him?"

"Cyborg unit designated 'Slant' carried standard-issue rifled-barrel fully automatic rocket launcher, model ARR-eleven."

"Anything else?"

"Negative."

"Maybe it really is some kind of mutation then — but I doubt it. That was probably just another lie. Besides, if Slant was using it, it couldn't be a local mutation, could it? He wasn't born here." She snorted quietly. "Oh, well, we'll figure it out."

She knew what she wanted to do before she called her ship down and got back on board. It wasn't necessary, since the ship now had enough nukes to obliterate all human life here, but she wanted to kill someone face to face. She had never done that before. It might be better than watching the mushroom clouds. Killing the squirrel had not been much of a relief for her tense need for vengeance, but people might be better.

She might even be able to kill the one she really wanted, the man on this planet who had actually betrayed her. She had told him that she might kill him with her own hands, and she might.

She liked that idea.

She stood, stretched in the peculiar way they had taught her back on Mars, and then kicked at the dead squirrel with a booted foot. Dark blood smeared the toe.

"I'll get you, Slant," she muttered. "I'll get you somehow."

ELEVEN

Cautiously, Turner emerged from the forest, and stepped forward to stand by the wreckage of his ship.

The blast of the other ship's main drive had left a long teardrop of bare, blackened ground in the clearing behind the shattered tail section. A broad line of white ash lay around the cleared ground, and around that was a band of black cinder that faded gradually into the surrounding undergrowth. Half the wreck lay exposed amid drifting ash, eleven years of accumulated plant life burned away in seconds, leaving bare, pitted metal.

Turner peered up at the sky for a moment, but could see nothing but clouds. He could no longer make out any trace of Flame's ship or its trail.

He wondered why Flame had ordered the ship to leave. Had she been afraid he would find a way to destroy it?

If so, she had certainly found the right defense. Obviously, he was not going to be able to hurt it, either single-handedly or with the help of every wizard on Dest, unless it landed again. Magic simply could not reach it in orbit, nor could any other weapon he had available.

If he could not stop the ship, then he had to stop Flame. Loose on the ground, she was, for the moment, the more immediate menace.

He turned around, studying the surrounding forest.

Flame would surely have stayed with her ship long enough to oversee the salvage of the missiles and warheads, and that would have taken some time. She had probably not left the clearing until that very morning. How far could she have gone since dawn?

Not very far, he was certain. She was on foot, and despite her training she was not really familiar with this forest. He would have a horse as soon as he could retrieve and calm the animal; he might be able to catch up to Flame if he could pick up her trail.

Of course, a cyborg could move much faster on foot than an ordinary person, but Flame would have had no reason to hurry. Even if she had expected pursuit, she could not have known that he would have a way of locating her.

He was not sure he actually could locate her, but as a wizard he had a possible method, and he intended to try. He reached out, seeking for some psychic trace of her passage.

His horse whinnied from somewhere amid the trees, and he felt the pale mist of energy that was its nervous system. He called for it, both vocally and psychically, and was gratified when it obeyed.

He stepped forward, turned to his left, and found a direction that somehow felt right. He took a step, then stopped.

There was no sense in walking off and leaving the horse; he crossed the clearing to meet it halfway, found the reins, and then swung himself into the saddle. Once astride, he again located the faint trace he had sensed, and guided the animal to the southwest, hoping, but by no means certain, that he was following Flame's trail.

He rode on through the afternoon, eating in the saddle. The psychic trace he was following came and went, so that at times he had to wander around aimlessly until he could pick it up again, but he never lost it completely.

He hoped that the trace was actually Flame, but he was still not certain, and on two or three occasions, before he could regain sufficient concentration to continue the pursuit, he had to stop and convince himself that he was not following a stray goat or dog.

Whenever he could sense it at all the psychic residue seemed to grow very gradually stronger, but he could not be sure he was reading that correctly. He had attempted no magical tracking since his apprenticeship, and had never taken the time, even then, to become good at it. He found it much easier than telepathy or several other wizardly arts, but had never expected to need it.

At nightfall he had found no physical trace of Flame, though his psionic tracking sense still led him on. The orbiting computer, although perfectly willing to talk to him, would say nothing of her whereabouts or actions.

He dared not rest, for fear he might lose her completely, or, worse, that she might double back, find him sleeping, and kill him.

When he first glimpsed the orange glow on the horizon, an hour after sunset, he was unsure whether it was visible light or something impinging on his wizard-sight. As it grew brighter, however, he realized that it was definitely visible. He smelled smoke, as well. Something was burning, something big. He hoped it was only forest that was afire.

Worried, he urged his tired horse forward; the beast obeyed reluctantly, and moved no faster than Turner could have moved on foot.

He cursed, then swung down out of the saddle and, although weary himself, drew on his reserves and levitated, rising quickly to treetop level. It meant leaving the horse behind for the moment, but he thought speed might be essential, and he could fly a good deal faster than he could walk. He refused to worry about what Flame's computer might think about his flight.

The computer said nothing about it, and he flew on toward the spreading glow.

Moments later he was sailing over a blazing village, fending off the billowing smoke as he tried to see what was happening on the ground. Even at his altitude of twenty meters or so the heat of the flames drove away the winter's chill, and he could feel himself sweating inside his heavy sheepskin coat.

He could see about two dozen homes, and a handful of assorted other buildings and outbuildings. In a town of such a size, in the event of fire, he expected to see several people running about, either aimlessly panicking or making desperate attempts to rescue their friends, their families, or their more precious possessions. The rest of the townspeople, he thought, should be watching from the relative safety of the nearby woods.

So far as he could see, only darkness filled the spaces between the trees, and the streets were empty.

He dropped to the ground to one side of the village, landing on a sparsely wooded piney hillside upwind from the burning buildings. He could still feel the heat, though, and the firelight painted the trees in stark orange glare and black shadow. The roar of the flames was like a strong gale.

"IRU 247," he called, "There's a village burning here, probably endangering friendly civilians. Do you know anything about it?"

"Affirmative. Cyborg unit designated 'Flame' set fire to destroy rebel outpost."

That was exactly what Turner had feared. *"What* rebel outpost?" he demanded. "There *are* no rebels on Dest anymore!"

"Cyborg unit designated 'Flame' maintains outpost was rebel-held."

Infuriated by the computer's mechanical calm, he said, "First off, that's no outpost, it's a village — or it was, anyway. Second, what grounds does she have for calling its inhabitants rebels? Those people were loyal to Old Earth! And where are the villagers, anyway?"

"Cyborg unit reports all rebels terminated."

Turner felt the shock like a blow to his belly. The village could well have held a hundred people.

"She killed *all* of them?" he asked, horrified. "Already?"

"Affirmative."

"How? I know they probably weren't armed, but they must have tried to escape."

"Initial assault was made with snark, allowing for surprise. Survivors of initial assault surrendered, and were ordered into large central structure, which was then burned. Persons attempting escape were killed."

Turner's stomach wrenched, and acid filled his throat. In his own years in the military he and his ship had killed hundreds or thousands of people, but even at the worst he had never carried out a pointless, vicious massacre like this. He looked out across the patchwork of burning thatch roofs, and the billowing black smoke. "How could she *do* that? Why did you let her? These people were loyal!"

The computer seemed to hesitate, as if uncertain, before replying, "Insufficient evidence exists to allow complete analysis of this situation; therefore, due to ongoing situation, cyborg unit has full discretion. Probability of inappropriate action not sufficient to justify risking loss of ship and mission in the event of cyborg-computer disagreement."

"So you didn't want to argue about it, and maybe have to blow Flame's head off? You let her kill innocent villagers instead. Aren't you supposed to make sure that your cyborg only kills the enemy?" Turner knew that the anger and bitterness in his tone would mean nothing to the computer, but he spoke aloud anyway.

The pause this time was so long that Turner wondered whether he had lost contact with the ship somehow. "Affirmative," it said at last. "Computer dysfunction remains within acceptable parameters."

"Oh, my God," Turner said, his anger suddenly washed out by fear and dismay. His own computer had used that very phrase, "computer dysfunction remains within acceptable parameters," when it began behaving irrationally. That had been bad enough for him, as a cyborg dealing with a demented computer, and this time it would surely be worse. This time both the computer and the cyborg appeared to be insane.

The missiles could be launched at any time, if the computer's insanity ever happened to coincide with the cyborg's.

"What dysfunction are you talking about, exactly?" he asked cautiously.

"Computer is marginally dysfunctional as a result of damage inflicted by enemy action, and as a result of long-standing internal programming conflicts caused by present situation, and as a result of general wear. Damage is suspected or known in programming and memory relevant to linguistics, cultural information, and procedures for dealing with civilian populations. Other damage may also exist."

Turner shuddered, took a deep breath, and then coughed as he took in a wayward puff of smoke.

When he could breathe freely again he said angrily, "Well, listen, I've lived on this planet for ten years, and there's nothing wrong with my programming or my knowledge of this planet. I'm an expert on the local culture and fluent in the local language, and I'm telling you, the people here are loyal to Old Earth. Don't let Flame kill any more without good evidence to the contrary. Understand?"

"Acknowledged."

That did nothing for the dead in this village, of course, but it was the most Turner could do. Hoping for further clues to how the two halves of IRU 247 thought, clues that might help him prevent further disaster, he asked, "What evidence did Flame have that these people were rebels? What did she ask them?"

The computer hesitated again — more evidence, if Turner had needed any, that it really was damaged. Military computers were not supposed to hesitate over simple questions of fact. He wondered what the internal programming conflicts were, and guessed that they resulted from the computer's knowledge that the war was over, combined with its inability to surrender. His own computer had never acknowledged such a conflict, but Turner suspected that it had existed.

He had no idea that Flame had booby-trapped her own ship.

"Information insufficient," the computer said at last. "Request cyborg unit designated 'Slant' discuss situation directly with cyborg unit designated 'Flame'."

"Fine! I'd be glad to!" he said, genuinely pleased that the computer was finally going to break through the barrier it had placed between the two cyborgs.

He wondered how she could possibly justify her actions. The villagers had been human beings, just as deserving of life as she was; how could she think she had the right to kill them?

As he waited for Flame's words, it suddenly occurred to Turner that Flame must be somewhere close to him, somewhere in the vicinity of the burning village. She could possibly have gone a few kilometers away, but not more than that, as the destruction of the village would have required a good bit of time. She might even have stayed to observe the results of her handiwork. She could be anywhere in the area, was perhaps watching him even now. The computer would not tell him where she was, but it would probably be glad to tell her his own location. He looked around, but could sense nothing over the heat and glare and roar of the flames; he stepped back, away from the village into the shelter of the trees, just in case. She *had* threatened to kill him, after all.

"You wanted to talk to me?" Flame asked abruptly, the voice in his head startling him.

Before he could reply, she continued, "I don't know how you convinced my computer to overrule me, you bastard, when it knows better than to argue with me, but however you did it, it won't do you any good. If you won't let me kill these people one way, I'll do it another — I'll burn every village on the stinking planet. It might even be better — slower, but more fun."

"But damn it, they're friendly!" he said, exasperated. "Didn't you ask them? Didn't they tell you which side they were on?"

"You're kidding, right?" Her strange cackling laughter came over the communications circuit, and he thought he heard it with his ears, as well, faint but audible. "I couldn't understand a word these damn rebels said!" she continued. "I yelled at them in every language I know, just in case, but they never answered me with anything but babble."

"Probably all they speak — all they *spoke* — was their own dialect. It's descended from Anglo-Spanish, but it's got added diphthongs and dropped consonants..."

"I don't care *what* it is, Slant — it's not anything I know and it's not anything the computer could interpret, and if these people were loyal they'd speak something we could understand."

"That's ridiculous!" A thought struck him. "If you couldn't speak to them," he asked, "how did you get them to surrender so you could herd them into the building you burned?"

"Oh, that was easy," Flame said. "I used sign language. A snark isn't very impressive, since it doesn't make any noise or flash, so to get their attention I shouted at them until they all came out into the streets to see what the fuss was, and then I cut someone in half." She laughed again. "That scared the crap out of the little bastards; all I had to do after that was wave and point, and they went where I told them."

Turner choked back vomit. He knew what a snark could do, and his imagination conjured up the scene all too clearly. "Oh, God," he said.

He found himself unable to stop thinking of the old schoolyard joke that he had heard as a boy — What's worse than finding a worm in an apple you just bit? Finding *half* a worm in an apple you just bit.

He forced down an urge to laugh hysterically, like Flame, and told himself that he was being foolish. He had seen plenty of gruesome things in his time, and had no excuse for letting a mere description upset him. His stay on Dest had weakened him, softened him up.

But then, he had never expected to need to be strong and hard again. He was a husband and father, a wizard, not a warrior.

And now, whether he liked it or not, he was Dest's protector. He did not yet know whether he would be called upon to be a warrior once again, but his role certainly called upon him to face reality and to make what decisions had to be made. He could not afford any illusions about Flame. He was facing an utterly ruthless opponent.

He might have to be equally ruthless to save the planet.

As he was recovering his composure, Flame demanded, "Where are you, anyway? How did you know about the village?"

Turner didn't bother answering. It seemed pointless. Talking to Flame at present was useless, he saw that plainly. She was simply beyond reason.

At least, this personality was. She presumably had seventeen others.

If they were similar to the ones he had had, several of them would appear only in specialized circumstances and would be incapable of reasoning about anything outside their own specialties. Others, though, would be more complete, and somewhere in the fragments of Flame's original mind a sane personality might still linger. If it ever came out, Turner might be able to settle things peacefully — but that seemed unlikely. This personality did not seem inclined to give way, and Dest, with its relatively primitive technology and social structure, was not likely to provide a situation where a cover personality was called for. Most of the non-technical personalities were intended to be used as deceptions in dealing with complex societies; at least one existed only in order to be ignorant under torture. Flame's attitude toward Dest's society made such subtleties unnecessary.

Besides, even if a friendly personality did come to the fore, Turner would have no way to keep her from switching identities again, and sooner or later this paranoid killer would almost certainly re-emerge, particularly if, as he believed, it was the default persona.

He had no idea what to do. It was easy to tell himself that he had to be ruthless, but what could he do? If he found Flame and killed her, her ship would retaliate by nuking cities.

"Hey, computer, I want to talk to you privately," Flame said, breaking into his thoughts. "I've got..." The rest was cut off, as the computer stopped relaying to Turner, leaving him listening to dead air.

He cursed, and unslung the rocket rifle and held it ready, the barrel gleaming dully in the glow of the burning village. Cutting off their communication channel was clearly a threatening move. Flame was somewhere nearby, he knew, and she might well be coming after him, intending to kill him. Her private business with the computer might have been to ask it to tell her exactly where he was.

If she came after him in her combat persona only fantastic luck would keep him alive, and that luck would need all the help he could provide, such as having his weapon out and ready. He was faster and stronger than any normal human, the equal of any of Flame's other selves in a fight, but even so, an IRU combat personality would completely outclass him. The combat persona was more efficient than any of the non-specialized selves. Since its decisions were limited to such basic choices as whether to fight or flee, and what weapon was closest at hand, it was able to operate much more quickly than a fully conscious person, even a person with spliced neurons. It was also able to completely ignore pain, and automatically kept adrenalin pumping at full force whenever it moved, so that it did not tire. An IRU cyborg with the combat personality dominant was really more a machine than a person, with a machine's unthinking efficiency.

Convincing the combat persona to take over without a direct and obvious threat, however, was not always easy, and it might not agree with the default personality about which target to attack, so that she would probably have to come looking for him as herself — if that mad killer could be considered anybody's true self. The two cyborgs would then be on roughly even terms until Turner did something that threatened Flame sufficiently to bring out her combat self.

If it came to a fight, he would have to kill her as quickly as possible, with a single shot, before the combat personality could take over.

And if it came to that, what would her ship do?

He could have little doubt of that. It would assume that Turner had lied, that Dest was enemy-held, and it would then set out to destroy as much of the planet as possible, firing every weapon it had — including the missiles it had salvaged from his own wrecked ship — before finally destroying itself, preferably by crashing into a final target with the fusion drive overheated to the point of explosion.

That was what the standard programming called for in the event of the cyborg's death on an enemy planet; he remembered that clearly.

That meant that he did not dare kill Flame, even if he could; it would mean the end of the world, the destruction of Dest, of his family, and of himself.

He knew that, but he kept the rocket rifle ready. The sight of it might deter her somewhat.

If she died in some other way, by accident or with her head blown off by the computer, but not killed by an inhabitant of Dest, his problems might well be over, since that would make him the computer's only available ally. He thought he would be able to convince the computer that Dest was friendly easily enough once Flame was no longer around to argue with him. That was something worth considering; if he could somehow kill her so that the computer accepted her death as an accident, Dest would be safe.

Better still would be if he could somehow convince the computer itself to kill her. If he could convince it that Dest was friendly, and that Flame knew that, then that would, to the computer's way of thinking, prove that Flame was a traitor. It would probably respond by detonating the thermite charge in the base of her skull.

That would solve the problem, certainly, but killing her would be a shame, in a way; Dest might have uses for another cyborg. If she were not a dangerous lunatic her death would not be necessary.

That started him wondering — *were* all her personalities deranged? If he had, as he thought, been dealing exclusively with her default personality so far, and if that had been the dominant personality during her entire time in space, the isolation had probably been what had driven her insane. Her other personalities, having been suppressed all that time, might not have suffered. Was there some way he could bring a different one to the fore, to see?

He sensed movement off to his left, something other than the flicker of firelight, and with superhuman, unthinking speed, the cyborg speed that he had believed lost and forgotten, he rolled to the side, bringing his rifle to bear on what he had glimpsed. A soft clatter sounded, barely audible over the fire's crackling roar.

Something had fallen; somewhere deep in the recesses of his mind that sound touched on a simple ruse that his combat personality had been taught back on Mars, so long ago. He spun around on one hip, boots scraping up pine needles, as he reached out desperately with his psychic senses.

TWELVE

Flame had at least one snark, he knew; she had used it to cut an innocent villager in half. No other weapons had been mentioned, though she might have some. He had to be ready for anything, but could take as a working hypothesis that Flame preferred to use her snark.

A snark broke down molecular bonds, reducing almost any solid matter to dust and loose ions. It was absolutely silent. It was also extremely limited in range, due to interference from the atmosphere. Flame had made something fall off to one side, probably while she was on his opposite side, perhaps by throwing whatever it was over his head, perhaps to get him to look the wrong way while she came close enough to use the snark on him.

Of course, she might have other weapons as well as the snark, and the pebble, or whatever it was, might have had another purpose entirely. He simply didn't know.

He fired his rifle out into the forest, away from the village, a single warning shot aimed high.

The rocket-shell whistled away, burning a yellow trail through the cold darkness, scattering pine needles and twigs as it passed through a treetop. He hoped the warning would delay her for the instant he needed to draw his breath.

"I know you're there, Flame!" he shouted. "Listen, you don't want to kill me yet — I know too much about this planet that you don't! I know what the gravitational anomalies are!"

His voice was lost in the trees, unanswered. A long second later a distant report and a flicker of light told him that the rocket-shell had spent its fuel, fallen to the ground, and detonated on impact.

Physically, he saw nothing but the forest, lit by the glow of the burning village. The sky was a solid blackness overhead, the stars hidden behind heavy clouds. He heard nothing but the crackling of the flames and the night breeze hissing through the pines.

His psychic awareness, however, was another matter. His every wizardly sense was alert, and he knew where Flame was. She was crouched a dozen meters away, behind a conjoined pair of trees. She was listening intently and watching him closely. He guessed that she was probably out of snark range — after her work on the village her snark would be low on charge. Even if she had brought two or three snarks, none were likely to be at full power if she had had to confine a hundred people in a burning building.

She might have other weapons, but he could not sense any. If she did have others, she was not using them. She was not attacking; she was waiting.

"Computer," he said, "Don't let her kill me. Not yet. You understand? *Don't let her kill me!*"

He waited for what seemed an eternity before the computer replied, "Affirmative."

That was what he had wanted to hear, but somehow it was not as reassuring as he had hoped it would be. He was still terrified.

"Flame," he called aloud, "Listen, you don't want to kill me. I'm what you came here to rescue, remember? I'm an IRU cyborg, the same as you — or I was, anyway, I'm decommissioned now, but even decommissioned, I'm still a Terran citizen, and you don't have the authority to kill me without a trial unless I do something that endangers you or your ship. I'm not doing anything like that. If you kill me, it's murder — and that's aiding and abetting the enemy. You know what your computer will do if you do that; that's what the thermite in your head is for. Neither of us wants to die. Let's talk this over."

"*Me*, aiding and abetting!" Her voice was higher than he had expected, and harsh. "*You're* the traitor helping the enemy, by preventing me from destroying everything! That's grounds for killing you, isn't it?" Switching to subvocalization, she repeated, "Isn't it?"

"Affirmative," the computer answered.

"But only if Dest is enemy-held! You haven't got any evidence of that!" Turner shouted.

"We don't *need* any evidence!" Flame insisted. "Old Earth's gone!"

Turner called desperately, "But these people don't even *know* that!" Except, he could not help adding to himself, for a few dozen he or his friends had told.

Frustrated at her inability to come up with an answer to that, Flame stepped out from behind the paired trees and fired the snark.

Turner glimpsed her, a shadow moving against the darkness beyond, and sensed the spray of disruptive energy. Instantly he dove for cover, ducking behind a young pine for what little protection it might provide. He saw powdered wood sparkle like gold dust in the firelight as a tree caught by the beam began to disintegrate. The trunk creaked and started to buckle.

The weapon could not reach him. He saw immediately that he was well beyond the snark's limited range. His dodging would have done no good otherwise, since even with the normal delays clipped out of his nervous system, with augmented muscles, with bones reinforced so that his increased speed and strength would not snap them, he could hardly have avoided a beam that moved at the speed of light.

"Computer, stop her! Override!" he demanded. "She's trying to kill me, and that's murder!"

"Affirmative," the computer replied, as the damaged tree slowly leaned over and fell, loudly tearing its way through the branches of its neighbors.

Beyond the toppled pine Flame suddenly jerked spastically. Even in the gloom, Turner could see her motion clearly. The snark fell from her hand as her fingers twitched uncontrollably. "No!" she shouted, "Goddammit, you stupid machine, don't duh-duh-duh..." Her jaw locked.

The computer, Turner knew from bitter personal experience, was attempting to override her brain's control of her body. If she had been hooked up to a control cable on her ship the computer could have taken over smoothly, completely, instantly, but at this long range she was able to put up a real fight; the ship's signal could not be much stronger than her brain's natural electrical output.

Her head turned toward him — the fire's glow was spreading, and he realized he could see her with his eyes as well as his mind, and not just as a shadow. She was short, heavy-bodied, wearing a worker's one-piece jumpsuit. Pale tangled hair, red in the firelight but probably blond by day, trailed down her back. The heat had not reached her, and her breath puffed from her mouth unevenly, visible as a pale golden mist. The hand that had held the snark was open and clutching, and she was bending down toward the fallen weapon, moving in small jerks, like a broken machine.

She was reaching for the snark. She was winning her battle for control of her own body.

He could not allow that.

"Computer," he called. "Can you induce a switch to a different personality? One of her cover identities?"

"Information insufficient," the computer replied. "Transition is regulated by conditioning of cyborg unit, not by computer control. However, application of appropriate internal stimuli may trigger transition."

"Try!" He held the rocket rifle pointed at her. "If she picks up that snark I'll have to kill her in self-defense. I don't want to do that." Even in his desperation, he wanted to make a point. "I *am* loyal, or I'd kill her now — you see that, don't you?"

"Affirmative."

He knew he did not dare to actually kill her. If he did the computer was likely to retaliate, whatever the exact circumstances. He was suddenly very unsure indeed that he could convince the computer that Dest was friendly if Flame died.

Her hand was on the snark, but her fingers would not close. She was staring at him, her entire body tensed.

"Then if she tries to kill me, it's murder, it's treason — you'll have to blow her head off. And that would mean she was wrong about this planet, it *is* loyal."

Her fingers were trembling, trying to close on the plastic grip.

"Information insufficient. Possibility of disloyalty of cyborg unit designated 'Slant' remains. Reasons other than loyalty to the Command may prevent destruction of cyborg unit designated 'Flame'."

He had not wanted the computer to figure that out. He aimed the rifle. "I'll shoot if I have to."

Then, suddenly, Flame relaxed. Her entire body lost its tension. The transition was so abrupt and complete that Turner lowered his own weapon slightly in startled response.

Moving casually, she stooped, picked up the snark, glanced at it, then looked back at Turner. He did not fire; he knew that he was no longer facing the same person. Her broad face was calm; she reached up and brushed back her hair with her free hand.

"*Zdrastvuytye*," she said in Russian, her voice almost an octave lower than before. "Do I know you?"

Turner hesitated, keeping the rocket rifle ready; he was unsure what to tell her, or even what language to use. She appeared to have completely abandoned the idea of killing him, but he knew better than to trust an IRU cyborg. Even if the current personality was sincerely friendly — which was not yet established — another personality might take over at any moment.

Flame studied him for a moment as he groped unsuccessfully for words. "Oh, of course I know you," she said, still speaking Russian. "Foolish of me. Forgive me; my head was only seeded sparingly. You're Slant." Even in the dim light, Turner could see the puzzled expression that crossed her face. "I was trying to kill you, against orders, wasn't I?"

Turner had to struggle to follow this; he had not heard Russian spoken for over twenty years of subjective time. "Do you speak anything besides Russian?" he asked in polyglot.

"No," she replied thoughtfully, still in Russian. "Only the Russian language. My native tongue." Puzzlement crossed her face again. "But I can understand you. I remember what my other self learned, regardless of what language was spoken. That seems strange."

"Not really," Turner said conversationally, trying to keep the mood light. "If you're a cover personality, it might have been done intentionally to keep you from slipping up, if you claim to only know Russian. You could still listen to anything, but couldn't speak anything you aren't supposed to know." He added silently, "Is that it, computer?"

"Affirmative."

"Who are you?" he asked, still speaking polyglot. "I mean, who are you supposed to be?"

She shrugged. "A technician. No one special. I could blend in in any number of industrialized societies. Quiet, obedient, no trouble." An instant of worry narrowed her eyes, then vanished. "What am I doing here? Is this a mistake? They do not speak Russian here, and there is no industry that I have seen; I should not have been called upon."

"It was an emergency," Turner explained. "We needed to get the default personality out of control for a time; she's become unbalanced. You can probably remember what I'm talking about. We dislodged her, and you came to the fore, and here we are. That's all." He could sense a wordless questioning over the internal communications circuit.

The computer replied, "Affirmative."

"If you think there's a better personality, you could switch, I suppose, just so long as you don't bring up either the default or the combat one." Turner still held the rocket rifle pointed at her; his grip had relaxed, but as he made this suggestion it tightened again.

He said it because he was trying to stay in his role as a loyal citizen of Old Earth, and because he had to struggle to understand her Russian, but in truth, he hoped that this personality would stay. She seemed much more pleasant and tractable than the default self. She was calm, relaxed, non-threatening.

But then, he realized as he looked at her over the barrel of his weapon, that was her purpose, as a cover personality, to be dull and non-threatening so as to allay suspicion. She was undoubtedly skilled at espionage or sabotage, and the combat personality still lurked just below the surface.

This was the first chance that Turner had had to get a good look at IRU 247's cyborg. He moved slightly, without lowering the rifle, to get a better angle on her.

The firelight had peaked a moment before and was beginning to fade, as the flames were running out of fuel; they had been unable to leap the gap from village to forest, and all the more flammable elements of the village, such as thatched roofs and old awnings, were now no more than fine ash. Still, Turner had enough light to see his recent antagonist reasonably well.

Flame was short, stocky, with a hard square face and dirty blond hair that hung raggedly down her back; Turner guessed that she probably really was of Russian descent. Her eyes were hidden by shadow.

Before, when she had been crouched in a fighting stance, or strained against the override, she had seemed muscular, powerful despite her small stature. Now, in her casual slouch, the gray jumpsuit hanging loose on her, she looked old and flabby and quite harmless.

He knew, of course, that she was not harmless.

"There might be a better personality," she said after an instant's hesitation. "But I don't want to leave. I have not been dominant since I finished training back on Mars. I'll go if I have to, but could I stay for now? Computer?"

"Affirmative."

"*Khorosho*!" She smiled, then suddenly frowned. "But now what do we do? Why am I here? I mean, what was I doing in this place, and why did I seek to kill you, Slant? All I remember is a need to destroy enemies." She hefted the snark, then shrugged and put it in a pocket. "But I see no enemies," she said with a bemused smile.

"There *are* no enemies..." Turner began.

"Unconfirmed," the computer said. "Mission status unclear, pending determination of loyalty of inhabitants of this planet."

"What the computer means is, this planet stayed loyal to Old Earth — they never even heard that the Rebellion had taken place, let alone that Old Earth was destroyed — but your default personality wouldn't believe that. She wanted to wipe out the local population. Naturally, since I know they're loyal, I wanted to stop her. That's what led to our disagreement and your emergence."

"*Are* they loyal?" she asked. "Those in error are corrected, but traitors are destroyed. Old Soviet proverb."

"They're neither in error nor traitors. Ask anyone." He hoped that that would prove to be true.

She stared at him, considering.

"You mean," she said, "that anyone I ask will tell me that this planet is loyal to Old Earth?"

"That's right," Turner said, fervently hoping that it was.

"And you want me to ask someone?"

"That's right." He nodded. He had only been using a rhetorical turn of phrase, but, perhaps because she thought in Russian rather than polyglot, the cover personality had taken him literally.

He had no objection to being taken literally, none at all. That might well settle everything peacefully, if he could establish to the satisfaction of the computer and any of Flame's personalities that remained sane that Dest was indeed loyal.

"To ask someone that we must find someone, yes?"

"Yes, of course," Turner agreed, pleasantly startled. She seemed to be cooperating completely; the change from the default personality could not have been more drastic.

"Then we will do that. We will find someone and ask whether this planet serves Old Earth or the rebels." She smiled wryly, again brushing her hair back. "And when we do, I suppose I must go, and let another personality emerge. From what I have seen, what my other self has seen, the people of this land speak no Russian, and I cannot question them in anything else. Until then, I will stay. Is this satisfactory?"

"Affirmative," the computer said.

"*Da*," Turner, said smiling slightly in return.

"Which direction, then?" She waved at the surrounding forest.

Turner looked around at the darkness, and realized that the movement hurt his neck, which was stiff with tension and fatigue. A wave of weariness swept over him, and he worried suddenly if he was doing the right thing. People chosen at random would probably have no idea whether they were loyal to Old Earth, and he wanted time to rest, to think over the situation, to see if he could devise a way to be sure that he and Flame got the answers he wanted. "I think perhaps it would be better if we waited until morning," he suggested.

"Of course," Flame replied, nodding. "I, too, am tired." She glanced around. "Computer, wake us if there is danger," she said aloud. "Watch particularly that the fire does not spread beyond the village." A troubled expression flickered across her face. "That village — I did that? Not good."

"*Nye khorosho*," Turner agreed; he could still speak enough Russian for that. He watched as Flame sank to the ground, folding her legs under her, then settled herself back against the bole of a tree and closed her eyes.

When he was reasonably certain that she was not going to leap up again and attack him or flee, he dropped the butt of the rocket rifle to the ground and gradually lowered himself down beside it.

He had not been using a psionic heat-field, but excitement and the heat of the burning village had kept him warm until now. A chill was creeping in. He pulled his coat more tightly about himself, hoping that the cold would not bother him too much while he slept.

He leaned back against the nearest pine and closed his eyes.

As sometimes happened when he was exhausted, he did not fall asleep immediately; he was too wrought up from the day's events. He idly reviewed what he had done.

It occurred to him for the first time that he could have telekinetically prevented Flame from picking up the snark. He could have snatched the weapon away from her fingers while she was struggling against the override. He had not thought of any such stunt, though; he had been thinking in cyborg terms, not wizardly ones, despite his use of wizard-sight. He had treated his psionic perceptions as a sort of substitute for his computer's sensors, rather than as what they were. If he had been fully alert he would have thought of telekinesis, and would probably have been able to sense Flame's actions before they happened by reading her aura.

It had been a very long day, though, and he had been tired. He forgave himself his lapses, all the more because they had resulted in bringing this far more pleasant personality of Flame's to the fore.

He had never had any Russian-speaking cover personalities. He had had a nondescript technician, but that one spoke Anglo-Spanish and had never been called upon. He wondered idly how close the correspondence was between the eighteen fragmentary selves he had once had and the eighteen Flame presumably still possessed.

It was odd, he thought as he looked across at the sleeping Flame, that it was the cyborg who was giving him so much trouble this time, and not the computer. His own computer had decided that Dest was hostile entirely on the basis of the "gravitational anomalies" that magic created; it had had no record of any friendly research being done in the field of anti-gravity, and had therefore concluded that this apparent antigravity had to be enemy research.

He wondered if Flame's computer would have reached the same conclusion had he not been on the planet to say otherwise. How similar was the programming for the two machines?

Had they had the same basic mission? It did not appear that they had. His own assignment had been to scout out planets whose loyalty was uncertain, to determine whether they were friendly, neutral, or hostile, and, if they were neutral or hostile, to destroy or cripple their offensive capabilities, if any, to make sure they could not attack Old Earth. That was all; he had never been ordered to attack civilian populations without provocation.

Flame's mission, from what he could make out, had been more retaliatory in nature, more vindictive. She seemed to have orders to destroy as much of the enemy as possible, whether civilian or military and regardless of potential threats to Old Earth. She and her ship came from a later series than his own, when the war was going badly; Turner guessed that by the time IRU 247 received its orders the Command might have been growing desperate.

The computer's programming, then, might be very different in some regards. Its acknowledgment of internal programming conflicts agreed with that. The basics should have remained the same, however.

If he gave this one its release code, would it commit suicide, as his own had?

That would solve all his problems, right there. With the computer gone, Flame's release code would trigger hypnotic conditioning that would merge her eighteen personalities back into one. If that one was still determined to wreak havoc, he could simply kill her.

Once she was decommissioned, taking it upon himself to kill her might be a little drastic, but she was an exceptionally dangerous person, and had already murdered the entire population of a village. Besides, quite aside from any pragmatic reasoning, as a wizard of Praunce he had the authority to execute a murderer in the name of the imperial government.

For the first time in years it occurred to him that that was an exceptional privilege for him to have, when he was not an elected or appointed official, but simply someone with unusual skills. Praunce's laws left much to be desired. What right did he have to the power over life and death?

Of course, in his present situation, anything he might do to prevent Flame from killing him or anyone else would qualify as self-defense. Even if he were not a wizard, he would not be committing a crime if he killed her.

If she was insane, though, without being aggressive or destructive, what would he do? She would still have a cyborg's superhuman strength and speed, would have the *potential* to be horribly dangerous.

He dragged his thoughts away from such speculation. Worrying about what might or might not happen after Flame's decommissioning was pointless until he knew how to decommission her.

Was there any way he could get her release code?

He had no idea. The code would be her civilian name, repeated three times; did she remember her civilian name? Would she tell him if he asked? Back on Mars he had had his own memory suppressed as part of his conditioning, but bits and pieces had surfaced during his years in space, and he had remembered his name now and then. All the buried memories had come back when his personalities had recombined.

Did Flame remember anything of her past? Were bits of it coming back to her, as bits of his own had come back to him?

Did that past have anything to do with her destructiveness, or was her sadistic viciousness a result of her long isolation in space, and the loss of her home?

He opened his eyes and contemplated her.

She appeared to be sleeping comfortably. How odd, he thought, that less than an hour ago they had been trying to kill each other, yet here they were, sitting peacefully a few meters apart.

He had not given up the idea of killing her, if it became necessary, and he was sure that on some level, beneath the cover personality, she still wanted to kill him.

Was he safe sleeping near her, he wondered, or would he wake up to find the default personality back in control? Would he wake up at all? Should he try to slip away, even though the unsleeping computer would be watching and could track the machinery in his body anywhere?

He had dozens of questions, and no answers. He told himself that he might find answers to some of them in the morning, but others would probably go with him to his grave. None were likely to be answered before dawn. He sighed, gave the dying flames of the burning village a final glance, then snuggled down more closely against the tree and fell asleep.

THIRTEEN

He came awake suddenly, unsure what had disturbed him.

Seeing where he was, he remembered the preceding night's events in quick succession. He had reached the two ships; Flame's vessel had refused him entrance and had then, at Flame's command, abruptly launched itself back into orbit. He had tracked Flame to the village she had burned, whose people she had killed.

It troubled him, somehow, that he did not know what the village's name had been.

Flame had found him there, and their confrontation had ended in a weird anticlimax when the computer forced a cover personality to take over Flame's body.

He looked for her, and saw her still quietly sleeping, her back against a tree. Whatever had awakened him, she was not responsible for it.

Dest's primary was still below the horizon, but the sky had faded from black to a pinkish gray. True daylight would arrive in a few minutes. He did not think his abrupt wakefulness could have been triggered by the approaching dawn; it seemed too sudden for that.

The village fires had died away, and the heat and light had faded with them, but the biting cold did not seem a likely cause, either. Like the daylight, it had crept up gradually, and he felt very strongly that he had been awakened by something *sudden*.

Had the computer spoken to him?

No, the computer would have known that he was asleep from the telemetry from his internal equipment, and would not have disturbed him without a good reason. If such a reason existed it would have kept yelling at him until he answered.

The forest was dark and still around him, gray and black in the dim light. He could see nothing strange.

Could he have heard something from the village, perhaps?

He looked down the slope, listening intently.

He heard nothing. He had not seen the bodies, but he had no reason to doubt that Flame had, indeed, killed every man, woman, and child in the place. She was an IRU cyborg, a warrior of Old Earth, and could be trusted to do the job competently.

Besides, the village simply *felt* dead, and as a wizard he trusted that.

It had probably been a chipmunk that disturbed him, he decided, or if chipmunks hibernated — he had no knowledge of their winter habits — then perhaps a spider had tickled his foot. Whatever it might have been, he could see no sign of danger. He allowed himself to relax.

As he did, he wondered, as he often had before, why the original colonists had brought chipmunks and squirrels and other such useless animals to Dest. He was glad that they had, as the little creatures made Dest's endless forests seem a trifle friendlier, but he was still puzzled by their reasons. Surely simple aesthetics would have been outweighed by the limited space on their ships! They could not have brought every species on Old Earth; how had they made their choices?

Had they based it somehow on the planet's original ecology?

No, he told himself, they could not have known anything about the planet's ecology. The decisions would have been made utterly in the dark, since in those days no one could afford the luxury of waiting decades for an advance probe to report back. The colonists had probably arrived knowing nothing of what to expect save that this star ought to have planets.

Their supplies and equipment had probably contained everything they could imagine needing, everything they would need to face whatever hostile environment they might encounter. Chipmunks and squirrels, or at least the DNA to create them, might have been brought with some purpose in mind. He could not guess what the purpose might have been, since from a human point of view they seemed to be useless animals.

They did, however, add a little life to woods that would have been dreary without them.

Had Dest ever had any life of its own? That was a question he had pondered before, but he had never found an answer. The planet's recorded history, as the current inhabitants knew it, started with the Bad Times, long after the entire continent had been covered by terrestrial flora and fauna. No one, neither Turner nor anyone else, had any idea what the planet had been like before humans had colonized it. Perhaps it had been a ball of bare rock, or a small gas giant, or some other unlivable environment that had had to be terraformed. Perhaps it had had completely alien life that had been destroyed by terraforming.

Or perhaps it had had indigenous life so similar to Old Earth's that Turner simply had never noticed the surviving native species among the imported ones.

He shook his head. Dest's past history did not matter; he was more concerned with its future. How could he waste time on such irrelevancies as squirrels and chipmunks when there was a starship overhead with almost three dozen nuclear warheads ready to drop?

The thought of whatever had awakened him was not so readily to be dispelled, however. Could it have been a chipmunk? For some reason he could not define he found himself determined to know what had aroused him.

He thought of asking the computer, but then decided against it. He did not care to risk an argument with the computer just now. Besides, as he remembered telling himself last night, that was cyborg thinking, and he was a wizard as well. He stood and looked about, then reached out psionically, studying the carpet of pine needles around him.

Something forced his gaze upward and to the east. From a corner of one eye he saw that smoke still trailed up from the smoldering ruins of the village, but that was not what had drawn his attention. All he could see to the east were treetops, turning from black to green and brown in the growing light, but he knew that somewhere beyond those trees something was moving.

"Ongoing gravitational anomalies approaching cyborg units from east, at an altitude of approximately twenty meters and ground speed of approximately one point five meters per second; distance from cyborg units approximately three kilometers," the computer said, suddenly and without preamble.

"Good morning to you, too," he replied with half-hearted sarcasm. He knew now what had awakened him.

Parrah had called to him telepathically. She and at least two other wizards had flown out from Praunce looking for him. He could sense them faintly in the distance.

The computer could also sense them, of course.

Turner suddenly realized why Flame had ordered her ship to take off when she did; he had been studying it psionically. Naturally, the computer would have told Flame, and she would not have liked the idea at all. In effect, Turner himself had driven the ship away.

But why had the computer not pointed the "gravitational anomaly" out to him? He had been ready to make glib explanations, but he had never been given a chance.

That, he guessed, was Flame's doing. She must have told the computer not to tell him.

This, he thought, could prove inconvenient. Whenever he used almost any sort of wizardry, Flame and the computer would know it. Even if the computer did not tell Flame about every instance, she would, he realized, be able to sense it directly, once she knew what to look for. She was a cyborg like himself, and he had always been able to sense magic, even before he became a wizard. She, too, would presumably feel its presence as an electric tingle in the air. Apparently whatever energy magic used — a matter of considerable debate among the wizards of Dest, with a hybrid of electromagnetism and the weak nuclear interaction credited by the most currently fashionable theory — interfered slightly with cyborg systems.

His wizardry could be a useful secret weapon against Flame, but only if he used it very cautiously. Any use but the very subtlest would not be secret. Flame and her computer might not be able to tell what he was doing with his wizardry, but they would know wizardry was in use. If he *had* telekinetically disarmed her while she struggled against the override the computer might have decided that he was using an enemy weapon and must therefore be an enemy himself. That might have been disastrous.

On the other hand, the computer might not have leapt to that conclusion at all. He simply did not know enough about its programming to be sure one way or the other.

He also did not know what Parrah thought she was doing, coming after him this way. The previous day he would have welcomed her aid, but now he felt that he had things more or less in hand, and that her presence could only be a nuisance. Annoyed, he pulled away from her psionic attraction and looked at Flame, still asleep against her tree.

If he called to Parrah the computer would detect his use of wizardry, and he might not even get through clearly, since he was lousy at telepathy. If he did not call to her, she and her companions might blunder in and make some fatal error in dealing with one or the other of IRU 247's component parts. Parrah was a good, intelligent woman, a talented wizard, a delightful wife, and a good mother to their children, but she could rarely leave well enough alone. For years she had been his adviser in matters of everyday life on Dest. As a result, she had little faith in his ability to deal with anything without her help. Ordinarily that was no more than a minor annoyance, since she truly did know Dest and Praunce and wizardry better than he did, but she knew nothing about Old Earth's military except what he had told her. Any meddling now might complicate the situation beyond his ability to control it.

He settled on a compromise between doing nothing, thus risking Parrah's interference, and calling to her and possibly upsetting the computer. He flashed an instant's psionic broadcast as loudly as he could, a non-verbal warning to stay back, to go away. By not taking the time for words, limiting the message instead to a single emotional concept, he hoped that the computer would decide that the associated gravitational phenomenon was a matter of instrument error, rather than something he was causing.

Flame stirred, then blinked up at him. He saw for the first time that her eyes were a dull, washed-out green.

"Ongoing gravitational anomalies have stopped moving; maintaining altitude of twenty meters, approximately two point one kilometers from cyborg units," the computer informed him.

That was better, but not very good. Parrah, and whoever was accompanying her, had not gone away, but had only stopped approaching.

He felt a sudden tug of undefined urgency, and realized that Parrah was responding to his call in kind, saying wordlessly that she had an important reason for coming after him.

Maybe she did, he told himself. The possibility that one or more of the children had fallen ill, or been injured, sprang immediately to mind, but he pushed that aside for the moment as he watched Flame stretch. Whatever had concerned Parrah would have to wait, as he was facing a much more immediate threat right where he was, a threat not only to his family but to the entire planet. Flame was awake.

What personality would she have? And was her waking at that particular moment a coincidence, or had she somehow felt his telepathic broadcast?

At most, he thought, it should have registered as that faint tingling he remembered. He had become so accustomed to it that he no longer felt it himself, really. He was usually aware of wizardry being performed in his immediate vicinity, but that was because he could sense it psionically, not because of his cyborg nature.

He would not have thought the tingling would be enough to awaken her. If she had felt anything more than that, though —

He broke off his thought there and started a different one.

He was an abysmal telepath, by the standards of Praunce's other wizards, because his aura was so different from a normal one that he had difficulty in meshing it with any other. The differences were the result of the rewiring of his nervous system. This had also meant that other wizards had always had difficulty in reading his mind, even when he made no attempt at privacy and thought slowly and clearly in the Prauncer dialect.

Flame's nervous system had been reconstructed along the same lines as his own. Her aura would also be distorted and abnormal — but should be a close match for his own.

Therefore, he should be able to read her mind easily, where no other wizard would be able to, even though he could not read ordinary, undefended minds, or even coöperative ones, very well.

This resonance, if it actually existed, would explain why she might have felt something when he broadcast his message.

He forgot completely about Parrah's message of urgency as he considered the possible implications of his theory.

If he could read Flame's mind, then he had an advantage in any future confrontations. He would know what she was going to do before she did it. He could look in and see which personality was dominant at any given time. She could keep no secrets from him.

He had never been very enthusiastic about telepathy before, since he had been so bad at it and others so much better, but now he saw all the possibilities laid out enticingly before him.

He could learn what drove her, and maybe talk sense into her. He could listen in on her private conversations with the computer. He could find her real name and use it as her release code — that would settle matters *very* quickly. If the reintegrated personality was sane, the threat to Dest would be ended; if it was as mad and bent on destruction as her default self, he could kill her without bringing on a holocaust, since the computer would be released from its military programming by the code, just as Flame would be.

That was too good a possibility to pass up, even though the computer might notice something was going on. He would, he told himself, approach the matter gingerly, working his way gradually, carefully, under the psychic blocks her trainers had set up, until he found the suppressed memories of her civilian life. Eventually he would find her name, and he could then convert IRU 247 from a fighting ship to harmless war surplus.

Assuming, of course, that he could, in fact as well as in theory, read her mind.

He eyed her appraisingly. She eyed him back, in no hurry to say or do anything.

A trial, he told himself. I need to see if it works.

He reached out his senses tentatively, feeling his way across the intervening meters until he could sense the aura of psychic energy around her. He tried to see the shape of her aura, see which personality looked up at him from those dull green eyes, see if she was still thinking in Russian.

Something shrieked in his head and his concentration shattered; old reflexes flung him sideways, groping for the rocket rifle. "Mayday! Mayday! Mayday!" the computer screamed. "Gravitational anomalies centered on both cyborg units! Enemy action assumed responsible! Mayday! Mayday! Mayday!"

Flame was moving, rolling sideways in a motion similar to his own, a snark already in her hand and her finger on the button. Somehow, despite the disruption of his own thoughts, or perhaps because of it, he could feel what was going through her mind — not merely guess at what she saw and felt and thought, but *know* as surely as if her mind were a part of his own.

There were no thoughts, not really, no more than there might be in the mind of some lesser animal. There were only reflexes and a constant intent awareness of everything around her.

The combat persona was in charge.

She had not yet classed him as the enemy who had attacked her, but she was evaluating the situation, entirely on a non-rational, unconscious level. The threat was continuing, unseen and unfelt, but made known to her through a signal from the computer, a signal that was not in words but in a simple continuing tone on a particular frequency, a mental "sound" that her other personalities would have taken for little more than background noise. This personality, such as it was, accepted that single message as an infallible indication of some deadly danger that she had to either fight or flee.

If her enemy had been completely undetectable she would have fled, perhaps striking out at random as she did so. In the present situation, though, another person was present, a person whom she could not immediately classify as either friend or foe. The memories left by other personalities disagreed. He was armed, but not attacking her with his visible weapon.

She was, however, under attack.

The village nearby was dead. The attack presumably did not originate from there.

Except for herself and Turner — she knew him as Slant, of course — no one else was present.

She was not sure Slant was a friend — or rather, an ally, as a warrior personality has no friends.

That was all the thought necessary. The entire evaluation had lasted less than a third of a second. She swung the snark and pressed the button, twisting into a running crouch that would let her reduce the range.

Turner, however, had followed everything that flashed through her primitive mind during that fraction of a second, and his own thoughts and reflexes were still superhuman, despite a decade of peace. He did not dare kill her, even if it was possible; the computer would retaliate. Instead he fled, using all the speed he could muster, dodging among the trees, grateful that snarks had such a limited range.

Flame had not allowed for Turner's speed. She had unthinkingly acted as if he were an ordinary human. He remained out of range.

However, his actions seemed to confirm his hostility. Since he should not have been able to see her attack in time to react, he must have started to flee before she made any threatening move, which implied that he had been an enemy before she had done anything.

She thought this out not in words, but in a single conceptual image — fleeing equals enemy.

And fleeing enemies were to be pursued, so she pursued, the snark ready, but her finger no longer pressing the button.

FOURTEEN

Turner's foot twisted as he stepped on a root; he staggered slightly, then righted himself and ran on, trying to think.

She was still after him, still in the almost mindless combat persona. He had not expected it to last this long. They were well out of sight of the burned village — even the rising smoke was nothing but a smudge on the horizon now — and Flame was still relentlessly pursuing him.

He knew that it was partly his own doing. He had realized a kilometer back that his attempt at telepathy — his *successful* attempt at telepathy — had been interpreted as an attack. The tingling sensation would probably have been accepted as non-threatening after a moment or two, but the computer was monitoring the "gravitational" effect and keeping Flame alerted to its presence. It would not listen to explanations until the anomaly ceased; instead it kept on transmitting the danger message. As long as Turner maintained his telepathic contact, the computer would keep Flame feeling threatened, thereby maintaining the combat personality in control.

And the combat personality had marked him as an enemy.

If he dropped the telepathic contact, though, he would no longer have any warning of her actions, and that, he suspected, would quickly be fatal. She was not tiring, as he was; the combat personality could draw unchecked on the body's reserves until she fell over dead, while he had only his own will power driving him on. She was already faster than he was, now that he had begun to feel the strain of the chase. Only the fact that he knew what she would do, before her own limbs knew, allowed him to continue dodging.

Once again, as he stumbled on, he thanked God and the Prauncer trinity that snarks were so limited. Their limits had given them their name, he knew. Even as he dodged behind a tree to avoid her latest charge he remembered the story as he had heard it, long ago, when he had first volunteered for the military, even before the Command had shipped him to Mars.

Once, a few years before he was born, a general somewhere back on Old Earth had been put in charge of a team of physicists and engineers working on developing disintegrators. The general had set forth what she wanted, and when she wanted it, and when the deadline arrived the physicists and engineers brought her what they had done. It was the best they could come up with, but it did not live up to her high expectations. They had been unable to lick the problem of atmospheric interference.

That problem never had been licked, really — at least, not before IRU 205 had been launched.

The general, however, had taken this failure as a personal affront.

"I wanted something that would be *dangerous*," the general had told the scientists in angry disappointment. "Something that would be really frightening. Something that nobody could face, that would make anyone who went up against it softly and suddenly vanish away, like in the old poem. I asked you people for a boojum, but you gave me just an ordinary snark."

Turner was very grateful, as he peered back at his pursuer, that those physicists and engineers had never found a way to build boojums.

At that particular moment he wished that they had not bothered with snarks, either. The tree he had used for shelter leaned abruptly to one side as Flame cut into it with her weapon, but he was already moving away, keeping himself out of range.

He remembered his idea of taking the snark away telekinetically; since Flame and the computer were already aware of magic in the area, his major objection to the scheme no longer applied, but nonetheless he still could not put it into practice. She held the gadget tightly, too tightly for him to pry it loose without serious concentration, and she had two more snarks with her besides. He could see clearly in her thoughts that she had three snarks and no other weapons; a combat personality always kept in mind exactly what weapons were on hand.

And in any case he was too busy running and dodging to spare the effort for telekinesis.

Once again, he stumbled slightly on an exposed root; one hand flew up as he struggled to keep his balance, and he felt Flame hesitate. He would never have *seen* that hesitation, but linked to her mind as he was, he perceived it.

A sudden realization dawned; he stopped suddenly, flung his rifle to one side, and turned to face her, arms raised over his head, fingers spread. As he did, doubt flashed through him, and he waited, unsure whether he had guessed right or whether he was about to die an abrupt and grisly death.

Flame also stopped. Though she kept the snark pointed directly at him, she did not fire.

The combat personality could accept an enemy's surrender. It did not need to kill. He had forgotten that at first. He had thought of Flame as if the irrational hatred of her default personality would drive her on to destroy him, even when that personality was not in charge. The combat personality was incapable of hate, though, or of any other emotion. It was little more than a set of programmed responses. And one of those responses was to allow an enemy to surrender.

Given this respite, he was able to drop his telepathic link and force himself to suppress his psionic abilities for the moment. With that threat gone, and with her "enemy" putting up no further resistance, Flame's combat personality would yield control to another self.

Turner had not yet had time to consider which personality would come to the fore, however. In an instant, as he felt her thoughts through the last fading remnant of the telepathic linkage, he knew which identity it would be. He dropped flat to the ground as he shouted aloud, "Computer, don't let her kill me!"

The snark's beam passed harmlessly overhead, reducing a few pine needles and twigs to powder, and before Flame could lower her aim to Turner's new position the computer override sent her arm into convulsive jerking.

She fought it for a second or two, then gave in. She dropped the weapon. "All right!" she said aloud. "Let go! I'm not going to shoot him!"

The jerking stopped. She lowered her arm and rubbed it with her left hand, soothing the abused muscles, as she glared at Turner.

"All right, bastard," she said, "You win for now. I won't shoot you until we settle this." She glanced upward. "And you, computer, you just remember what's going to happen in another sixty hours or so, if I don't stop it. Don't push me too far."

Turner got carefully back to his feet, watching her every move, very much aware of the two snarks still in her pockets as well as the one she had dropped. One, he believed, was out of charge, but the others were both still dangerous.

He wondered what she was talking about with her sixty-hour deadline, but had no way of guessing. He shoved it aside as irrelevant.

The two of them, he realized, had reached a sort of stalemate. They had absolutely contradictory goals, with no hope of compromise — she wanted Dest dead and he wanted it alive. Each of them had advantages — he his psionic abilities, she her greater access to the computer and ship and the threat of nuclear weapons — but the net result was a close balance of power, maintained by the computer's refusal to side completely with one over the other. Each move that either of them made the other could counter; using wizardry against her would bring the combat personality out again and convince the computer to let her fight unhampered, while any direct, unprovoked hostile move on her part would cause the computer to use the override or to force a personality switch, or possibly even to kill her.

So far as he could see, only settling the question of Dest's actual loyalty could break the deadlock, by bringing the computer down on one side of the fence or the other.

That was what he had intended in the first place, of course, before he had gotten the idea of digging for her release code. He had intended to somehow prove Dest's loyalty, probably by the simple expedient of asking people. He had gotten the Russian-speaking technician personality to agree to that, at least provisionally, and then he had blown the whole thing by trying to read deeply enough in Flame's mind to find her release code.

That attempt had not worked out very well. He had not been able to look through her memories much while he was busy following her surface thoughts in order to stay alive. He had glimpsed one or two stray items, without really meaning to. He now knew what her ship's control cabin looked like. He knew that odd bits of her civilian life were there in her mind, slipping out from under the artificial barrier the Command had built, memories that would be readily accessible to a telepath, though Flame herself might not be aware of them. Turner had caught glimpses of them in what he thought of as the cracks between her several identities.

Her real name, however, was still a mystery. He had not happened across it. He did not have her release code, nor did he dare make another attempt to find it.

With that settled, he fell back upon his earlier plan.

"Listen," he said. "Let's find some of the natives and ask them about Old Earth and get this whole misunderstanding cleared up. They'll tell you they're loyal. Could we do that? Would that be all right with you?"

She watched him intently for a moment, then shrugged.

"All right," she said, "Let's do that." Her eyes narrowed. "I'll be watching to see what sort of trick you're pulling, Slant, I warn you, and if I catch you trying anything, that will prove once and for all that you're a traitor, and that the whole thing about this place being friendly is a sham, and then we can go ahead and blast this planet. Right, computer?"

"Affirmative. No deception may be permitted."

"Fine!" Turner said, smiling, hiding the doubts he felt. He noticed that Flame did not mention the possibility that the natives would support him without any trickery, and for a moment he considered demanding that she promise to accept at face value whatever evidence they found.

He decided not to press the issue. Flame would probably not give such a promise, or keep it if she did, and besides, the computer was the important one, not Flame. She could go on thinking whatever she liked.

The override and the thermite charge would keep her in line once the computer made its decision.

"So where do we find some of these natives to talk to?" Flame asked.

Turner had no ready reply. Before he could either admit this lack or devise a suitable lie, the computer interrupted.

"Ongoing gravitational anomalies are maintaining altitude of twenty meters, approximately two kilometers from cyborg units," the computer said. "Query: Advisability of investigation by cyborg units."

This, Turner saw, was a perfect opportunity. "I think that it's very advisable," he said. "If people there are using that mutation I told you about, then they must be wizards, as the natives call them. I can show you what the mutation is, and you can talk to them, and you'll see that they're friendly. That should kill two birds with one stone, shouldn't it?"

He knew that they would be friendly enough, since his wife was one of them. The only problem would be in getting them to say the right thing without any obvious coaching. He thought his problems with IRU 247 might be almost over.

"I don't trust you," Flame said, frowning.

Turner shrugged. "I don't trust you very much, either. You keep trying to kill me."

"Give me that rocket rifle," Flame said decisively. "Then we can go take a look at those mutant things, whatever they are. But I need the rifle first. I want something with some range."

Turner was not at all happy with that suggestion. "I don't dare give you all the weapons and leave myself unarmed," he said. "You *have* been trying to kill me, after all."

"Well, I'm not going up against anti-gravity with nothing but snarks," Flame insisted. "The computer said those things were twenty meters up, and these stupid snarks only have a range of three or four meters."

Turner had to concede that she had a point, and after a moment's hesitation he made a suggestion. "All right," he said, "We'll trade. You give me the snarks and you can have the rifle. For now, anyway." The alternative, which she had apparently not thought of yet, was to call the ship down so that Flame could re-equip herself from its armory. Turner did not like that idea at all. Giving her the rocket rifle was the lesser of the two evils, and would not, he told himself, be impossibly dangerous. The weapon's ammunition was not limitless, after all, and telekinesis ought to be able to deflect the missiles if the target wizard was alert enough.

In fact, Flame had made no mention of extra ammunition for the rifle. It held a single magazine of fifty rockets — no, he corrected himself, forty-nine, since he had fired one as a warning round the night before. He had four more magazines in his pack, but he had no intention of telling anyone that until he was asked.

He wondered how much charge the snarks still had. Flame might be effectively disarming him if they were low enough.

It was worth the gamble, he decided.

"The rifle is right there," he said, pointing out where he had thrown it. "You put all three snarks on the ground where you are now, and we'll trade places and arm ourselves."

She hesitated, then nodded, and reached into her pockets. Alert to any treachery, he watched intently, ready to simultaneously dodge and lash out psionically if she tried to kill him.

She picked out each snark, and dropped it to the ground.

When the third had fallen, and lay motionless on the frost-whitened pine needles, Turner allowed himself to relax. He moved almost casually as he walked over to where the deadly little things lay.

Flame made no pretense of nonchalance; she moved swiftly and smoothly to the fallen rifle and snatched it up, checking it over quickly and efficiently as Turner picked up the snarks, turned them to SAFETY, and stuffed them into his coat pockets. A glance at the dull red of the power dials before he switched the control settings showed him that one held a charge of five percent, another thirty-five percent, and the third seventy percent.

It would not be tactful to crosspatch them and run the best one up to full charge, he decided. That would look too much as if he really expected to use the thing. "All right," he said, "Let's go."

Only at the last moment before he turned did he remember to ask the computer, "Which direction?" He knew perfectly well which direction to take, since he could sense the wizards' presence quite clearly, but he judged demonstrating this seemingly unaccountable knowledge to be unwise.

When the computer had given them a bearing he marched off, and Flame followed a few paces behind. She was plainly not willing to let him get behind her.

That seemed illogical to him. After all, he had had chances to kill her, and he had not done so. Why should he kill her now, when she was doing what he wanted?

Besides, he was not particularly happy about allowing *her* behind *him*, and he glanced back frequently to make sure the rocket rifle was still held loosely before her, and not aimed at his back. He would have been much more comfortable had she slung it on her shoulder, but a single quick look at the hostile expression on her face put an end to any thought of suggesting that.

He watched his breath puffing out in the cold air as they walked, and gradually became more and more aware that he had not had breakfast, or much of a dinner the night before, and had already spent the better part of an hour in violent action this morning. He was ravenously hungry.

Food could wait, he told himself. He would deal with this meeting between the cyborgs and the wizards first. Flame was liable to misinterpret his actions if he stuck his hands in his pockets looking for something to eat.

He felt a slight tug as Parrah tried to call to him again; he ignored it. He did not want the computer to notice anything. If he did not actively listen, and did not answer, Parrah's transmission should not register on the ship's sensors as being connected to him at all.

After several seconds the call ceased.

"Gravitational anomalies are descending," the computer announced a moment later.

Turner glanced up, looked back at Flame, and kept walking.

"What are they doing, traitor?" Flame demanded.

"How should I know?" he called back over his shoulder. "They probably got tired. Or maybe they know — " He cut himself off short. He had been about to suggest that they might know the cyborgs were coming, and were landing to greet them. Flame, however, would probably have interpreted that to mean that she was walking into a trap.

"Maybe they know what?" Flame demanded suspiciously, her grip on the rocket rifle tightening.

"Maybe they know it's time for breakfast," Turner finished weakly, his hunger still on his mind

Flame did not seem to be worried about food; she snorted derisively.

"Gravitational anomalies have ceased," the computer said.

Flame stopped dead. Turner, automatically recognizing the difference between her normal walk and the sound of her final footstep, halted and turned.

"What's going on?" she demanded.

"They're resting, I guess," Turner said.

"They didn't just disappear?" Her grip on the rifle tightened.

"How could they disappear?" Turner asked placatingly.

Flame was not willing to be placated. "How should I know?" she said. "You're supposed to be the expert on this planet."

"People don't disappear here any more than on any other planet," Turner said, disgusted. "They're just resting, I guess, not using their magic — I mean, not using the mutation — at the moment. Your ship can't very well see a few individuals through all these trees."

"How do I know they aren't going to ambush us?" Flame asked suspiciously. "What is this mutation, anyway?"

"Why would they ambush us?" Turner knew that was a stupid question even before he finished asking it; Flame did not bother to answer it.

"What is this mutation?" she demanded again.

Turner could think of no answer that would serve better than the truth. "Psionics," he said.

"What are psionics?" Flame asked. "I've heard the word, but I want to know what you mean by it."

"Well, it's mental powers, sort of," Turner said hesitantly. "Levitation, mostly. That's how they can fly." He was careful to make no mention of telepathy or any of the other psychic senses; he was sure that Flame would violently object to the idea of such scrutiny.

"Levitation?" she said, "It *is* anti-gravity, then?"

"I don't know," Turner admitted truthfully. "Maybe."

Flame remained dubious. "It's not all just a lot of mystical tricks?" she asked skeptically.

"I don't think so." Turner thought that leaving a little doubt in Flame's mind might be useful later. He certainly did not want to admit that he, himself was a wizard.

"We had one of these anomalies centered on us before," Flame said, still skeptical. "We didn't levitate."

Trapped, Turner shrugged. "I can't explain that."

"Oh, I'm sure — just as sure as crayfish whistle," she said sarcastically. "You're lying, you bastard, and we both know it."

"Query: Evidence for assertion of untruthfulness," the computer interrupted.

"The whole general pattern," she replied silently. Turner heard her over the open communication channel. "His entire behavior. Besides, didn't he say earlier that he knew all about the anomalies? Now he's saying he doesn't. That's a contradiction."

"Affirmative."

"I can explain!" Turner called quickly. Shifting to subvocalization, he continued, "Computer, I lied for security reasons. I don't trust Flame; she destroyed a friendly village. After that, how can I trust her with information that might be extremely destructive to our side — to Old Earth? The psionic abilities here are probably unique in all the colonized worlds, and if she *is* a traitor she might sell them to the enemy."

"Cyborg unit designated 'Flame' is incapable of disloyalty, due to presence of termination systems."

"You mean the thermite in her skull. But that's just it! Psionic abilities allow the *removal* of security mechanisms like that! How long do you think she'd stay loyal if she could —"

"That's enough of that!" Flame shouted, the rifle pointed directly at Turner's belly. Her voice trembled with rage; her hands, regulated by computerized micromechanisms, did not. "I won't have a piece of filth like you impugning *my* loyalty!"

Turner held up his hands placatingly. "All right, calm down; if you shoot me now you'll just prove what I say, and the computer will blow your head off. Right, computer?"

"Affirmative."

"There, you see?"

Flame's face contorted in wordless fury; after a long silent moment she spat out, "It would almost be worth it! After I went, the ship would nuke your precious planet back to the Stone Age, Slant!"

"But you wouldn't be around to see it, would you?" He forced himself to speak calmly and quietly, calling on the emotionlessness that some of his personalities had been taught so long ago, back on Mars.

"Destruction of planetary installations in the event of termination of cyborg unit for insubordination is not definite," the computer put in. "Further analysis required. Circumstances might result in destruction of ship before attack could be carried out."

"See? You might not even destroy the planet. Now, calm down. I'm sorry if you feel I insulted you, but I *don't* trust you — you're too violent." His tone was that of an adult soothing a child, though his gut twisted at the memory of the burning village.

Turner watched as Flame silently struggled with herself, her face working. He wondered whether more than one personality might be involved, but easily resisted any temptation to look into her mind and see. He was attuned to her aura, but did not make the effort to listen, for fear the computer would notice and disapprove.

"All right," she said at last. "Keep walking. I want to see these psionic marvels." The thought that followed was so intense that Turner, quite inadvertently, picked it up telepathically.

"And when we see them," she thought, "I'll blow them to hell!"

FIFTEEN

Turner quietly slipped the snark with the greatest charge into his hand as they walked and dialed it from SAFETY to HIGH, keeping it carefully hidden from Flame. He did not intend to let her kill any wizards, and most particularly not his wife. He hoped fiercely that Parrah and her companions would be alert and ready to defend themselves when he and Flame arrived.

All he could do was hope. He did not dare try to warn them about the rocket rifle, or anything else, while Flame was walking a few paces behind him with her finger ready on the rifle's trigger, and while the computer was watching closely for any psionic activity.

As he rounded a tree he glimpsed a clearing ahead. Three robed figures stood in the clearing's center. He glanced back at Flame.

"I see them," she said. "Keep going."

He kept going, down a short, needle-covered slope, his breath rising in clouds above him as he descended. His shoulder felt curiously empty without the rocket rifle's weight on it, as if his coat were hovering about him unsupported. Cold gray daylight filtered through the trees and speckled the dark ground with dull colors.

Parrah was sending again, and at her present range he received part of her message without trying, not as words but as concepts and images.

She wanted something; she was here representing the Council, and they had sent her to tell him that they wanted something.

Exactly what they wanted was not clear; Parrah's imagery was of something bright and shining, hidden by something dark and unspeakably hideous.

He decided he really didn't care what the Council wanted, and he resented their use of his wife as a messenger. He had far more important concerns than what the Council, that short-sighted, elitist, arrogant bunch of psionic freaks, wanted. He looked down at his feet.

Parrah stopped sending.

The slope ended in a ditch, a dry streambed; he could see ice crystals on the bottom, in the cold shadows where daylight never shone directly. He climbed the other side, then stepped around a thicket into clear view of the waiting wizards.

They had all known he was coming, of course, and were looking directly at him, their gaze friendly and open.

"Hello, Sam," Parrah called aloud. She stood between Arzadel and Dekert, whom Turner knew to be not only old friends, but two of

Praunce's most powerful wizards, as well. If any wizardry should be needed, she had chosen her companions well — she, or the Council.

"I left the children with Haiger and Ahnao," she added before her husband could answer. "I thought you might like a little company out here."

Turner needed an instant to switch his thoughts from polyglot to the Prauncer dialect, and to comprehend that Parrah was giving no outward sign of her actual reasons for coming. He had still not phrased his reply when he was distracted.

Flame, close behind him, had stopped abruptly. "What the hell is this?" she cried. "Slant, that's your wife!"

He turned, startled. How had Flame recognized Parrah? The two women had never met, he was sure of that.

Then, with sudden clarity, it dawned upon him that when he had spoken with Parrah in their kitchen — when was that, just three days ago? — the computer had been watching, taking in the telemetry from his still-functioning systems, and it must have seen and recorded everything he saw. At some point before Flame left her ship she must have played that recording back, including the visual. With the control cable plugged into the back of her neck she could have experienced the entire thing exactly as if she had been there, in Turner's place — assuming that all the telemetry was still functioning, which seemed unlikely.

Obviously, though, the feed from his optic center still worked.

"You're right," he admitted in polyglot. "That's Parrah."

"What's *she* doing here? She should be back in that city of yours!"

"Why?" Turner demanded, honestly annoyed by Flame's arrogance. "She has a right to go where she chooses, just as we do! Normal life doesn't stop for everybody just because you're here, you know."

"Sam, say something we can understand," Parrah called.

Simultaneously, the computer was saying, "Gravitational anomalies detected in immediate vicinity of cyborg units."

Before he could respond to either Parrah or the computer, Flame said, "Oh, come on, Slant, this has got to be a trick of some kind! I didn't expect anything this obvious, but I'm still not going to wait around here for you to close your trap!" She swung the rocket rifle up and squeezed the trigger.

At some point in their walk, Turner realized, she had switched the rifle from single-fire to automatic. A stream of rockets screamed out, drawing lines of red fire across the clearing in a stroboscopic flicker.

The miniature missiles' explosions were out of all proportion to the size of the projectiles. The blasts came so quickly, and so close together, that the sound resembled a high-pitched roll of thunder; the glare was so sudden and intense that Turner blinked involuntarily, and even so he was partially blinded. Acting on a trained reflex he had had drummed into him throughout his apprenticeship, he flung up a defensive shield without thinking, a telekinetic barrier against anything solid that might come his way.

Nothing came his way save light and sound and a few tiny flecks of debris. Flame was concentrating her fire on the wizards — on the *other* wizards, not on him.

The roar subsided abruptly, replaced not by complete silence, but by a soft patter as fragments of rocket casing and pine tree fell to the ground all around him.

When his ears had stopped ringing, when he had blinked away the red blotches of after- image that had marred his vision, when the cloud of smoke had dissipated somewhat, he looked around.

His three fellow wizards stood unscathed in the center of the clearing, blinking and befuddled, looking about themselves in dumbfoundment; around them the ground was pockmarked with assorted small craters and strewn with a variety of litter. The trees around the clearing were a shambles of splintered branches and broken, blackened trunks. Several small fires flickered in the carpet of pine needles. Tiny shards of metal and plastic, all that remained of the rockets themselves, glittered on all sides like multicolored dew.

Flame was nowhere in sight, either by eye or by the quick psionic scan that was the best the rather shaken Turner could manage. She had apparently fled immediately after firing her burst.

"Oh, damn!" Turner muttered. He drew a deep breath, then let it out slowly, before silently asking, "Computer? Are you still there?"

Parrah started to say something; Turner held up a hand for silence.

"Affirmative," the computer said. "Ship is dropping from synchronous orbit in preparation for landing to recover cyborg unit designated 'Flame'."

"Damn," Turner said again. "Listen, computer," he subvocalized, "it was all a mistake. I admit that it was a pretty strange coincidence, my wife being one of the wizards we went to talk to, but that's all it was, a coincidence. She probably got worried and followed me. I wasn't trying anything deceitful. You've been watching me ever since we first made contact, I'm sure; I ask you, have I had a *chance* to arrange any tricks?"

"On four occasions since initial contact communications contact between ship and cyborg unit designated 'Slant' has been terminated due to ship's location in non-sychronous approach or departure orbits," the computer told him.

"It has?" Turner's surprise was genuine. "I didn't know that."

"Affirmative. Cyborg unit designated 'Slant' was not informed of termination of communications contact."

"But then I didn't *know* I could have planned something. I couldn't have set up any tricks because even if I had known you'd be out of contact, I didn't know *when*. You see?"

"Affirmative. Evidence indicates no conspiracy existed between cyborg unit designated 'Slant' and any local inhabitants."

"Tell Flame that!"

"Affirmative."

"Thank you." That eased Turner's mind somewhat, and he was able to turn his attention to his wife and her companions.

"Sam," Parrah called immediately, in Prauncer dialect. "We came to see if we could do anything to help."

That was not what Turner really wanted to hear just then.

"*That's* what was so urgent?"

"Well, no," Parrah began.

Arzadel interrupted, "Is that demon still around?" He pointed to his ear, and Turner knew that what he actually meant was, "Is the demon listening?"

"Probably."

"Then it can wait."

Turner shrugged. Whatever their reasons for coming, they were here, and he had to deal with that. The first objective had to be simply to keep them alive.

"Stay alert," he called. "Keep your defenses up; Flame might sneak around for another attack. I don't really think she will, but she might."

Arzadel nodded quickly, while Parrah began studying the surrounding pines intently, as if expecting Flame to leap out at her at any moment.

"Request cyborg unit designated 'Slant' refrain from conversation in unidentified language," the computer said.

Turner had been expecting that request at any moment, but that did not make it any more enjoyable to actually receive it. Annoyed, he forced himself to think in polyglot as he tried to devise an intelligent response to that. It was irritating that Flame and her computer could not understand the local version of Anglo-Spanish, when so far as he knew nobody on Dest, except himself, spoke anything other than that tongue or variations on it as a native language.

It was worse than irritating, he suddenly realized; it might be disastrous. It could mean that there was nobody on Dest who could tell either half of IRU 247 that Dest was loyal to Old Earth.

He might well be the only person on the planet who could speak to both sides.

This also meant that he could have conspired with Parrah or anyone else without worrying about being discovered by the computer. He fervently hoped that neither the computer nor Flame would think of that.

That was relatively unimportant, however. The important thing was that no one on Dest could attest to the planet's loyalty.

Was that true, though? Simply because he had never heard anything but dialects of Anglo-Spanish spoken didn't mean that all knowledge of other languages had been lost. In fact, thinking back to his earliest days on Dest, he remembered seeing books in other languages in a library in Teyzha. Might any of the scholar-wizards of that city know either Russian or polyglot, or some other language that either Flame or her computer could understand?

And if they did, would they agree that Dest's people were loyal to Old Earth? Teyzha was not part of Praunce's empire, at least not yet; it ruled its own little piece of turf, several hundred kilometers away in the eastern hills, and had its own unique culture. It was a wizard-dominated oligarchy, like most of Dest's city-states, but it had a good many cultural and social distinctions.

Teyzha had been founded well after the Bad Times, by people who had wanted nothing to do with the past, while Praunce had been built on ruins by people determined to restore as much of the past as they could. Prauncers had put up with the constant damage caused by lingering radiation for the sake of salvage and history, and the loyalty to Old Earth professed by much of the educated elite was a part of the heritage that they sought to preserve. Teyzhans, less concerned with heritage, might not feel that way. They might well feel that Old Earth had abandoned them and deserved no loyalty.

Certainly, they had abandoned Old Earth's customs. They made no pretense of representative government in Teyzha, or of social equality, or any of the other democratic or egalitarian habits Old Earth had passed on to its colonies. The Council of Wizards ruled the city outright, and guarded their prerogatives and the city's territory zealously.

He remembered that long ago, in the course of an audience before the Teyzhan Council, he had mentioned his loyalty to Old Earth — at the time his computer had still been operational and had been diligently enforcing that loyalty. One of the councilors, a middle-aged woman, had reacted to that, had started to demand an explanation, but the eldest of the councilors had brushed the matter aside as irrelevant.

He silently cursed the old man; the question was certainly relevant now. If the old councilor was still alive his life could depend on it.

Because the subject had been shoved aside, Turner had no idea whether Teyzha considered Old Earth friend or foe, whether the Teyzhans thought of their ancestral home as the long-lost motherland, or a trivial anachronistic legend, or even as the bitter enemy that had betrayed them and destroyed the planet's original civilization. Save for his own friends and family, no one in Praunce's empire knew that the fleet that had bombed the cities had come from Old Earth, but the people of Teyzha might be better informed.

And he did not really know whether anyone in Teyzha spoke Russian or polyglot. He could not recall, after more than a decade, whether either language had been present in that library. He had the feeling that he had been unable to read any of the books that were not in dialects of Anglo-Spanish, and if that were so, then Flame would probably be equally ignorant.

He could not be certain of his memories, but Teyzha did not seem promising.

What of the other eastern cities, such as Orna?

Turner shook his head. He knew less of them than he did of Teyzha. At least he had once been inside Teyzha; he had never visited Orna or any of the others.

There were still independent city-states on the western plains, as well as in the east, but from what he recalled of Awlmei, the only one he had seen directly, the western towns were very much a rough-and-ready sort of culture, one that had diverged from the old Terran model at least as much as Teyzha had, though in a different direction. It was unlikely that anyone there would speak a language Flame could understand.

Somewhere on the eastern coast, beyond even Teyzha, was the ancient museum city of Setharipoor, the only pre-war city that had never been nuked. It was a small town by pre-war standards, which probably accounted for its survival, but it had always been considered a city by those who survived the Bad Times. There could well be people there who spoke the old languages.

Setharipoor was well over a thousand kilometers away, though, and again, he was unsure of the city's loyalties. The people of Setharipoor *should* be loyal to Old Earth, he thought, but he simply wasn't sure. Although the city had never been bombed, it had been abandoned for decades after the Bad Times had disrupted everything.

He was not eager to risk the entire planet's fate on a mere probability, but if necessary, he decided he might resort to taking Flame to Setharipoor and hoping that no one there said the wrong thing.

Of course, Flame might wonder why she was being taken to so distant and obscure a city and assume it to be a ruse of some sort, but it was probably about the best he could do, as far as finding natives of Dest who could speak to IRU 247.

As he came to this conclusion he realized that he had been standing silently and staring at the three wizards for several seconds. They were staring back uneasily, apparently not sure it was safe to speak.

And something was tugging at his mind. Parrah had been trying to speak to him, telepathically, for several minutes, but had been unable to get through the interference his cyborg modifications created.

He hesitated, wondering if CCC-IRU 247 might possibly be able to intercept telepathic transmissions, then let himself hear her.

"Sam," she thought at him when she realized he was listening, "you mustn't destroy the ship if you can help it. The Council wants it intact."

"*What?*"

"*Stop the demon, of course, but if there is any way you can capture the ship, instead of wrecking it, capture it. Do it as little damage as you can.*"

"*Why?*" he demanded.

"*I don't know,*" Parrah answered, flustered. "*They just want it.*"

"Gravitational anomaly in immediate vicinity of cyborg unit designated 'Slant'," the computer interrupted.

"Yes," Turner said in silent polyglot, breaking his telepathic link, "I know."

"Request explanation."

"My wife is using psionics to check for damage from Flame's unprovoked attack."

"Query: Civilian designated as wife of cyborg unit designated 'Slant' possesses mutation responsible for gravitational anomalies."

"That's right." He could hardly deny it, under the circumstances.

"Query: Reason for survival of civilians."

"Psionics," Turner replied succinctly. "It can be used to defend against projectiles."

"Request detailed explanation of psionics."

"You're talking to the demon," Parrah said sharply.

"Yes, I am," Turner said, "Wait a moment."

Parrah watched him closely, but said nothing further, and Turner switched back to subvocalization. "I won't explain psionics over this channel. I told you that."

The computer did not reply immediately, and Turner knew that he had been standing and staring for an unnaturally long time. He broke eye contact, then looked back casually and tried to restore a semblance of normality.

"Are you all right?" he called in the Prauncer dialect.

"I think so," Parrah replied aloud, as Arzadel nodded beside her, "Are you?"

"I'm fine," he said, before the computer interrupted again.

"Request cyborg unit designated 'Slant' refrain from conversation in unidentified language," it repeated.

"It's not unidentified; it's the local dialect of Anglo-Spanish," Turner retorted.

"Request cyborg unit designated 'Slant' refrain from conversation in language not known to this unit," the computer said.

Ignoring the silent exchange, since she could not follow it or participate in it, Parrah asked, "What were those things that exploded everywhere? And how could that demon throw them so fast?" She waved a hand at the blasted clearing around her as she stepped gingerly toward her husband, picking her way carefully among the smoking bits of wreckage.

"Those were miniature missiles," Turner explained. "Rockets, each with its own propellant and warhead. That thing she was carrying can spit them out at several hundred a minute; I don't remember the exact rate of fire."

"Request cyborg unit designated 'Slant' refrain from conversation in language not known to this unit," the computer repeated.

"Oh, shut up!" Turner replied in silent annoyance, "I'm a civilian, and I have a right to talk to my wife!" He knew that part of his irritation was not actually with the computer, but with Parrah. What was she doing, turning up here with this mysterious request — or was it an order? — from the Council, complicating matters when he was struggling to keep their entire world alive.

"That weapon she used — isn't that the one you had?" Parrah asked hesitantly. "Or did she have one, too?"

"Oh, she probably has one, too," Turner said, hiding his anger, "but that one was mine."

"How did she get it away from you?" Parrah asked, worried.

"We traded," Turner explained. "And you can be glad we did, because if she had been using a snark and had gotten close enough to get a shot at you, your protective shield wouldn't have done anything to help you. I shot someone right through a shield once, in Teyzha." He smiled, an attempt at reassurance that became genuine pleasure. Seeing Parrah's familiar face, even when she wore her present worried look, even when she had no business being here, even when she was interfering dangerously, was wonderfully comforting.

"Uncooperative attitude of cyborg unit designated 'Slant' has been noted. Therefore, request matter of planetary loyalty be settled immediately."

"Fine," Turner said, slightly startled. "But how?"

"Suggest interrogation of random sample of population."

"The population doesn't speak polyglot around here," Turner said. Reluctantly, thinking of Setharipoor and hoping that the people there would profess loyalty to Old Earth, he added, "I think I know a place where they do, however."

"Negative. Due to uncertainty regarding loyalty of cyborg unit designated 'Slant,' sample must be chosen without reference to input from cyborg units."

Turner tried to think of some clever counter to that, but could not. "But you won't find anyone you can understand!" he finally burst out in frustration.

"Sampling will continue until sufficient evidence for determination has been accumulated."

That, Turner thought, was exactly the sort of idiocy one could expect from a computer. "How much of a sample do you need?"

"A minimum of three isolated responses will be adequate, or if both cyborg units reach agreement."

Parrah watched her husband for a moment as he stood, silently arguing. With a stifled sigh, she turned away. He was obviously going to be too busy to talk to her for a while, distracted by that incomprehensible machine that he called a computer and that she considered a demon.

She had delivered the Council's message, and had seen that her man was still alive and coping. There was nothing more she could do until Sam instructed her, and right now he barely saw her.

The demon obviously still controlled its ship and its city-destroying weapons, the prizes that the Council hoped to capture.

She wondered where the ship was. She saw no sign of it anywhere nearby.

She looked around, first at the forest, where she half expected to see that dreadful yellow-haired monster leap out at her with some new and hideous weapon, and then at the clearing.

Arzadel and Dekert were systematically stamping out the last few smoldering fires left by Flame's barrage. Parrah joined them, taking out her helpless frustration at the demon's existence and her husband's distraction by grinding harmless charred pine needles into black powder beneath her booted heel.

SIXTEEN

The discussion in Turner's head seemed to drag on endlessly. He could think of no clever new arguments, but could only repeat that if the selection were left entirely to random chance it would take years to find anyone on Dest who spoke polyglot or Russian.

That prospect did not seem to trouble the computer in the slightest. It seemed perfectly willing to devote years to the task.

When the computer stated as much, even Flame broke into the conversation to protest, but with no more effect than Turner had had. Her interruption served only to prove that wherever she was, she was listening in, which Turner had already suspected.

The details of the computer's plan gradually became clear. After picking up Flame and allowing her to re-equip herself, it would choose population centers at random. It would transport Flame to each in turn, and wait at each until Turner could make the journey overland to join them. The two cyborgs, working together, would then question the inhabitants, in either polyglot or Russian.

The computer required both cyborgs to be present, in order to prevent any sort of deception. It had been programmed to be aware of its own ignorance of large areas of human psychology, and knew that either cyborg alone might be able to distort the responses to suit his or her own preferences. Turner did not think it actually understood the concept of slanting evidence, but its programmers had, and had guarded against it.

The computer assumed that if either cyborg attempted any trickery, the other cyborg would be able to detect or prevent or counter any deceit where it, the computer, might not be aware that anything was amiss. It wanted an honest survey.

That was heartening, Turner thought. Flame might be paranoid, committed to bending facts to fit what she chose to believe, but her computer still seemed genuinely impartial.

When three responses supported one side, with none for the other, the computer would consider the matter settled in favor of that side. If either cyborg unit, at any point, were to acquiesce and accept the other's point of view, the computer would likewise accept that point of view. Uninformative responses, whether in unintelligible languages or simply not clearly supporting one view or the other, would be ignored. If positive responses were obtained on both sides of the argument, the entire method would be thrown out and another would be found.

What that other method might be could not be decided as yet. A simple majority would not serve, though; the computer wanted a unanimous decision.

The whole thing was quite clear, simple and direct. Turner and Flame both understood it immediately, and neither of them liked it at all. Since Turner was sure that only a handful of scholars spoke any language either Flame or CCC-IRU 247 could understand, and most of those scholars would probably be vague on matters of planetary loyalty, the survey would in all likelihood take the rest of the cyborgs' lives.

Spending the rest of his life tramping from one town to another interrogating strangers was not the future Turner had planned for himself; he said as much, to no avail.

He did not say that he was afraid that the results, if any were ever obtained, would be inconclusive, or contradictory, or that they would support Flame's position, but that was a very real concern.

He could not imagine what alternative method the computer might eventually devise if this one failed, but since this was, the computer said, the best, simplest, fastest, most immediate method, he did not want to find out.

Wandering hither and yon until he dropped dead of exhaustion was certainly preferable to dying in an immediate nuclear holocaust, of course. He had to concede that.

Once the computer had stated its irrevocable position, and he and Flame had run out of objections, the discussion degenerated into a debate between Flame and himself over who should acquiesce and put an end to the project. She maintained that he should give up his treason, join her aboard the ship, and watch as Dest was blasted into lifelessness. He suggested that she could afford to err on the side of mercy and leave Dest and himself alone.

The argument was still going on, with Flame holding forth on the vileness of all surviving humans, when the computer abruptly said, "Termination of communications contact imminent. Will continue determination of course of action upon resumption of communications contact in approximately fifty-five minutes."

"Nice of you to tell me this time," Turner said sarcastically.

The break in communications meant that the ship was about to drop below the horizon. It was in a steep descending orbit on its way to pick up Flame, but the approach was not so steep that it could avoid passing around the planet on its way down. It could not simply drop straight down; that would require a ridiculous amount of braking.

Turner started to wonder just what sort of an orbit it was following, but dismissed the matter as irrelevant. The computer certainly knew what it was doing when it came to piloting the ship, no matter how confused and stubborn it might be on other matters.

The break also meant that he would be able to talk to Parrah privately, even more privately than the computer's ignorance of Anglo-Spanish already assured. He could find out more of what the Council had in mind, or enlist her aid in any schemes he might devise. He did not need to worry about Flame overhearing on the communications circuit; he could not speak directly to Flame even if he wanted to. Everything had to be relayed by the ship.

Flame certainly had no way to tap into anything he did not want to transmit. Only the computer had access to his body's telemetry.

And he did not need to worry that Flame might sneak up undetected and eavesdrop with her own ears. No one could sneak up on four alert wizards undetected.

He realized suddenly that he had been assuming that the computer genuinely did not understand the language, and was not simply shamming ignorance in hopes that he would slip up and say something incriminating. The computer would never have thought of such a ruse — but Flame might have. He wished he had considered the possibility earlier.

For that matter, even dropping below the broadcast horizon might be a deception. The ship might still be somewhere overhead, listening to everything.

He gave the matter another few seconds' consideration, then decided to ignore it. He doubted that any of it was trickery. Flame did not strike him as being that subtle. If she had been clever, she would long ago have professed to accept Dest as friendly, while secretly conspiring with the computer, letting it know she was lying. She would then have found some trivial contradiction, cited it to the computer as proof that Dest was enemy territory, and killed Turner, probably by shooting him while his back was turned.

That would have been easy, and he could only be glad that Flame had not thought of it. Whether she was simply not very bright, or whether her apparent insanity had damaged her ability to scheme, or whether some other cause entirely had prevented her from devising and carrying out such a deception, he had no way of knowing.

Of course, now that he had thought of it, he would be alert for any such attempt, ready to head it off. Of the two cyborgs, he was definitely the tricky one. Flame was right about that.

He needed trickery, when faced with the ship's overwhelming firepower, and he knew he was capable of it. He had had years of practice in fooling his own computer in a myriad of small ways, and he had abilities as a wizard that IRU 247 could not imagine. He would find a way to counter any scheme Flame might devise — though with the computer's insistence on its interrogation plan, he was not sure she would be concocting any schemes.

He intended to concoct his own, however. He was determined to find a way out of spending the rest of his life questioning people. Already, an idea was stirring somewhere in the back of his mind.

"Termination of communications contact," the computer said.

Tearing his thoughts away from the communications circuit and back to the world around him, Turner found himself staring fixedly at a thick clump of long dark pine needles that dangled from the tip of a broken branch, just at eye level. He took a deep breath of the frosty air, looked around, and saw his black-robed wife seated on a fallen log, chatting quietly with Arzadel while Dekert studied a handful of missile fragments.

Was Dekert's action simple curiosity about something novel, or was it an unhealthy interest in the old military technology? Why did the Council want the ship?

He shoved that aside. He couldn't spare the time to worry about it. The ship would be back in contact soon.

"Parrah," Turner called.

Parrah looked up, startled, then broke into a smile as she realized that she could detect no sign of the demon.

"Hello, Sam," she said, "Did you get rid of the demon yet?"

"No," Turner said, "Not yet. I have an idea, though. Come here, I've got to talk to you."

SEVENTEEN

Parrah was not smiling any more.

"Are you serious?" she demanded. "You want me to learn an entire language telepathically in the next forty minutes — from you, the hardest mind to read on the entire planet — and then teach it to three whole towns?" She stared at him in open disbelief.

"That's right," Turner agreed, nodding. "Can you do it?"

Studying his face, she realized he was completely serious. She sighed, and thought for a moment.

"I don't know," she said finally. "I doubt it. I can read your mind when you cooperate, but I never learned another language before, telepathically or otherwise." She shivered slightly at the thought; the very idea of any language but her own was unpleasantly alien. Her entire world had always spoken a single tongue. She knew other languages existed, even on Dest, but she had never encountered them. Her apprehension at the prospect, and Sam's intensity, distracted her from any consideration of other matters, such as whether Sam's scheme, whatever it was, would capture the ship intact.

Turner, for his part, was grateful that she had accepted his brief explanation and was not demanding unimportant details, or arguing about the necessity of learning polyglot, or otherwise wasting precious time. "You don't need to learn *all* of it," he said. "Just enough to make yourself understood on a few subjects."

"I can *try*," Parrah said reluctantly. "You'll have to think through everything you want me to learn, and I'll need to be in a trance. Dekert and Arzadel may be able to help."

Turner glanced up from his wife's face and realized that both the other wizards had been listening intently; he had forgotten they were there at all. Arzadel nodded agreement with Parrah's suggestion.

He had gone to Parrah because she was his wife, the one he trusted above all others, but it occurred to him that Dekert and Arzadel might actually be better qualified for the task he proposed. They were both somewhat more powerful — but Parrah's specialty was telepathy, while the others preferred other skills.

Turner looked up at the two of them. "Do you think one of you two might do better?" he asked uncertainly.

"No," Arzadel replied, "Parrah knows your mind far better than we do — or she should, at any rate, as your wife."

"She's as good a telepath as anyone," Dekert put in.

"We will help, though, as much as we can," Arzadel added.

"All right, then," Turner said, "Go to it." He closed his eyes, thought back to his earliest language lessons, and concentrated on translating Prauncer Anglo-Spanish to polyglot.

Back on Mars his training had included techniques for learning languages quickly, with or without computer assistance. The Command appeared to have skipped that with Flame, further evidence that her series of IRU had been a rush job. Turner, along with the rest of his slightly earlier group, had been given careful instruction in the best, most efficient methods of either learning or teaching a rough working knowledge of new tongues. He was able to run through the essentials of the two grammars very quickly, and then to review the basic vocabulary, starting with pronouns, then covering the most common verbs, and then the nouns he thought might be needed, such as "world," "war," "loyalty," and a few dozen more.

He could feel Parrah's mind touching his own, taking in at least part of the information, but whether she would be able to put it together and use it he could not tell. She had never spoken any tongue but her own, had never even *heard* any language but her own save for a few odd sentences spoken almost in jest, and learning a language was not just a matter of knowing a few hundred words and some formal rules of sentence structure. He forced himself to think every thought in both Anglo-Spanish and polyglot, almost simultaneously.

He knew that he would have been able to acquire the rudiments of a new language from what he was giving Parrah, but he had spoken three different tongues by the time he started college, not counting machine languages, and had learned bits and pieces of at least half a dozen more later on. Each new language learned was easier than the last; that had been a recognized fact for centuries. Parrah did not even know any dialect of Anglo-Spanish but her own.

He forced himself not to worry about that, but instead ran over the polyglot vocabulary again. He let the grammar slide this second time around; it was similar enough to Anglo-Spanish grammar that he thought Parrah could get by, if Flame kept her sentences simple. The vocabulary was another matter; although Anglo-Spanish and polyglot were both largely derived from Old American English, they had gone in very different directions in what they did with that ancestral tongue. The people of Dest had modified their speech still further, of course, so that even the few words with the same roots were hardly recognizable as cognates.

He was starting on a third run-through when the mental voice of Flame's computer broke into his thoughts. "Gravitational anomaly exists in immediate vicinity of cyborg unit designated 'Slant'."

Turner immediately forgot about language lessons and waved Parrah away.

She was deep in trance and ignored her husband's gesture, but Dekert was more alert, and forced a break in Parrah's concentration. The mental link between the wizards vanished instantly.

"Gravitational anomaly has ceased," the computer said immediately. "Query: Advisability of further investigation."

"Not necessary," Turner said. "We were just passing time."

"Acknowledged. Site selection for determination of planetary loyalty completed. Initial interrogation site will be population center located approximately one hundred and forty-three kilometers south by southeast of present location of cyborg unit designated 'Slant'."

"Where?"

"Initial interrogation site will be population center located approximately one hundred and forty-three kilometers south by southeast of present location of cyborg unit designated 'Slant'."

He tried to estimate his position and figure out where that would be, but gave up. "I'll need my horse," he said. He had left the animal somewhere back near the burned-out village.

The computer made no reply. Turner realized he had not asked a question.

"What about Flame?" he inquired. "Will we be traveling together?"

"Negative."

The computer had no need to explain further; even before Arzadel shouted in surprise and pointed, Turner saw the blazing streak burst out of the clouds and burn its way across the sky as the starship came in hot for a fast landing approach. As the computer had said before it looped around the far side of the planet, it was coming down to pick Flame up.

Flame and her ship certainly seemed to like showy landings. Turner shook his head slightly in disapproval. His own computer would certainly have objected to so blatant an approach, even in its later, suicidal days.

His own computer had liked to take its time and circle in slowly, or simply to start in a much lower orbit. It would glide in silently, at subsonic speeds that did not even warm the hull. Once it had refused to land at all, and had delivered him by parachute.

Flame's computer had obviously been programmed differently.

The line of fire vanished behind the treetops, and a moment later the sound of the starship's passage struck like a thunderclap.

"Not very subtle," Turner said aloud, in polyglot, thinking of his own arrivals.

"No," Parrah agreed, "It wasn't."

Turner looked at her, startled.

She smiled and nodded, but before she could say anything he held up a hand for silence.

She hesitated, then nodded again.

Turner relaxed slightly. The computer probably believed Parrah did not speak polyglot, and letting it learn otherwise might well be a serious tactical error. This was obvious to Turner, while Parrah trusted her husband enough to accept his command without fully understanding its reasons.

She had something she wanted to discuss with him, however, so she switched back to her native Prauncer dialect. "Sam, we came partly because the council talked it over and decided that —"

"We don't have time," Turner began, in Anglo-Spanish.

"No, this is important," Parrah insisted. "We want the ship — if you can get rid of the demon without wrecking it, do it. That's what we came to help you with — " She had intended to go on to explain that for her, that was only an excuse, that she had come because she loved him, but before she could say that he interrupted her, gesturing angrily.

"You told me that! Don't worry about it. First we need to deal with the demon! Get moving!"

He did not enjoy saying that. He wanted very much to get a clear explanation of just what the Council wanted the ship for, and why they had sent Parrah, and why she had agreed to come, and any number of other things — but the computer was listening, and Flame might be as well, and they wanted an immediate resolution. He had no time to spare.

"Request cyborg unit designated 'Slant' refrain from conversation in language not known to this unit," the computer said.

Turner ignored it.

There was no need to say more. Parrah knew what to do. Turner had explained it before beginning the language lesson. She was to go to the site the computer had chosen and teach as many as possible of the people there to say, in polyglot, that they were loyal to Old Earth. She would be able to reach the village quickly by flying, arriving long before the computer could expect Turner to arrive.

Turner suddenly saw two flaws in his scheme, flaws that had somehow eluded him before.

First, the ship might fly Flame directly to the site and let her wait for him there, in which case Parrah might not be able to get in to teach anyone anything. Even a wizard flying at top speed could not match the starship's velocity.

He could do nothing to prevent that, however, and could only hope it would not happen.

The second, more serious flaw was that if Parrah flew, the computer would be able to track her the entire way. Her flight would create a moving "gravitational anomaly."

That would ruin everything; that would make the entire scheme woefully obvious even to something as stupid as a computer. Flame, suspecting conspiracies everywhere, could not possibly fail to denounce this one if Parrah's flight path made it so blatant.

"Parrah," he said, "There's a problem." He still spoke in Anglo-Spanish, so that the computer would not understand him.

"Request cyborg unit designated 'Slant' refrain from conversation in language not known to this unit," the computer said again.

"I'm just saying goodbye to my wife," he replied, then hesitated, waiting to counter further objections.

The computer said nothing.

"You mustn't fly or use any other magic," he told Parrah quickly in Anglo-Spanish, "Or the demon will know where you are. But you've still got to get there ahead of me, so you'll have time to teach people polyglot."

Parrah nodded. "I'll try," she said, "But Sam, I don't even know where I'm going!"

Turner cursed himself. Of course, Parrah had not heard the computer's directions, which had been given silently over his cyborg communication circuit. He repeated the description of the chosen town's location to her, intentionally using peculiar phrasing so the computer would not recognize the cognate words. He was relieved that Dest had not lost the metric system in the Bad Times. He did not think he could have managed if he had had to convert kilometers to some other unit.

Parrah nodded understanding. "I have it," she said. "Seven score and three kilometers southeast by south."

"Yes," Turner said. On a sudden uncontrollable impulse, he pulled her to him, embraced her, kissed her, then let her go. "Go now," he said, "Hurry!"

"I will," she replied. "I love you. Be careful. And try not to wreck the ship!" Before she could say any more, he turned and trotted into the forest, back toward where he had left his mount.

He had covered less than half the distance from the clearing to the burned-out village when the overcast sky lit up ahead of him, and IRU 247 lifted off, ascending into the heavens atop a tower of flame.

He stared at it for a moment, but even before the starship had vanished into the clouds he was marching onward once more.

In the woods a kilometer or so to the southeast of the blasted clearing, in an area where evergreens began to give way to the leafless branches of maples and oaks, Parrah was baffled. She was fairly certain the town of Killalah, on the old Etorrian highway, was her intended destination. How could she get to Killalah before Sam did, if she could not fly?

Killalah was where she was headed, following Sam's instructions, and she was fairly confident that she understood where she was going, and why, and what she was to do when she got there, but she had no idea at all of how she could reach the place in time.

For the present she simply ran, trotting south through the forests at a steady pace, trying to keep her wizard's robe from tangling in the bushes and trying to think of something she could do to speed her passage. She had left Arzadel and Dekert back in the clearing and set out on her own, wasting not a moment in explanation, so she had no one to ask for advice.

She did not really understand why she was not to fly or use any other magic. Sam had not had time to explain how her magic could tell the demon anything. Magic left no traces that she was aware of. The only way she could detect magic in use was through her own magic, and she knew that demons did not use wizardry, but something else.

If Sam said she was not to use magic, though, she would not use magic. She trusted him, and was determined not to fail him.

She wished she had had more time with him. At least, she thought, she was helping now, not just sitting at home with the children.

She knew her husband well enough to be sure that he would give her every chance. If he wanted her to reach Killalah first, he would do what he could to see that she did. He would undoubtedly dawdle along the way, keeping his horse to a walk, but still, she needed to have reached the town, taught people a strange ancient tongue and what they were to say in it, and then departed without a trace before either Sam or the yellow-haired, baggy-garbed demon with Sam's weapon arrived.

If she could find a horse herself, that might be all she needed. She risked a quick magical scan of the surrounding area.

A brilliant golden light appeared to the west, and for a moment she thought she had found something. She quickly realized, though, that she was seeing the demon's ship take off, with her eyes more than with her magic. That was nothing that could possibly help.

The roar reached her a few moments later, like a distant explosion or the echo of thunder.

The thought of thunder gave her an idea. She thought for a moment, then decided that a little more wizardry, more powerful this time, was needed. Sam had told her not to use magic, but she *needed* her magic if she was to accomplish anything, and she chose to risk it. Concentrating, she made a long-range mental call to Arzadel, straining herself badly to do it.

Her feet slowed, and stumbled, and she completed the message — semi-conscious and in a light trance — lying on her face on the cold, damp dead leaves that carpeted the ground.

When she was sure that Arzadel had heard and understood, she sent him a final warning that he was not to fly until he was well away from the blasted clearing — if it was not safe for her, then it would not be safe for the others. When she received an acknowledgement, faint with distance, of both her message and her final warning, she broke contact with a rush of relief and lay still for a few seconds, the warmth of her cheek melting the frost from the cold leaves.

After a moment's recuperation, she forced herself back to her feet, brushed off her robe, and began walking, gradually picking up speed until she was again running, not flat out, but at a pace she could maintain for kilometers.

She was no longer quite so worried. She had found a way to ensure that she would reach Killalah first.

If she could not go quickly, then Sam would need to go slowly. The demon would not want him to dawdle, but it could scarcely blame Sam if the weather turned bad enough to slow him down. That thundering sound the demon's ship had made as it took off into the sky had reminded her that the magical techniques that her comrades used to keep dangerous storms from damaging Praunce could make storms, as well as break them. The clouds were thick, and the winter had been dry, so that plenty of raw material should be available to work with.

Arzadel and the other wizards of Praunce should have no trouble in creating a fair-sized blizzard, its location carefully controlled. She herself would go around it, along its eastern edge, unhindered. Sam, farther to the west, would catch its full force. Even her Sam, strong and fast as he was, would be slowed by a blizzard.

Building and controlling a blizzard called for a really heavy use of magic, of course, but not in Killalah, or moving in that direction. If the demon saw it it would have no reason to connect it with Sam's mission.

She hoped that Sam would not have too rough a time with the storm, and that he would forgive her for not finding a less strenuous way.

She spared little thought for capturing the demon's ship intact.

EIGHTEEN

Turner was puzzled by the blizzard's sudden arrival. The clouds had thickened and darkened with incredible speed, turning the sky from pale gray to black, and the snow had begun falling even before the last light had vanished into the gathering gloom.

He knew immediately that the storm was magical in origin. He could sense it, even had its suddenness not been a giveaway. The magic that piled up the clouds put a tingle in the air as if it were a thunderstorm to break a long summer drought, rather than a midwinter snowfall. This storm, beyond question, was made by wizards.

But why would wizards be creating a snowstorm?

Turner had no idea. The wizards in the area were strangers, he was sure, and no doubt had their own reasons. Perhaps water supplies were running low somewhere. He could have signaled or tried to mind-speak to someone, but the computer would have noticed his use of psionics. Instead, he simply shrugged, and rode on.

A few moments after the first flakes sprinkled his brown hair with white, the computer asked, "Query: Reason for high concentration of gravitational anomalies in and around center of winter storm system."

Turner sighed, his breath swirling away in the wind, lost in the snow.

"I don't know," he lied. "I suppose the local wizards must be trying to break the storm up."

He saw no point in revealing that wizards could create storms, since that would establish beyond question the possibility of using psionics as a weapon. It might also bring up questions of whether the wizards might be trying to interfere with Turner's own actions. Flame and her computer were quite suspicious enough without adding any such unnecessary complications.

Although he would never have mentioned it to the computer, he wondered inwardly whether there might actually be some connection between the storm and his own activities, despite his failure to guess at what the connection might be.

The more he thought about it, the more he suspected a link of some kind. He had never before heard of anyone intentionally creating a blizzard. Certainly wizards often gathered clouds and supersaturated them to create rain, for crops and drinking water, but nobody ever made snow.

The sudden appearance of such a unique event, directly in his path, seemed an unlikely coincidence. When presented with two extremely unusual occurrences so close together as this snowstorm and his conflict with Flame, only a fool could be certain that one was not cause and the other effect. The blizzard had hardly brought Flame to Dest, but he could not really rule out the possibility that Flame's arrival was somehow responsible for the snowstorm. The local wizards were strangers, but they were all, he supposed, loyal subjects of Praunce. His compatriots might well have a hand in the storm.

He had no idea why they would want to, though.

Could it have anything to do with the Council's request that he try to capture Flame's ship intact?

He began to wonder whether the storm might be an act of war, or the start of a rebellion against Praunce. Neither one seemed likely. Turner tried to keep up with current events, and so far as he knew, the area had been completely peaceful for years. In fact, he was fairly certain that the region he was crossing had not been forcibly conquered, but had joined Praunce's empire peacefully and willingly. Such an area did not seem likely to rebel without warning, and any external enemy would have surely attacked either Praunce itself or somewhere along the border, not a thinly settled expanse of forest nowhere near either the city or the frontier.

But if this blizzard *were* an attack of some sort in a new, no-holds-barred war, might Praunce want a starship to retaliate against hostile wizardry?

That made no sense. No war had been brewing when he had left the city; no one could have known that any extraordinary defenses might be called for. Besides, magic could easily suppress hostile magic, which was why wizards had proved to be of very little use in combat, leaving warfare to the swordsmen and archers; a single defending wizard could usually suppress three or four attacking wizards. Magic was delicate stuff, easily disrupted. Wizardry was of military use only in intelligence, or if the other side had no wizards — or if the element of surprise was present.

If a storm could be conjured up without the enemy noticing, Turner supposed that it might have its uses.

But that was fantastically unlikely. Wars did not simply happen without warning. And nobody would be stupid enough to attack Praunce, not even with total surprise on his side. Even if Praunce had not had more wizards than any other nation, and more powerful wizards, it would still have no need of the starship to counter hostile magic. A handful of competent wizards would be enough for that, and Praunce's regular army was the largest and best on the planet.

But if the Council didn't want the ship to defend against magical attacks, then why *did* they want it? For attacking the city-states that remained unconquered? For quick transportation? For its computer, or its arsenal, or the technological knowledge it could provide?

Actually, he realized, they might not know exactly why they wanted it. They might simply see an opportunity, one they did not want to miss. They might not yet know just what they would do with the ship; after all, they knew very little about it.

If they had it, what would they do with it? Unite all of Dest under their dominion? That seemed the most probable use.

What right did they have to ask him for it? Why should he give it to them?

Was there any connection at all between the ship and the snowstorm?

He puzzled over the matter for a few minutes longer, then gave it up. He had no answers. He resigned himself to that and forgot about the mysteries as he concentrated on directing his mount through the thickening snow.

The storm worsened quickly and steadily. The wind picked up from a moderate breeze to a screaming gale, and the snow began falling in heavy white masses, rather than gentle scattered flakes. Visibility decreased quickly, and the footing deteriorated, so that Turner soon had to dismount and lead his horse.

The surrounding forest provided little shelter. The heavy, wet snow quickly exceeded what even the evergreens' branches would hold, and tumbled down to the ground beneath. Turner could not recall ever having seen so fierce a storm, and certainly not one that had achieved such ferocity so rapidly. The wizards responsible had certainly outdone themselves.

Within half an hour of the first flakes Turner found himself plowing through meter-high drifts, unable to see anything but blowing whiteness ahead except once, briefly, when he came within centimeters of walking into a tree's trunk. As he tugged at the reins, pulling his frightened horse along, he could feel the stallion's trembling through the wet leather. Even over the mounting howl of the wind he could hear branches above him creaking under the weight of the snow. A limb snapped loudly somewhere off to his right.

He began to worry that he would become lost, and wander endlessly in circles in the manner described by innumerable old stories, stories told on both Dest and Old Earth. The possibility of freezing to death or walking off a precipice seemed less absurd with every step.

"Computer," he asked as he fought through a drift, "Am I still headed the right direction?"

"Affirmative," the machine answered immediately and clearly. Turner was relieved to learn that the storm did not interfere significantly with either transmission or reception.

"Let me know if I veer off, all right?" he said.

"Affirmative."

Somewhat reassured, he struggled onward.

Assuming that the faint magical aura that permeated the entire storm would cover his own minimal output, he risked using his own psychic senses to guide him. The computer said nothing. With that little bit of magical assistance, and the computer's tracking as back-up, he fought his way on into the storm.

Within fifteen minutes of first asking the computer's aid, however, he was forced to admit that he was lost and exhausted. His coat was layered with snow, his beard frosted with his own frozen breath. Moisture from the snow and his own sweat had frozen into the reins, making them stiff and awkward, and the horse put up more and more resistance with every step. Unable to use any high-energy magic for fear the computer would find it suspicious and change the entire plan for determining Dest's loyalty, he had done without a heat-field, and as a result he could no longer feel anything in his toes. He still dared not warm them.

He could no longer perceive much psychically, and nothing useful at all. The storm and his own weariness blurred his senses. He did not know the area.

The computer, however, would have routinely recorded every visible detail of the entire planet ever since its ship entered orbit. He knew that. He had been relying on the computer to guide him to the target village, but now it occurred to him that he might have a better, more immediate use for the computer's stored data.

"Computer," he asked, "do you have any record of human habitation in my immediate vicinity — within a kilometer, say? It doesn't have to be a real town, or even a village; a farmhouse or an inn would do just fine."

"Affirmative," the computer replied immediately. "Isolated building located approximately two hundred and forty meters west by southwest of present plotted position of cyborg unit designated 'Slant'. Evidence indicates an individual dwelling."

"That's great," Turner said, sincerely. "Direct me to it, would you?"

The computer complied. Several long moments later, Turner's outstretched hand struck the side of a building.

He groped along until he found a door, and tried the latch.

The door was barred, which was hardly surprising. An ordinary latch could easily have given way before the wild gusts of wind, and whoever was inside would not have wanted to risk snow blowing in.

The fact that the door was barred from the inside meant that someone was inside to have barred it. Turner pounded on the snow-spattered oak as enthusiastically as he could.

Not until the door opened suddenly and he fell forward into a cozy living room was Turner able to verify that the computer had been right, that it was indeed a house, and not an inn or some other structure. The snow had hidden all exterior details so thoroughly that Turner believed he could have walked directly under an inn's low-hanging signboard without seeing it.

A short, middle-aged man in brown homespun had opened the door. A woman stood behind him, a long knife ready in her hand. Turner had fallen to the floor when the door had given way beneath his weight, too tired to bother about such details as breaking his fall. As the man shoved the door past Turner's feet, closing and barring it, Turner smiled up at them both from where he had landed.

"Hello," he said, "I hope you don't mind, but I lost my way in the storm. Could I stay here until it breaks?"

He smiled again, cracking the ice on his beard, not so much in an attempt to reassure his new hosts as in genuine relief at getting out of the wind for even a moment.

Until he noticed how good it felt to lie there on the floor, Turner had not realized how tired and battered he was. It was not entirely the storm's doing. He had not really rested since he had stupidly tried to read Flame's mind that morning. He had fled through the forest, and taught his wife polyglot, and fought his way through the storm, all in a single day.

Getting off the floor would be difficult.

The man and the woman glanced at each other, and then both began speaking at once.

No one would turn a man out into such a storm, he was assured in a confused volley of words. The two before him were the owners of the house, Hellegai and Turei by name, and they had many questions. They wanted to know who he was, where he came from, whether he knew anything about the storm, and virtually everything else up to and perhaps including the meaning of life itself.

Turner told himself that he could not lie on the floor indefinitely, and reluctantly acknowledged to himself that this was true. He had responsibilities. He had to save the world, among other things — and Praunce's wizards thought it would be nice if he could give them a starship while he was at it.

Right now, though, he had smaller, more immediate commitments. With a sigh, he rolled over and struggled slowly to his feet, thanking Hellegai and Turei profusely while completely ignoring their questions. Once upright, he took a deep breath of the warm air, asked directions, then pulled his coat tightly about him, hunched his shoulders, and fought his way back out to his horse.

He led the unhappy beast into the stable adjoining the house, tethered it to a post, then found a bucket and manger. The bucket was mostly full. He broke in the ice with the heel of one hand, then placed it where the stallion could reach it.

Fodder was a little more difficult, but eventually he simply stole a portion from the manger of the other horse in the stable, which presumably belonged to his hosts.

He was too tired to bother with any elaborate care, but he did at least manage to get the saddle off his mount.

He left the blanket on. The stable was cold. The walls kept out the snow and most of the wind, but provided little warmth.

When he was satisfied that the beast was not about to fall dead, he took a deep breath and opened the stable door.

The storm blasted at him. He would have groaned, save that he could not spare the breath. Instead he hunched himself forward and marched back out.

He reached the safety of the house's front door, where he was once again admitted. He staggered in, closed and barred the door, and then collapsed gratefully onto the hearthrug to warm his face and hands before the fire.

Once he had thawed out a little, he could worry about other matters, such as what Flame might be doing, what Parrah might be doing, and why Praunce's wizards wanted the ship.

NINETEEN

Flame lay back on the acceleration couch and closed her eyes. The control cable was securely in place in the socket in the back of her neck, and it felt almost comfortable there, linking her to her ship. She relaxed, enjoying the good feeling of a solid meal in her stomach and the familiar, well-worn shape of the couch beneath her.

Her adventures planetside had been exciting, an exhilarating change of pace, but the ship was her home, and she was glad to be safely back aboard, away from the cold and the dirt and the wind and the damp, secure where Slant and his treacherous allies could not get at her.

She only wished she could convince the computer to launch the missiles. That would make her pleasure complete. She had argued with the obstinate machine throughout the launch, and off and on throughout her subsequent leisurely shower and meal, but it had refused to yield. She had delayed resetting the timer on her little doomsday device, but when it became obvious that the computer was not going to yield, she had relented. The computer insisted on carrying out its scheme to question people at randomly selected sites, and would have let her destroy them both rather than doing the sensible thing and nuking the planet immediately.

Now that she had been back aboard for a few hours, and was rested, calm, and fed, she felt that she was ready to get down to business. She could yield gracefully. If the silly machine was determined to interrogate villagers, she might as well accept the fact and get on with the farce.

It would only mean a delay, after all. Sooner or later the truth would become apparent, and the computer would acknowledge that Slant was a traitor, and that the planet was run by rebels. Then she could nuke the cities and move on to the next target.

There was no hurry. This planet would get its just desserts eventually, she was certain. She judged that about fourteen warheads of varying yields would do the job, and then she would head for the next system. She would live long enough to see her entire arsenal fired, she was sure. She was still young — or at any rate not old — and even with the missiles salvaged from IRU 205, she could wipe out only a few more worlds, at best. One heavily populated planet would take everything she had, and then she would have nothing left to do but die. There was no need to hurry. Wasting a few days, or even months, on this planet could do no lasting harm.

"All right," she thought to the computer, "Where is this village you've picked out?"

The computer fed her its answer visually, through the control cable. Dest's one inhabited continent appeared in her mind, spreading out before her like a rug unrolling. A tiny spot glowed a vivid red amid the greens of forest and grassland. She saw nothing special about it.

"Has it got a name?" she asked.

"Information unavailable."

She stared at the map for a moment, then, on a sudden whim, she asked, "Show me all the gravitational whatever-they-ares."

Innumerable golden sparkles appeared, scattered here and there across the map, some blinking instantly into existence and then vanishing a moment later, others burning steadily for extended periods of time. Some were stationary, while others moved about randomly. A few of the cities were almost invisible beneath liberal coats of yellow-gold light. The big central city, however, seemed to be only lightly infested.

Generally, the dots were either gathered in the cities or strewn sparsely across the countryside. Outside the towns very few of the golden dots appeared in groups, with one exception. Several of them seemed to be gathering in an area to the north of the red dot that represented the computer's chosen interrogation site, not in a tight bunch, but in a loose ring, several kilometers across.

That looked suspicious.

"Where's Slant?" she asked.

A blue dot appeared to the northwest of both the red dot and all but the outermost of the gathered golden ones. It did not appear to be moving. She concentrated on it for a moment, thinking it might be moving very, very slowly, but it still appeared motionless, and she decided that Slant must be resting. The center of the cluster of gold lay directly between Slant and the village.

What could that mean?

She studied the situation for a moment. "Is there any anti-gravity activity right around Slant? I mean, within half a kilometer or so?"

"Negative."

Then it was not anything Slant was doing directly, she told herself. Slant had friends, though.

"What about his wife? Is she doing any of that?" she asked.

"Information insufficient," the computer replied.

"Why?"

"Present location of civilian identified as wife of cyborg unit designated 'Slant' is not known."

"Why not? Can't you find her?"

"Negative. Forest cover prevents visual tracking. Attempt at infrared tracking possible, but inconclusive results highly probable due to forest cover and presence of other heat sources, and no attempt was made prior to loss of contact. Possibility exists of tracking gravitational anomaly congruent with her position while such anomaly exists, but no such anomaly has been present. Subject does not radiate significantly in any other quantity detectable and measurable from ship's present altitude. No reason was known to attempt tracking."

"You've lost her, then." Flame was, for once, not accusing, but simply getting her facts straight.

"Affirmative."

"Is there a chance she could be connected with all that stuff I'm seeing, between Slant and the village? That looks awfully suspicious."

"Information insufficient. However, no evidence exists to suggest connection. Anomalous activity occurring at distance from last known position of civilian subject not consistent with lack of vehicular transport observed on planet."

"You mean she couldn't have gotten there that fast?"

"Affirmative."

"What if she levitated?"

"No gravitational anomalies observed departing last known position of civilian subject."

"Could she have walked partway, and then levitated?"

"Hypothesis is possible but not fully consistent with available data. Both gravitational anomalies originating within possible walking distance of last known position of civilian subject originated to east of last known position and procceded southwest at high altitude. Behavior not consistent with human psychology."

"Both? There were two, not three?"

"Affirmative."

"High altitude?"

"Affirmative."

Flame thought that over. She was still suspicious, but if the two anomalies were two of the three psionicists she had shot at, where was the third? And why were they at high altitude?

"Plot me their courses."

Two pale blue lines appeared on the map. They did indeed originate near the spot where she had encountered Slant's wife, but from there they diverged. One had headed straight toward the concentration of anomalies, while the other had swerved off to the north and vanished in a small town. Neither went anywhere near the target site.

If they were part of some deception Turner was arranging, she could not guess what it might be.

"Then you think that yellow stuff is all just a coincidence?" she asked.

The computer hesitated before replying, "Non-urban concentration of gravitational anomalies coincides with major winter storm activity. Cyborg unit designated 'Slant' theorizes an attempt by planet's inhabitants to disrupt storm system by use of psionics, to prevent possible damage and loss of life."

"A storm?" That sounded interesting. "Show me the weather, then," she demanded.

The calm green map was suddenly overlaid with swirling masses of white cloud. The area Flame had been watching vanished completely beneath a heavy grey blanket that spiralled and spun as she watched.

"*Bozhe moi!*" She started, and opened her eyes for a moment, then quickly closed them again. Adding the beige background of the carpeted ceiling did nothing to improve the image she was seeing.

"Where did *that* come from?" she asked. "It was cloudy when we took off, but nothing like that!"

"Information insufficient."

Flame stared for a moment. "A corner of it is over that village you picked, too," she remarked.

"Affirmative."

The storm system was huge and obviously powerful. "Could you land in that?" she asked.

"Affirmative."

She stared for a few seconds more.

"I don't think I want to," she said at last. "I'd rather stay up here where it's warm. We can land when the weather clears."

"Affirmative."

That storm did seem like sufficient reason for the concentration of psionics, she had to admit. The two dots that had passed near the clearing had probably been on their way to the storm. Tracing their course back she could see a village where they might have started. The one who turned away had probably gone for more help.

They probably had nothing to do with Slant or with herself.

She willed the map-image away. "I think I'll take a nap," she said. "Call me when that storm is gone."

"Affirmative."

The computer observed the slowing of Flame's breath and heartbeat, and charted the shift in brain waves as she fell quickly asleep.

Somewhere in the computer's processors, a fraction of a second after Flame passed the point the computer recognized as the line between sleeping and waking, the conclusion was reached that the storm could not be considered consistent with normal weather patterns.

That did not necessarily mean much. The computer's programming in regard to weather allowed for a great deal of latitude, since different planets had different climates, and any number of odd variables might intrude, from volcanoes to chemical waste from manufacturing, or from the tidal effects of moons to the fallout from supernovas.

The computer could detect no sign of such phenomena here. This planet had a rotation, axial tilt, gravity, diameter, shape, temperature range, orbit, and atmospheric composition well within normal ranges. Its weather, as far as the computer could see, should behave normally. The only abnormality was the concentration of what it had been told was "psionics," a concentration that had appeared *before* the storm really began.

The presence of psionic activity could be coincidence, or the result of good predictive methods, or causal.

It ran this information through its standard programming, and arrived at the string of "if...then" statements that related to informing its cyborg unit of the facts.

Flame had announced her intention of napping until the storm had passed. That kicked in a standing order she had given long before, that she was not to be disturbed unless something critical came up.

Therefore, the information on the storm's origin was run through tests of criticality.

Weather was not recognized as enemy activity, by definition, no matter how destructive. Certain sorts of weather, such as nuclear winter or volcanic eruptions where an impact had holed a planet's crust, could result from enemy activity, but were not in themselves enemy activity. This storm was not recognizably connected with enemy activity unless psionics were enemy activity. Slant had said that psionics were a mutation in friendly civilians, and no evidence to the contrary had been produced, so the computer did not consider psionics to necessarily be enemy activity.

Flame had said that the ship would not land until after the storm had subsided, so it was not critical to navigation.

The possibility that the psionicists had merely predicted the storm was very strong, and new methods of weather prediction, while interesting, were not critical.

Test after test came up negative, or brought in a sub-test that in turn, either came up negative or brought in a sub-sub-test. Quantification after quantification came within a point or two of testing positive, but none quite reached critical level.

Several tests yielded no decision. The termite damage to the computer's programming, during that long-ago attack, had been quite serious, far more serious than the computer itself realized.

One of the electronic termites in particular had been destroying computer memory for almost eight minutes when Flame finally got to it. It had wiped out vast quantities of essential data, most particularly data concerning the computer's own design and capabilities. The damage had not been judged critical only because the computer had been unaware that the destroyed programming had included most of its standards for judging criticality in any number of situations — including damage assessment, and also including judging when to override its cyborg.

Flame had remained blithely unaware of the extent of the damage, and in any case her own judgment was no longer entirely sound. She had done nothing about the computer's impairment beyond rigging her salvaged termite as a doomsday device.

The computer had carried on, and was still carrying on, applying its remaining tests to the question of whether it should treat doubt about the storm's origin as an urgent enough matter to report to Flame during her nap.

It drew no conclusion regarding any effect that the storm might have on the loyalty of the civilians who were to be interrogated. It could establish no link between the storm and the Slant cyborg.

The information was not reported. Had Flame taken another third of a second before falling asleep, the computer would have mentioned it.

By the time she awoke the computer had filed the information as inactive data, available should the subject be brought up, but not to be volunteered. Flame never learned that the storm might have been artificial, never had a chance to guess why it had been created, to apply her conspiracy theories to the question.

On the planet below, as he ate Turei's thick vegetable stew and listened to Hellegai's pointless anecdotes while he finished thawing out, Sam Turner had no way of knowing how close to falling apart his schemes had come. He was still far more concerned with what Parrah had meant about keeping the ship intact. What *did* the Prauncer wizards intend? Whose idea was it to capture the ship — Shopaur's? He was chairman of the Council at present, but Turner had not thought him sufficiently inventive to have come up with the idea. Arzadel was more likely. Dekert might well have thought of it, but would probably not have suggested it aloud. Haiger? Parrah herself? Pleido?

Wirozhess? If that young idiot was responsible, Turner was sure that the idea was to use it to conquer the planet. Wirozhess thought that way.

He puzzled it over as he savored the stew.

And at that same time, several kilometers to the east, Parrah stared in awe at the piled clouds on the western horizon. She had asked Arzadel for a blizzard, true, but this storm was more than she had expected. She could sense its fury readily from where she rode. She was very glad indeed that only a few isolated flakes and random gusts of wind were reaching her as she hurried on toward Killalah. She rode a horse she had bought on her credit as a wizard of Praunce, purchased at the first inn she had been able to locate after leaving Arzadel, Dekert, and Sam.

Killalah itself, she knew, had not been as fortunate as she, and was catching considerably more than isolated flakes and random gusts. She dreaded having to fight her way in if she reached the area before the storm had died.

She also shivered at a thought she could not suppress. A storm of that magnitude could easily kill someone. If anyone died in that howling maelstrom, she would be a murderess.

Furthermore, a storm of that size, for all she knew, would be enough to wreck the sky-ship she had been sent to preserve. Her entire mission might have been a mistake.

And worst of all, her husband was somewhere in the middle of the blizzard, and despite being a cyborg and wizard, he, too, could die, as a result of her instructions to Arzadel. That thought, had she allowed herself to entertain it for more than an instant, would have been enough to bring on nightmares.

She rode on toward Killalah free of snow, but in a thick fog of worry and desperation.

Somewhere in between husband and wife, in the fringes of the blizzard, Arzadel stared in horror at that same storm, towering above him as he hung in mid-air above the forest. He had started the cloud-building himself, before Dekert's local recruits began arriving, and had been concerned that the storm might not form quickly enough. Therefore, as the other wizards had arrived in twos or threes, he had urged them all on to the greatest possible speed, and had not really counted the newcomers, or kept a close watch on the storm system's overall development.

They had obviously overdone it. The storm had burgeoned out of control, until it was now far and away the most powerful storm ever created by wizardry on the face of Dest.

Even considering the wizards' haste and their numbers, Arzadel did not really understand how the blizzard had grown so big so fast.

Of course, the winter had been exceptionally dry. He guessed that he and his fellow wizards had unwittingly tapped into a pressure system that had been sitting there, waiting and building. Parrah's message had stressed urgency, so Arzadel had allowed no time to study the situation closely. He had simply started gathering clouds and ramming them together, piling them up and sweeping moisture up from lakes and rivers, until the sky could no longer hold the accumulated mass. The other wizards, as they arrived, had done the same.

And, apparently, they had triggered something, as much as they had built anything. A storm that might have come days later, or not at all, or as a series of storms spread over a much larger area and much more time, had all come at once, concentrated into one small area.

The result was quite impressive.

Now, the problem was not building the storm, or sustaining it, but disposing of it. Arzadel was unsure whether the best approach would be to shred away pieces, or just to keep it contained until it blew itself out, or something else entirely.

A message formed in his mind, and the decision was taken away from him. Dekert and the others were already shredding it, tearing away the outer cloud masses, deflecting winds, and trying to wear it down.

Arzadel looked at the roiling clouds and felt his heart sink. The thing was huge and looked stubborn. Killing it might take days.

But, he asked himself rhetorically, what choice did he have?

He gulped, gathered his strength, and reached out with his mind to pull away the nearest clouds.

In all, it took four days to kill the storm they had built in an afternoon.

TWENTY

The skies were still gray, but no longer particularly dark or threatening, when Parrah rode into Killalah. The snow had finally stopped falling there a few hours before, and already respectable paths had been dug out along most of the streets. Several people were now turning their attention to clearing the roofs, lest the weight of well over a meter of wet snow cave them in.

The storm had delayed Parrah somewhat after all. She had been able to skirt its edge for more than a hundred kilometers, but for the last fourth of the journey she had had to fight her way through the remnants of the once-mighty storm. She had made her way through two days of meter-deep snow and three- meter drifts, at times on horseback, at other times leading the way herself, practically dragging the beast along in her footsteps.

Now, though, she had reached her destination.

"Hello!" she called, "Who is in charge here?"

Several people stared at her, some of them openly hostile at the sight of a stranger in winter, when they had better things to do than cater to an uninvited guest.

Parrah wore the robe of a wizard, however, and wizards commanded respect. Many of the townspeople suspected that so sudden and heavy a storm could only have been the work of wizards, and had said so to anyone who would listen, but that was just gossip. Wizards commanded respect. People who failed to respect wizards had a tendency to suffer for it, in one way or another.

Accordingly, when Parrah asked her question, half a dozen hands pointed to a nearby rooftop where a rotund figure was vigorously shoving snow out over the eaves with a manure scoop. Parrah gathered from various phrases shouted through scarves and mufflers that this person was the town's imperial agent.

"Thank you," she said, nodding politely. She urged her horse forward until she sat near the building — though well clear of the overhanging eaves, as she had no desire for a faceful of snow.

"Hello!" she called again. "Are you in charge here?"

The person on the roof turned his head, saw her, and nodded, the manure scoop still in his hands.

"I need to talk to you!" Parrah shouted.

The plump figure, so heavily bundled in blue wool that Parrah could make out nothing but a vaguely manlike shape, rammed the scoop upright into the snow and turned to face the newcomer. A gloved hand reached up and pulled several layers of wool away from a thick black beard and a smiling mouth.

"Talk, then," a cheerful tenor voice replied.

"I would much prefer to speak on the ground," Parrah called, "Or better still, indoors somewhere warm. It's very important."

The figure peered speculatively around at the roof. Roughly a third of it had been cleared down to a depth of a few centimeters. The empire's representative obviously wanted to stay where he was and finish the job, but he, too, had seen the wizard's robe Parrah wore. Although Praunce's wizards theoretically served only an advisory role in government, everyone knew where the real power in the empire lay.

Since this woman wore no coat amid the snow and cold, yet appeared warm and comfortable, it seemed a safe assumption, despite her request to speak indoors, that the robe was not fraudulent or stolen.

He sighed, his breath puffing out of the woolen bundle like the steam from a kettle. "I'll be right down," he called. "Meet me inside."

The building on which the empire's representative stood, Parrah saw when she dropped her gaze from the roof to the facade, was a public house. She tied her horse to a rail and found her way to the taproom, where the plump man joined her a moment later.

Unwrapped, the imperial agent in Killalah proved to be of medium height and large, but not really excessive, girth, with a round smiling face and big stub-fingered hands. He refused to speak until warm cider had been provided for both himself and his guest, but then settled back comfortably and said, "My name is Tagyi, and I'm in charge around here as much as anyone is, so what can I do for you?"

Parrah hesitated; she had been so concerned with reaching Killalah that she had not really thought out what she would say.

"I'm here on an urgent errand," she said at last, "I need to teach as many people here as possible a new language, as quickly as possible. Magically."

The agent made no attempt to disguise his puzzlement as he looked at her, still smiling. "Why?" he asked at last.

Parrah sighed. "There is someone coming — a demon, in human form. She controls weapons from the Bad Times, many of them. My husband...she wants to kill us all. I mean, she intends to destroy entire cities at a time, with Praunce the first on her list. My husband is with her. No, I don't mean that; he's not *with* her, he's trying to stop her." Parrah, aware that her explanation was garbled, struggled to make clear what she herself did not fully understand. "She...she's under a geas, a commitment, and she can't kill those who swear loyalty to Old Earth, you see."

"Go on," Tagyi said noncommittally.

"Well, she's coming here. She conferred with her other demon, or whatever it is that restrains her, and they chose this town as their sample. They intend to come here and question people, and if anyone denies loyalty to Old Earth, then she'll start destroying cities. We don't want her to do that, of course, we just want her ship. So you must all say that you are loyal to Old Earth, do you see?"

The agent stared mildly at her for a moment before replying, "We're loyal to Praunce here, my lady; we know nothing of Old Earth."

"That doesn't matter." Parrah gestured as if to sweep away such unimportant details. "*Praunce* is loyal to Old Earth, and that's what we need to convince this demon of."

"My lady," Tagyi said politely, "I apologize if you think me impertinent, but who are you? You haven't mentioned that, and as a representative of the government of Praunce, I take an interest in such matters as loyalty oaths, and cannot ask my people to give them based on nothing but the word of a stranger. I can see that you are a wizard — either a wizard or a truly gifted actress — but I know nothing more about you." He smiled gently, as if to make plain that he meant no offense.

Parrah was not offended by anything except the delay the agent's doubts would cause. "I am Parrah," she said, "and I am a member of the Council of the Wizards of Praunce. My husband is Sam Turner, also a member of the Council. I am here as a representative of the Council, on Council business."

"Ah." Tagyi nodded. "I believe that I have heard both your name and your husband's, though I have never before had the pleasure of meeting either of you. Killalah has never before been graced by your presence, and I have never had the good fortune to visit Praunce. I must therefore confess, reluctantly, that I am unable to attest that you are who you say you are, but accepting your identity for the moment, I will grant that you are well within your rights to ask a favor of our humble town. But what *is* this 'Old Earth' the Council wants us to swear allegiance to? Do you mean the country of the old myths? And what was that about teaching languages?"

Parrah hissed in exasperation.

"It doesn't matter what Old Earth is. I do mean the world of the old myths; it isn't mythical. That doesn't matter, though. What matters is this demon, and convincing it that all of Dest is still loyal to the government of Old Earth, so it won't destroy Praunce and so we can get its ship."

Tagyi remained courteous but visibly skeptical. "And what does this have to do with new languages?" he asked.

"The demon doesn't speak our tongue," Parrah explained patiently. "So I have come here to teach as many of you as I can the demon's tongue."

"A demon that can't learn our speech, so that we must learn its?" Tagyi asked politely. "I had thought demons were more versatile than that."

Parrah's patience was exhausted. "Yes, damn you, it's a demon that can't learn our speech, so that we must learn its! Hligosh, I don't have time to argue about it! I need to start right away; the demon could be here any minute!"

"All right," the agent said calmly. "You're the wizard; you pick who you want to teach, then, and I'll see what they say."

"I pick *you*, then, San take you to hell!" She reached out and forced her way into the agent's mind.

Aboard Flame's ship, several thousand kilometers above, the computer informed its cyborg, "Gravitational anomaly occurring in site chosen for sample interrogation."

Flame was bored, after days of inaction while waiting for the storm to die, and sunk in lethargy and depression. "So what?" she asked.

"Insufficient information," the computer replied.

It said nothing more, but Flame could sense that it was awaiting further action. She sighed and stirred herself sufficiently to ask, "Is Slant there?"

"Negative."

She thought for a moment, then asked, "Did one of those psychics I met levitate himself to the place, or one of the ones that was in the storm?"

"Negative."

"Then forget about it," she said. "Those stupid anomalies turn up all over the place." She did not feel up to arguing about it either way.

"Affirmative." The computer considered silently for a moment, and then said, "All winter storm activity near site chosen for sample interrogation has ceased. Query: Advisability of landing."

Flame shifted on the couch and frowned at the poster. "Is Slant there yet?"

"Negative."

"Oh, that's right; you already told me that." She thought for a moment. "Oh, hell, I don't feel like it right now. It must be cold down there, with all that snow they just got; I'd rather wait up here. You won't let me kill any of the bastards anyway, will you?"

"Information insufficient. Permissibility of termination of local inhabitants dependent upon circumstances."

She felt too tired and dismal to take umbrage at the computer's literal-mindedness. "I mean," she said, "you won't just let me go in and shoot some, will you?"

"Negative."

"That's what I thought. In that case I'd just as soon wait up here, where it's warm."

"Acknowledged."

A momentary flash of guilt for her own disinterest struck her, and she forced herself to add, "Let me know when Slant gets close, though — say, about a dozen kilometers away." After all, she thought to herself, all she had left was her mission; she did not want to screw it up.

"Affirmative," the computer said.

On the ground, still a good many kilometers north of Killalah, Turner overheard this entire conversation as he clambered over the drifted snow. Flame's earlier orders regarding what Slant was to be told had apparently expired, or been inadvertently countermanded somehow. The computer had informed both cyborgs of the psionic activity simultaneously, and in the absence of instructions to the contrary had simply kept both communication circuits open.

Turner did not say anything, preferring to simply listen and save his energy for moving. The snow was too soft and deep to make riding a horse practical, so when he had decided the day before that the storm had let up enough for him to travel, he had left his mount with Hellegai and Turei, the householders who had sheltered him through the worst of the blizzard.

At first they had insisted that they would keep the animal safe for him until he returned, but he had told them to keep it for themselves, as payment for their hospitality. He did not want to bother returning. So far as he knew, the horse was not anyone's particular pet. He would buy another mount if he needed one.

They had finally accepted, but having seen his bare head and face they had forced a sturdy hat and a long, thick black scarf on him in exchange. After only a token resistance he had accepted those gratefully.

Now, listening to IRU 247, despite the cold and the snow and his general weariness, he smiled, genuinely cheerful at what he heard. Parrah had reached the target community and was starting her education program, he was sure. Furthermore, if Flame stayed in orbit until he was within a dozen kilometers of the town, she would not be arriving to interfere for days yet. Parrah would have all the time she needed.

That assumed, of course, that Flame didn't change her mind. Turner was slightly puzzled by her apparent indifference. It was not so much that indifference in an IRU cyborg was surprising; on the contrary, it was to be expected. A certain dull passivity seemed to be essential in anyone who was going to travel interstellar distances alone. The IRU default personalities, from what he knew of them, were designed for just that. His own default personality — Slant's default personality, at any rate — had certainly tended toward passivity. In general, he had acted only when forced by his computer to do so.

What was surprising in this case was not the passivity itself, but the contrast with Flame's earlier manic behavior.

He thought that over as he fought his way through forests and fields buried in snow. Having something to think about helped him resist the temptation to fly despite the inevitable arguments he knew flight would inspire.

After some consideration, he theorized that her present dull indifference was probably more or less Flame's normal condition. Surely, no personality, no matter how deranged, could sustain the level of anger and hatred that Flame had previously displayed — not over the long, empty years of uneventful travel between stars. That anger and hatred must have been her response to the disruption of her shipboard routine. Her ferocity had been waiting somewhere below the surface until it had something to act on, and he and Dest had been a perfect target. When she had arrived at Dest she had been primed and ready to unleash all her pent-up fury on the planet's cities — and she had been balked.

And, balked, she had been unable to maintain her state of rage.

In short, she was sulking. She hadn't been allowed her way, so now she would sit in her safe little place until she *was* allowed to do as she pleased and obliterate Dest's population.

Turner liked that theory. It seemed to fit everything he knew of her. The hatred and anger surely still lurked just below the surface, ready to break out in a new tantrum at any time.

He wondered what sort of a person she had been before her mind had been splintered. His current analysis of her default personality made her sound childish. Had the whole person been childish?

It was entirely possible that she had been, of course. The default personality was generally supposed to be pretty close to the complete original, as far as behavior went. It had to be, in order to remain dominant most of the time; the mind would keep trying to heal itself otherwise. That was why it took a special sort of person to become an IRU cyborg in the first place.

On the other hand, the Russian-speaking technician personality had seemed mature enough during the brief period he had seen it.

That meant nothing, he reminded himself. Of course, a cover personality had to *seem* like a complete and trustworthy person in order to be of any use in undercover work. That personality might have turned out to be utterly shallow and vapid. Probably would have, in fact.

He remembered, though, the puzzlement the cover self had displayed at her own emergence, and the wistfulness when she had asked not to be sent away again, and doubted his own conclusions.

He sighed. He really had to find out Flame's real name, he told himself. Once he knew her name he could deliver her release code, and her eighteen personalities would automatically reintegrate. Reintegrated, she might be a perfectly reasonable and useful human being.

Of course, she might not be a perfectly reasonable and useful human being, even then, but the release code would also demilitarize her ship, which would be well worth his while in any case.

What to do with the ship in that case might be an interesting problem. His fellow wizards wanted it, but having thought it over at length during the storm, he was not at all sure he liked the idea of giving it to them. The wizards were quite powerful enough in Prauncer society already. Too powerful, perhaps.

That was getting ahead of himself, though. He could learn Flame's name only by telepathically prying deep into her unconscious mind, and he could not do that while the computer had doubts about his loyalty and believed that any and all psionic magic directed toward it had to be considered an attack.

As the situation stood any study of Flame's mind was impossible.

He sighed again, his breath warm on the inside of the thick black scarf he had wrapped around the lower half of his face. He hoped his little scheme to establish Dest's loyalty to Old Earth would work.

He floundered on through the snow.

Dekert hovered in mid-air, wearily shredding a few last lingering clouds while he waited for the other wizards to gather in the agreed-upon spot. His psychic sensitivity was high, as he wanted to detect his companions early so as to be able to greet them properly. He did not care to be caught off guard if one dropped unexpectedly out of a cloud bank.

Alert as he was, he was not surprised when he sensed someone nearby, but he *was* surprised that the new arrival, who definitely felt like a fellow wizard, was on foot, and not flying. He paused in his cloud shredding, glanced down, and spotted a man who, judging by his hair color and clothing, looked like Sam Turner.

Startled, he verified Turner's identity with a quick psychic scan, so quick and light that it went unnoticed by its subject.

Dekert tried to evaluate the situation. He knew Turner was going to meet the demon. He did not know exactly what was to happen at that meeting, or what might be happening now, but he could guess some of it. A demon or two might well be watching Sam surreptitiously.

Dekert decided that dropping down and greeting Sam, or calling to him telepathically, would be a serious mistake.

Besides, even at the best of times, mind-talking to Sam Turner was extraordinarily difficult and uncomfortable. His mind was shaped wrong, permanently damaged by his own long-dead demon.

Dekert watched contemplatively. The entire party of wizards responsible for building and then breaking the blizzard would be gathering shortly, in that very spot, to decide what, if anything, they should do next. Dekert and Arzadel, as the two with the most information on what was happening as well as two of the highest-ranking and most powerful, would have considerable say in the final decision. Dekert therefore watched Turner with interest.

Sam, he knew, could take care of himself. Looking down, studying his compatriot, he could see no sign of uncertainty or worry in Turner's appearance, either physically or psychically — though Sam's aura was always odd. Whatever Turner was doing, he did not seem to be encountering any unforeseen difficulties.

He deserved a chance to clear up the entire problem himself, before anyone else got involved, Dekert decided. After all, judging by their performance with the storm, the wizards of Praunce and its empire were not exactly flawlessly competent and inerrant, and Turner did seem to know what he was doing.

Taking the demon's ship intact was not really very important, compared to preventing it from destroying Praunce. He saw no need to burden Sam with any further problems by reminding him that a sky-ship would be of use to the empire, or by interfering in any way.

Dekert resolved that, when the wizards were gathered, he would personally see to it that none of them entered Killalah until Sam Turner had emerged, had called for help, or was proved dead.

Parrah was in the town, he knew, on some errand Sam had set her. She might emerge at any time. Impulsive as she was, she might then go back on some whim of her own. Dekert decided that he would send a party to watch for her, to find her at the first opportunity, and make sure that she behaved herself.

This affair's resolution was up to Sam Turner and no one else. Dekert watched silently, without interfering, as Turner struggled on toward Killalah.

TWENTY-ONE

Parrah looked out the window, suddenly inexplicably nervous. The weather-beaten houses across the street looked no different than they had when she had entered.

Her gaze rose from the houses to the western sky just in time to see the starship blaze a band of golden fire across the indigo heavens.

Parrah froze for a moment. "Hligosh! She's finally coming! I have to get away from here, quickly. If she sees me she'll suspect something."

The old woman she had been telepathically instructing looked up at her in mild puzzlement.

Parrah turned back to the Killalaher. "Remember," she said sharply, "if you talk to her, don't tell her I was here, and don't let her know we were expecting her! Act as if her arrival is a complete surprise. Do you understand?"

The old woman nodded and smiled toothlessly.

"Ftha," Parrah swore, as the boom of the starship's passage shook the walls, "Ftha and Hligosh." As the echoes faded she turned to the old woman and demanded, in polyglot, "Do you understand me?"

The villager nodded.

"Who are you loyal to?"

The crone licked her lips, then managed, "Old Earth?" Her pronunciation was abominable, even by Parrah's standards, but the words were intelligible.

"Good enough," Parrah said. "Don't forget it." She glanced at the sky again, then turned and dashed out of the house.

Aboard the starship Flame was arguing with the computer. "Land close in!" she demanded aloud. "Don't give them time to prepare!"

"Standard procedure — " the computer began.

"Standard procedure doesn't cover a case like this!" Flame interrupted. "Since when is there a standard procedure for loyalty checks?"

The computer, as usual, took her question literally. "Standard procedure for loyalty checks was developed over a sixty-day period betwee —"

"Never mind that," she said, interrupting again. The computer obligingly stopped in mid-word.

Flame gathered herself together, spat a few choice expletives in two different languages, and then said, silently, "Listen, computer, I want to get there before Slant does, to be absolutely sure he doesn't interfere with anything before we get there. He speaks their language, remember. I want to land right next to the town — or better still, inside it — so I won't need to waste time walking from the ship to the town."

"Travel time has been allowed for."

"But you can't be sure there won't be unforeseen delays."

"Acknowledged. Not relevant."

Flame swore again, this time entirely in Russian. "Why don't you want to land right there in the town?" she demanded.

"Presence of ship may affect response to interrogation."

"What do you mean? Affect the response how?"

"Local inhabitants may recognize solar origins of ship and present appearance of loyalty to avoid conflict."

Flame sneered. "How would they recognize where we're from, idiot? They haven't seen *any* ships in three hundred years!"

The computer considered that for a perceptible fraction of a second before replying, "Acknowledged."

"Does that mean we can land close and save me a long walk? I don't have to remind you about a certain timed device?"

"Affirmative."

Flame smiled. Sometimes winning an argument with the computer could be very satisfying; it yielded so completely when it yielded at all. "Good!" she said. "Then let's get my pilot personality up here and I'll put us down right in the middle of town!" She lay back on the couch and let her mind go blank, to make room for the emotionless pilot identity.

"Affirmative," the computer said, but no one was listening.

Below, in Killalah, Parrah had left her horse at the public house that had been her home for the past three days. The pub stood on the town's central highway, toward the eastern end. The old woman's house had been chosen as Parrah's latest teaching site because it stood in the northwestern corner of town, where she judged Sam would first arrive. The distance between the two places was the better part of a kilometer, but Parrah wanted her horse and the other belongings she had left in her room.

She was still hurrying through the winding streets, calling last-minute instructions in polyglot to those she recognized as her recent students, when the fiery glare appeared overhead.

This new light was not the single vivid line the starship had drawn from one horizon to the other. This was a dull crimson radiance that approached almost slowly, yet seemed to fill half the sky. A warm wind accompanied it.

She looked up to see the starship descending toward the village, a huge red-glowing barb that was gliding down as if to crush several houses beneath it.

The red light shimmered and the trailing edges of the triangular wings seemed to warp out of line. The ship slipped sideways, as if sliding from an invisible surface that had been tilted beneath it, and a roaring, something like a waterfall but not really like any sound Parrah had ever heard before, reached her.

Then the terrifying craft vanished behind the roofs of the houses that lined the street she stood on. The sound became a violent hissing, as if a cat the size of a tower were spitting, and then faded to silence. She saw steam billowing up over the rooftops, but where Parrah stood the warm breeze had passed and a renewed chill could be felt.

She had gotten her best look yet at the thing, and she had to admit that Arzadel had a point in wanting it intact. Flame's ship radiated sheer power. Possession of such a machine was very tempting.

Seeing it in the hands of an enemy was terrifying.

She realized, when she reviewed its movement, that the ship had landed, not out in the surrounding forest as she had expected, but somewhere very close to, if not in, Killalah. She guessed that it had settled into the market square itself. That would be the only open space in town large enough for it, and since almost all the people were busily digging out their homes, or else inside keeping warm, the market would have been empty.

Her horse stood in plain sight of anyone taking the east highway out of the square. She dared not go near the animal. Instead, she turned and headed north again.

Before she had gone a dozen paces, she stopped.

Going north was not safe, either. She did not dare risk meeting her husband. The demon was linked to Sam somehow, and sometimes could see whatever Sam saw. Panicky, she looked about as if hoping to find instructions painted on one of the snow-covered houses.

She saw nothing that helped at all.

Gathering her wits, she turned again and ran for the nearest intersection, where she headed more or less east, hoping to find her way out of town without using the highway, without being spotted by the demons or their devices, or by her husband, with his own diabolic ties. She did not concern herself with the horse, or her belongings, or with anything but her flight.

She had survived one encounter with the demon, and she did not care for another. Seeing a forest clearing blasted around her had been bad enough; if the demon were to unleash the same sort of firepower in Killalah, property damage would be inevitable, and someone might well be killed.

And if the demon had one of the other weapons Sam had told her about, the ones a shield could not stop, that someone might be herself.

She had done her part, had delivered the ancient language and the instructions to go with it. She had spent three days teaching Killalahers what to say and the language they were to say it in, and she had managed to educate a fair portion of the town's population. She had told Sam, however briefly, that the Council wanted the ship intact, even though she had had no time to explain why. That was more than she had thought she could do, but she had done it. All that remained was to get away unseen.

She fought down the temptation to take to the air, as she did not know if the demon would notice. Sam had not said anything about flying upon leaving the town, only that she must not fly *to* it, but she dared not take chances. She ran on, leaving the people of Killalah to fend for themselves with the knowledge she had given them.

That knowledge, she hoped, would be enough to save her world, her children, and herself.

When the starship landed, when Parrah turned and ran, Turner was still somewhere in the forest to the north, but he knew he was finally nearing the town. He saw the ship's approach. He saw it come in fast and hot, as Flame seemed to prefer, burning the air around it with the friction of its passage. He saw it veer suddenly from its normal descent path, swoop back up slightly, turn, and then vanish behind the trees heading the opposite direction, still red- hot.

He stared for a moment, then demanded, "What the hell was *that* about?"

"Cyborg unit discretion in choosing landing site," the computer replied immediately.

"So where is she landing?" Turner asked. "Isn't one piece of forest as good as another?"

"Cyborg unit has chosen to land in open area at center of inhabited area."

Turner absorbed that for a few seconds, then remarked, "Oh, hell." He wondered how much damage Flame was doing, bringing her ship down inside the town.

He could think of two ways to make such a landing. One was to simply land in the usual fashion, ignoring the obstacles posed by houses and shops, and the other was to stall the ship out over the intended landing site and allow it to fall the last few meters with only the belly maneuvering jets to brake.

The first method would reduce a significant portion of the town to burning rubble. He hoped the computer would not have allowed that. The second method did much less damage to the surroundings, but it was tricky, and could damage the ship. It also used up maneuvering fuel, and the ship's replenishment facilities worked slowly, so the Command had discouraged its use.

"She stalled it and dropped it in?" he asked, hopefully.

"Affirmative."

That was at least a minor relief. Flame apparently was not overawed by the Command's discouragements or recommendations.

He was, he judged, still a good two hours' walk away from the town — three hours or more with the snow. Flame would presumably emerge as soon as the ship had cooled enough. She had made a fast, hot landing, but the cooling would not take anything over an hour, at the very most.

He hoped that Parrah had done her work well. Flame would obviously be out of her ship and asking questions before he got there.

He struggled to pick up his pace, wondering if, with the ship in the town ahead of him, it might be safe to fly.

TWENTY-TWO

Still lying on the acceleration couch for a moment after the landing, Flame listened dubiously to the computer's assurances that Slant was still a few kilometers away. "I'm not taking any chances," she said, swinging her feet to the floor. "I want to talk to these peasants before he can interfere. I want to get this over with. I want to get *everything* over with."

"Query: Planned course of action."

"I'll show you," she said, as she ducked her head into the computer's access hatch and reset the timer. She checked the readout, and, satisfied, straightened up and headed for the airlock.

"Hull temperature is unsafe for unshielded cyborg unit," the computer informed her.

"I know that, stupid," she said. "So I won't be unshielded."

She found the door she wanted and opened it, then pulled the spacesuit from its locker and stepped into it. She had chosen out her weapons in advance, during the days she had spent waiting for the storm to break. They lay ready and waiting in a griprack on the corridor wall beside the inner door of the airlock.

A moment later, fully suited, she emerged and stood on her ship's wing, looking out over the square.

Her landing had been a good one, but not absolutely perfect. The tip of the wing she stood on had come down through the thatched roof of a shop, caving in a small portion of one of the supporting walls. The heat of the metal had ignited the roof's damp straw, and only a torrent of melting snow had kept it from blazing up and spreading. The wet thatch still smoldered. She could see a blackened area several meters across.

The wing, of course, was undamaged.

The ship's heat had melted or evaporated every trace of snow in the market. All that remained was a thin fog and a heavy dampness to the air. The ground beneath the ship had been baked hard and dry, but a few meters away, where the heat had not reached as intensely, the dirt had been transformed to mud by the melting snow.

Save for her ship, the square was completely empty. She looked about for signs of life.

The helmet got in her way, and the readout just above normal eye level showed a tolerable exterior temperature. She unlocked the neckseal, lifted the helmet off, and tossed it back into the open airlock.

That reminded her that the lock was open. She subvocalized a command, and the door slid shut.

That taken care of, she took a deep breath of the damp air and studied the square again.

She glimpsed faces peering from windows, but whenever she looked directly at one it would vanish behind curtains or corners. A few brave souls were just visible, watching her from a safe distance up one of the side streets. They looked like her best prospects for the planned interrogations.

She stepped forward and jumped down from the wing. The spacesuit made her clumsy, and she stumbled awkwardly as she landed. Cursing her clumsiness, she straightened up and glared at the villagers on the side street.

They had not fled. She counted five of them, all watching her intently, albeit somewhat doubtfully.

"You there!" she called in polyglot, though she knew they probably either could not understand it or would pretend not to understand it. "Wait right where you are!"

The five of them glanced at each other, but said nothing.

Flame stared at them for a moment, a rocket rifle in her hand — not Slant's, but one from her own arsenal — waiting for one of the villagers to make a suspicious move.

They did nothing suspicious. They simply stood, uneasily motionless.

"Where is Slant?" she demanded.

"Cyborg unit designated 'Slant' is currently on planetary surface approximately eight point four kilometers north by northwest of present location of cyborg unit designated 'Flame,' and approaching along an irregular course at a variable speed averaging approximately point nine meters per second."

"He has never been in this place?"

"Information unavailable."

"Have you ever tracked him here?"

"Negative."

"And you've been tracking him since we got to this planet?"

"Affirmative, when possible. Tracking was not possible when communication was occulted by planet."

"Good." She lowered the rifle. "I'm going to go question those people."

The computer paused perhaps half a second before replying, "Action marginally acceptable."

Flame hesitated. "Why only marginally?" she asked.

"Evidence exists to indicate that cyborg unit designated 'Flame' possesses emotional commitment to demonstrating hostility of local inhabitants regardless of fact or consequences. This commitment is counter to programming. Cyborg unit designated 'Flame' acting without presence of cyborg unit designated 'Slant' may be able to influence response of local inhabitants to increase probability of demonstrating hostility without allowing CCC-IRU 247 to detect this influence. Such action would be counter to programming. However, this interrogation site is not necessarily decisive in determination of planetary loyalty; therefore interrogation remains marginally acceptable."

"Not necessarily decisive?"

"Affirmative. Results of interrogation may prove inconclusive. Cyborg unit designated 'Slant' may be able to refute demonstrations of hostility."

"You think so?"

"Information insufficient."

Flame snorted. "If we get a clear statement that these people are rebels, will that satisfy you?"

"Information insufficient. Exact situation may modify final determination. Also, three sites required for decision in the event cyborg units continue to disagree."

"But we might be able to settle at least one of the three before Slant even gets here?"

"Affirmative."

Kilometers away, Turner overheard this entire exchange. Once again, he guessed, Flame had forgotten that the computer required a specific order to keep telecommunications private. Either that, or she simply did not care whether she was overheard.

Or, just possibly, the computer, in its damaged and confused state, was intentionally misleading her.

He could not guess why the computer might want to mislead Flame, but he did not want to rule out the possibility. He remembered how Flame had seemed to threaten the computer once or twice; the two halves of IRU 247 did not seem to get along well.

Turner debated for long minutes whether or not to say anything, but resolved to keep silent. If Parrah had been successful, Flame should, he thought, be forced to admit that Dest was friendly. He did not want to risk interfering in that. That would save them all the trouble of finding two more sites.

If more sites were needed, he was unsure how he could contact Parrah to send her on ahead. That might be a problem.

However, if Parrah had done what she was told, the people of this town should state unequivocally that they were loyal to Old Earth, and if that happened he could not see how Flame could fail to yield.

Of course, in the nine years of their marriage Parrah had hardly ever done what she was told. Ordinarily, he admired her independence, but he hoped that this time she had obeyed him.

If the interrogation went badly, he could still intervene over the communications circuit.

The five villagers were still standing, apprehensively awaiting Flame's next move. She forced a smile, ostentatiously slung the rifle on her shoulder, and marched toward them.

She expected them to turn and flee, whereupon she would be able to argue to the computer that that was hardly the act of friendly civilians, but to her surprise all five stood their ground. She stopped two or three meters away and studied them.

She faced three men and two women. Two of the men were young, and the other man, and both women, were well into middle age. All five were obviously frightened. The older man was visibly trembling, and one of the women looked faint. One of the young men was trying to look nonchalant and failing miserably.

Still, they had stood their ground, which impressed her. She knew, from everything she had seen on Dest, that the culture was fairly primitive. Thatched roofs and wooden tools could mean little else. For five near-savages, the sight of her ship landing, glowing red-hot and boiling away the snow, must have been awesome and utterly alien. Her own appearance in the metallic gray spacesuit could hardly be familiar. She guessed that she would seem more an apparition than a woman.

Yet there the five stood, right in front of her, growing visibly more nervous as the silence continued. They deserved, she decided, at least a chance to prove their disloyalty. She would talk to them, as the computer wanted, before she shot them.

She hesitated, unsure which language to try first, and then said, "*Zdra'stvuytye!*"

The heavy consonants and strong Y-glide of the Russian greeting sounded nothing like the rattling, nasal language the villagers had been taught, the language they had expected the demon to use. One of the women moaned and leaned heavily on her younger male companion. "San and Hligosh!" the other young man muttered in his native language. "I couldn't understand that at all!"

Flame, of course, could not understand what he said, either. Her hand slid up toward the strap of the rocket rifle.

The older man, his plump face now creased with worry, said hesitantly in bad polyglot, "I do not understand."

Thunderstruck, Flame stared at him, and her hand halted a centimeter from the rifle strap.

"What did you say?" she said at last in polyglot.

The older man looked to either side, but found no help. His four companions were determinedly silent. "Ah...I said that I do not... I mean, *did* not understand what you said," he managed. "The first thing, I mean." He stared at her pleadingly.

"You speak polyglot!" Flame said accusingly.

"Ah... a little, yes?"

She glared at him. "Where did you learn it?" she demanded.

Puzzled, the townsman said, "Here?"

"Here? In this village?"

Uncertainty was plain on his face; the word "village" was not in his limited vocabulary. "What?" he asked.

"You learned polyglot here?" She waved at the surrounding buildings.

"Yes," he said, nodding vigorously. "This is my place. This is Killalah. I am called Tagyi, and..."

Flame was not interested in introductions. She cut him short, demanding, "Who taught you? Was it Slant?"

"Who?" Tagyi's confusion was obviously genuine.

Flame was not yet ready to give up her conviction that only trickery by the traitorous cyborg could be responsible for the unexpected discovery of people who spoke polyglot. "Computer," she demanded, "what name does Slant use here?"

"Information unavailable," the computer replied immediately.

Flame snarled, then turned her attention back to the townsman. "A man?" she asked. "A tall man with brown hair, he taught you?"

"Oh, no," Tagyi replied. "No man. A woman."

"What woman?"

"A government... government person," he answered, unable to come up with a word meaning "agent," or "representative," or "wizard."

"What government sent this woman? What government did she *say* sent her?"

"Praunce," Tagyi replied immediately and confidently.

"Do you recognize the name?" she silently asked the computer.

"Affirmative."

"Is it a rebel planet?" she asked hopefully.

"Negative. 'Praunce' is the name used by inhabitants of city where cyborg unit designated 'Slant' was located upon ship's arrival within communication range to describe both that city and the political entity of which the city is a part."

"So Slant *does* have something to do with it, then!"

"Information insufficient."

"This person from Praunce — why did she teach you polyglot?" she demanded, focussing again on the townsman.

"So... so we could talk to... I mean, so we could talk in the language of Old Earth. Praunce is a loyal... uh... Praunce is loyal to Old Earth. I do not know the word for '*teibuitarro*'," he said apologetically, using a Prauncer word describing a conquered or colonized area that paid taxes to a central government in exchange for protection, but otherwise more or less governed itself.

Flame had no idea what the word meant, and therefore she ignored it. Fuming, she stepped forward and grabbed the man by the front of his fur-lined blue wool coat. The other four villagers stepped back in surprise and fear; Tagyi's mouth dropped open in terror. The woman-headed demon with the peculiar yellow hair and the strange gleaming garment had moved much faster than any human could move, and the grip on his clothing was as strong as granite.

"What did you say?" Flame demanded. "Did you say Praunce is loyal to Old Earth?"

"Ah... ah... yes," he said, nodding, certain that he was about to be eaten alive by the demon but determined to do as he had been told rather than risk making things worse.

"Damn it!" Flame said, as she flung the man to the street. "Damn it to hell! How did that bastard do it?"

"Rephrase question," the computer said.

Tagyi landed hard on a patch of ice, and his head snapped back against the base of a wall, dazing him. His head would ache for a day or two, and he would wear bruises for a week, but none of his bones were broken. Flame ignored him and the computer both, and grabbed the woman who had slumped, as if about to faint, earlier. "You!" she demanded. "Tell me about Old Earth!"

The woman moaned again, and passed out. Flame flung her aside brutally. She was not as lucky as Tagyi. Her right arm was broken just above the elbow when she slammed into a stone wall. Her other injuries were minor. Her head, fortunately, did not hit hard.

Again, the cyborg paid no attention. She grabbed one of the young men and shouted into his face, "Tell me about Old Earth!"

"Our fathers and mothers came from there, long ago!" the man babbled, terror-stricken. Parrah had not taught him a word for "distant ancestors," forcing him to improvise. "We are still loyal!"

"When did you hear from Old Earth?"

"Never! But we are still loyal, I swear!"

Flame was enraged beyond words, and now, for the moment, even beyond violence. She released the man disgustedly and turned back toward her ship.

"Evidence now indicates..." the computer began.

"Shut up!" Flame ordered. The computer obeyed instantly.

She stood for a moment, staring back down the street to where her ship loomed above the empty market stalls. The heat-glow had completely died away, and its metal skin gleamed a dull silver above, its belly black with shadow.

She was furious, frustrated beyond the ability of words to express. She *knew* that all of humanity was her enemy, and there before her stood her weapon against that enemy. Aboard that ship were thirty-four nuclear warheads.

But she could not use any of them. The computer would not let her. She could kill the computer easily enough, with the termite, but it might well blow her head off before it died completely, and even if she survived, she did not know how to launch the missiles without the computer's help.

Slant had beaten her. If he had somehow made this one town lie, he could make them all lie. He had beaten her.

Or had he? A thought struck her. She turned again, and stared at the five she had spoken to. Two of them still lay crumpled on the ground, and the other three were standing there, staring at her, not daring to flee.

This group had been obvious. They had stood here in the street and waited for her. They were most probably plants, shills, people Slant or one of his unknown accomplices had selected and trained.

Whatever trick Slant had used, he might not have prepared anyone else. He might have sent these five to meet her because they were all he had ready. He probably thought that after speaking with them Flame would give up in despair, or at least move on to another village.

He was wrong, she swore to herself. She would not give up that easily!

"Computer," she said, "I want you to make sure that Slant can't overhear anything. I'm going to find somebody around here who will tell me the truth!"

TWENTY-THREE

Turner slid cautiously down the final snowbank onto the shoveled-out street and looked around warily, studying the town.

The street was empty and silent. Long shadows stretched across it and up the buildings on the opposite side. Dest's primary was well down in the western sky, almost at the horizon, and the darkness of night seemed to already be gathering in the pools of shadow. No lights showed in any of the windows. No one was in sight in the street, or in any of the windows. He could hear nothing but a distant bird whistling a complaint about the cold.

"Computer," he asked. "Where is everybody?"

"Information insufficient."

"Where is Flame?"

"Cyborg unit designated 'Flame' is in a private residence approximately eighty meters southeast of present location of cyborg unit designated 'Slant'."

Before Turner could ask anything more a wordless scream reached his ears. He judged that it originated roughly eighty meters to the southeast of where he stood, around a corner on a cross street. Something about the voice sounded familiar, but he could not place it. It was not Parrah's, he was sure, and that was a small relief. After an instant's hesitation, he ran toward it.

Flame glowered down at her latest victim, who cowered in the corner, cringing in terror before this blood-spattered superhuman apparition. As with most of the others she had questioned, Flame had been unable to get this scrawny teenaged girl to admit to any understanding of either Russian or polyglot, or to speak in anything but that maddening babble the locals used. The cyborg's final wordless shriek, which had sent the girl into her moaning crouch, had been the result of pure frustration.

She had questioned dozens of townspeople. She could not recall the exact count. Somewhere between half and two-thirds had been, like this girl, unable to communicate at all.

All the others had insisted, no matter what Flame might do, that they and all of Praunce remained loyal to Old Earth. A few had died under her questioning, and more, perhaps a majority, had been injured in varying degrees. None of the blood that liberally adorned her face and spacesuit was her own.

She had tried everything she could think of to get a confession of what she knew to be the truth, that the whole town was lying, that they were rebels, that Slant had told them what to say.

She had tried surprise, bursting in through doors without warning and snatching up whomever she found inside. She had tried brutality, beating men and women to the verge of unconsciousness and sometimes beyond the verge. She had tried threats, smashing obviously prized possessions, abusing loved ones, displaying what her weaponry could do, once even demolishing an entire house with her bare hands to demonstrate her abilities. She had tried bribery, offering people gold, weapons, power.

None of it had worked. Everyone in the village who spoke so much as a word of polyglot attested to Dest's undying loyalty to Old Earth.

She was amazed that she had, so far, resisted the temptation to flatten the entire town. She was proud of her self-restraint.

This terrified girl would tell her nothing more, she decided. She turned and marched back out into the street.

"Flame!" someone called.

She spun, rocket rifle ready in her hands, and saw a man in a heavy sheepskin coat rounding the corner, running toward her. Her finger automatically closed on the trigger.

Turner saw the rifle swinging toward him and reacted without thinking. He dropped flat to the ground, raised a telekinetic shield, and screamed silently, "Computer! Stop her!"

Half a dozen missiles whistled over him. An instant later the wall of a tack shop behind him erupted into an inferno with an ear-shattering six-part roar. Dust and debris scattered across his legs.

Realizing whom she faced, Flame had released the trigger as quickly as she could, and immediately shouted aloud, "It was a mistake, computer! I didn't recognize him at first, I just saw someone attacking!"

The explosions and collapse of the damaged tack shop into its own basement drowned out her voice, but the computer did not rely on sound. It calmly replied, "Acknowledged."

She relaxed and lowered the rifle.

A moment later, when the debris had settled and silence had descended once more, Turner got slowly and carefully to his feet, ignoring the particles of glass and plaster that spilled from his back. He saw the smeared blood that darkened Flame's spacesuit, and did not allow himself to relax.

"I heard a scream," he said. "What happened? What's been going on here?"

Flame stared at him distrustfully. "How long have you been in the village?" she demanded.

"I just got here. Who screamed?"

"I did." Subvocally, she added, "Computer, is he telling the truth?"

"Affirmative."

"Why did you scream?" Turner asked, sincerely puzzled. He had assumed a townsperson had screamed in response to some act of violence Flame had committed. To discover that she, herself, had screamed disconcerted him. "Is something wrong?"

"No, nothing is wrong," she said. "At least, not as far as you are concerned. I was just angry. You did a good job on the people here, Slant; I couldn't get a single one to admit to disloyalty."

Turner resumed his puzzled expression, hoping that this fraudulent one looked as genuine as its immediate predecessor. "What job are you talking about? I just got here. I haven't done anything to the people here."

"You know what I'm talking about, you lying bastard," Flame said, struggling to keep from screaming again. "I don't know how you did it, but you did it somehow. Every one of them that could speak polyglot swore he was loyal."

"Oh, is that all?" Turner feigned relief. "I told you, they *are* loyal!"

"Oh, save it for the priests! You know as well as I do that not a single planet outside the solar system fought on Old Earth's side!"

"I never said they did," Turner said mildly. "I said they were loyal, not that their ancestors fought for Old Earth. They never knew there *was* a war."

Flame stared for a moment, then demanded, "Computer, did you hear that? He admits they didn't fight for Old Earth!"

"Affirmative."

"They didn't know there was a war!" Turner insisted. "Besides, that was their ancestors, three hundred years ago; what we're concerned with now is the people *now*. And they're loyal; if I understand you correctly, they told you so themselves, several of them."

"Oh, they told me, all right. They told me lies and more lies! This planet was never loyal. Their ancestors didn't fight. They were all traitors!"

Turner sighed. "But that was their ancestors."

"That doesn't matter. If their ancestors were traitors, then they are, too."

"Their ancestors' ancestors were all from Old Earth, though; if the generations don't change anything, then these people are all from Old Earth, so they can't be enemies."

Flame stared at him. "That's nonsense!" she retorted.

"No more so than yours," Turner replied.

Flame appealed to the final authority. "Computer, they're lying. They *can't* be loyal."

"No evidence exists to support that statement. All evidence acquired to date supports the contention that this planet's population has remained loyal to Old Earth and is therefore friendly. However, the plan agreed upon specified three separate interrogation sites. Query: Continue interrogations."

Turner watched Flame expectantly.

A string of expressions flitted across her features, first hope, then anger, then consideration, and finally despair. She slumped. "No," she said at last, reluctantly. "However he did it, Slant would just do the same thing at the other two sites."

"I didn't do anything," Turner insisted.

"Oh, you did," Flame said. "I know you did. But I give up. I can't argue about it anymore. You've beaten me, at least for now."

"You mean you're acknowledging that Dest is friendly?"

"I mean I can't prove it's not. You've got the whole planet on your side, and all I have is a computer that's damaged too badly to believe me without more evidence than I can give it, and that won't obey me even when I can destroy it."

Turner smiled, and subvocalized, "You hear, computer? She admits that she can't provide any evidence that this planet is hostile, while I, and all these other people, have been telling you it's friendly. What do you say to that?"

"Analysis: Cyborg unit designated 'Flame' has acquiesced on major points. All further objections are irrational. Planetary population is friendly."

"Then you can't nuke us, right? You won't let Flame kill or harm anyone else, except in self-defense?"

"Affirmative."

Nearly overcome with relief, Turner allowed himself to relax. As he did, he was suddenly struck by an overwhelming curiosity. "What happens now?" he asked.

Flame, whose gaze had sunk to the icy mud beneath her feet, suddenly looked up at him. "We leave," she said.

"Affirmative," the computer agreed. "Unit has no function in friendly territory. Unit is programmed to seek out and destroy hostile forces and populations. Mission must continue until receipt and acceptance of recall or release code. Therefore unit must leave friendly territory immediately."

"What about me?"

"Unit has no authority over friendly civilians except in the event of military action."

"So you'll leave me here, and go away, and never come back? You'll leave Dest alone?"

"Affirmative."

Turner knew that he should have been happy. That was everything he had thought he wanted from IRU 247. His world was safe. He could return home to his children, his wife, his secure position. He had not captured the ship for the wizards of Praunce, but he saw no reason why he should.

Something was still troubling him, though.

"Flame," he said, "is that what you want?"

She stared at him. "What the hell do you care?"

"Never mind my reasons; is that what you want, to get back in your ship and go on alone until you die?"

"No, that's not what I want, damn you." Her face twisted into a bitter smile. "What I want is to nuke this filthy planet into radioactive dust. I can't have this one, though; you've seen to that. But I'll find others. We were on our way to one when we picked up your message. I think we can get there from here in about two years of subjective time, and I can nuke *them*. And if we have any missiles left after that we'll find another planet, and another, and when we run out of missiles we'll use beam weapons, and when those burn out I'll land and use up the entire ship's arsenal, and then I'll kill people hand to hand, until I die of old age. And when that happens the computer will carry on as long as it can, until my termite eats its brain out. Maybe the termite will keep going after that, I don't know. You haven't stopped me, Slant; you've saved this planet, but I'll find others, and they'll all pay for what was done to me." She took a step, then another, not toward Turner, but heading around him, to return to her ship.

"Computer?" Slant said. "Is she right?" The mention of the termite slipped past him, unnoticed.

"Affirmative."

Reluctantly, Turner said, "I can't let you do that."

"Cyborg unit designated 'Slant' has no authority to interfere with military actions."

"What are you going to do?" Flame demanded. "Kill me?"

Turner began to reach for a snark, but then stopped when he saw Flame's grip on the rocket rifle shift slightly. "Computer," he asked, "if Flame were murdered by a friendly civilian, in a personal quarrel, what action would you take?" He had no desire to sacrifice himself, but he knew that he could never forgive himself if he allowed IRU 247 to go on destroying whole populations because their ancestors had left Old Earth. Even planets that actually had rebelled had done so centuries ago. Retaliating after so long a delay would be a meaningless, pointless injustice.

"Programming specifies that such action be immediately reported to the nearest civilian and military authorities. However, special circumstances may allow direct action. If cyborg unit designated 'Slant' destroyed cyborg unit designated 'Flame,' all data on this planet would be re-evaluated."

Flame was watching him closely.

"If I killed her, and you killed me in return, but then decided that Dest really was friendly, what would you do?"

"Mission would continue. Unit would leave friendly territory immediately. Unit is programmed to seek out and destroy hostile forces and populations. Mission must continue until receipt and acceptance of recall or release code, or destruction of unit. Therefore unit must leave friendly territory and seek out hostile forces or populations. With cyborg unit destroyed, mission programming requires ship to continue mission as long as possible, determining loyalty of potential targets by response to Command identification codes or voice transmissions. Present situation would require that action be taken to prevent destruction of unit before programming could be carried out."

His own computer's programming had been different. His mission had been different. CCC-IRU 205 would not have gone on seeking out new target planets once he was dead, but CCC-IRU 247 had no such limitation.

That statement about the "present situation" made no sense, but he attributed it to the computer's damaged state and ignored it. He had not put together Flame's references to time limits and termites. His own ship had never encountered breeder lampreys or cybernetic termites.

As far as he could see, sacrificing himself would do no good. The ship would carry on anyway.

"Just asking," he said, retreating quickly from his position. "Out of curiosity, that's all. I wasn't planning to harm her."

He knew that he could not allow IRU 247 to go on, but he could think of no way to stop it. He was alone in the area. So far as he was aware, no other wizards were near enough to help, and he knew that by himself he could not drain the starship's power or otherwise cripple it before the computer realized what was happening and retaliated.

By the time any other wizards could reach it the ship would be gone. He had to stop it himself, single-handed, and he could not. IRU 247 would go on to launch its thirty-four nuclear warheads against some other helpless planet.

With a twisted half smile at her recognition that Turner's victory was not complete, Flame strode by him. She knew that if she died, the ship would never reach another target before the termite destroyed it, but she was hardly about to tell Turner that.

His hand on the snark in his pocket, Turner watched her go, cursing his helplessness. He was a cyborg and a wizard, the only person ever to be both. That made him arguably the most powerful creature on the planet, yet he could think of no way to stop the ship.

He had stopped his own computer; why could he not stop this one? He was a wizard now, more powerful than he had been then.

He stopped and ran over that line of thought again.

He had defeated his ship's computer. He had fed it their release code, and it had shut itself down.

He did not know the release code for IRU 247, and no distress message was about to tell him what it was, but he was a wizard. He could find it out. He hastily improvised a plan.

"Computer," he asked hurriedly as Flame walked out of sight around the corner. "Could I speak to you privately, without Flame listening in?"

Flame, out of sight but still in earshot, stopped walking.

"Query: Reason for request."

"It's personal; I'll tell you once you cut her out of the circuit."

The computer needed a full second to decide the matter. "Affirmative," it said at last.

Flame called, "Go ahead, Slant, try your tricks on it. I don't care anymore. If it gets out of hand it'll die, and it knows that." She walked on.

Turner ignored Flame's retort, though he mentally filed this latest reference to her hold over the computer. He subvocalized, "I didn't want her to hear because I didn't want to worry her. You see, Dest has some unusual indigenous diseases."

"Query: Nature of indigenous diseases."

"I'll get to that. First, though, since it's been established that Dest is friendly, then I assume you'll now acknowledge that psionics are not enemy weapons activity?"

"Affirmative."

"Then may I do a psionic inspection of Flame? I want to make certain that she hasn't picked up any of the local diseases. I guarantee the inspection won't harm her."

"Query: Cyborg unit designated 'Slant' possesses psionic capabilities."

"Yes, I do — artificially induced mutation. May I make the inspection?"

"Query: Nature of indigenous diseases."

"There's a family of degenerative nerve diseases, bacterial in origin," he lied smoothly. "The natives here have bred in an immunity over time, but off-worlders, like Flame, are mostly susceptible. Massive doses of antibiotics can halt the disease if it's caught early. May I make the inspection?"

Again, the computer needed a measurable time to decide the matter, before replying, "Affirmative."

Turner did not allow himself any expression of his vast relief. He knew he had been taking a huge risk in revealing that he was a wizard, but over the past few days he had gradually become convinced that the computer was damaged to the point that it would agree to almost anything if asked correctly, and if no one else objected. Only his presence and objections, he was sure, had kept IRU 247 from nuking Praunce immediately upon arrival; the computer would surely have given in to Flame, with or without evidence.

Perhaps Flame's warped values had somehow warped its own perceptions of who and what to trust.

Whatever the reason, the computer had agreed. He wasted no time in gloating, but simply took off, lifting himself upward and flying directly toward the ship.

He spotted Flame walking quickly but unhurriedly along one of the town's main streets, and he reached out psychically, feeling her aura, trying to merge his own with it.

It was tricky, doing it while flying, but he managed.

He felt her surface emotions first, a tangle of pride that she was leaving Dest unscathed and shame that she had been partially defeated. He forced his way down through that.

Bitterness, surging, endless bitterness, that she had thrown her life away by volunteering for the IRU program, that she could not surrender, that she could not destroy Dest, that she had been trapped into her current empty existence, that she had not died long ago. She would have preferred death.

Pride, proud determination that she would not give in, that she would not go mad from the loneliness, that she would not despair, that she would not die yet, that she would carry on, that she would not die so long as she had her mission.

She had been tricked and trapped into becoming an IRU cyborg, but having become one, she was proud of that, proud and determined to carry out her mission without fail. Mars had failed, Old Earth had failed, Slant's computer had failed, everything that had ever fought against the rebel worlds had failed, but she would not. She knew that her mission was meaningless, but it was all she had.

Hatred and anger and a peculiar acceptance, a quick memory of the termite booby trap that came as a revelation to him, and then Turner was through the default personality.

The combat personality blinked past, a small, intricate complex made up of simple "if...then" concepts, with no real thought or emotion at all.

The pilot personality could not be described verbally, not even to himself. It was all images and abstract concepts for which no words existed.

The cover personalities flicked past, thin and superficial, all asleep. A saboteur identity was somewhat like the combat personality, somewhat like the pilot. The seductress personality, which he had known he would find as an equivalent of his own long-merged seducer personality, was an eerie mix of cold calculation and unbridled eroticism. It seemed out of place in Flame's unattractive body and hostile mind.

Of all the currently suppressed selves, only the one cover personality, the Russian-speaking technician, possessed any memories at all. He realized with a shock that except for brief use of the pilot, Flame's default personality had *always* been dominant, ever since the eighteen were first separated back on Mars, until her arrival on Dest. He had seen the combat identity and the Russian technician allowed to surface briefly, but that had been the very first time for each.

No wonder she was insane — and after reading her mind, he knew that she was indeed insane. Her reality was entirely internal, and in interacting with anything external she interpreted it entirely in terms of that inner reality. Anything that did not fit with her established view of how the universe operated was denied or ignored; she shaped facts to fit her beliefs, not her beliefs to fit facts.

Those beliefs included the certainty that the entire universe, everything outside herself, was hostile.

It had been a very long time, either subjectively or otherwise, since Turner had studied psychology, but he thought that he was looking at a case of paranoid schizophrenia.

Her other personalities did not appear to be mad, though he could not be sure of anything in their present inactive state.

The barriers between them were sharp and clear, but as he continued to pore over what he could sense — and as Flame neared her ship — he came across thin, faint wisps of thought, of memory, of identity, seeping in between the eighteen.

He latched onto these and followed them down into the depths of Flame's past, into the memories that she herself could no longer reach, the memories the Command had suppressed.

He saw through her eyes as, at the age of eight, she was teased by an older brother who held her new kitten out of reach above her head. When he finally relented and gave her her pet, the terrified animal scratched her face and fled in panic.

The scratch had become infected, and her parents had taken her to the hospital, blaming her for abusing the kitten, ignoring her accusations of her brother. Her father had declared the little cat to be ruined, turned against humanity, and had strangled it, wrung its neck in front of her so that it could not scratch her again. He was only protecting her, he had explained, and he had stared in angry astonishment when she had burst into tears.

The white-coated doctors had talked quietly and calmly to her parents, and one of them had then turned to her and said loudly, "So, Valentina, you've been a bad girl!"

She had cowered in confused shame and hurt.

Valentina, Turner repeated to himself. He had her first name. Valentina what?

He could not find any more of the incident with the kitten. Anything else that might have happened at that time was gone beyond his reach.

Flame was crossing the market square to the ship's access ladder, unaware that anything was happening to her mind. She was too full of emotion to sense the electric tingling, and the computer, struggling with its confused and contradictory damaged programming, had not bothered to mention Turner's little psionic check-up. Turner, straining himself to the fullest extent of his magical abilities, watched her surface thoughts with what effort he could spare, ready to react should she realize that magic was in use.

He was hovering above the ship, but she had not noticed his presence. She thought he was still somewhere behind her, in the streets of Killalah.

When she was seventeen a boy had taken her to a picnic beside a lake. She had been lying back, relaxing on the grass, when he reached out and touched her.

She had been feeling content, pleased with the world, and she did not want the mood broken. She was still a virgin at the time, and his attention made her nervous. She had pushed his hand away, saying, "Not right now."

"When, then?"

"Oh, later; right now I'm resting."

He had turned mockingly stern, imitating her father. "Resting, Valentina Mikhailovna?" he had demanded. "And what has tired you out so?"

Her answer was lost. The imitation of her father had been enough to break her mood completely, and she had turned angry, but the exact words she had spoken were gone.

For a moment Turner thought he had found her full name, but then he realized that Mikhailovna was her patronymic, not her surname. As an ethnic Russian she would have regularly used all three names, in various combinations depending on the degree of familiarity. He still needed her surname.

He flashed on through other memories, back to infancy, then forward again, through her idolatrous crushes on video stars, through the drudgery of her education in a backward town in the Urals, through her first kiss and her last, saw her brothers, mother, father, friends and friends and more friends, none of them close, none who stayed friends for more than a year or two. He saw her teachers, her relatives, her military superiors.

She stood before the sergeant. She was eighteen years old, reporting for duty, frightened but refusing to show any sign of it.

"Yessenina, V.M." she said, clearly and precisely. Her voice had been flat and calm and had not shaken at all, and she had been proud of her composure.

Yessenina. That was her name. That was all he needed. He broke the telepathic link and looked around, focusing on the real world once again.

Flame — Valentina Mikhailovna Yessenina — was swinging herself up onto the wing of the ship. He began descending, careful not to plummet down and startle her into thinking she was under attack.

The airlock opened and she vanished inside, more quickly than he had expected; he landed on the ship's wing just as the portal closed.

"Warning," the computer said. "Evacuate launch area."

It struck him for the first time that although Flame had been able to drop her ship neatly into the market without destroying the surrounding buildings, she would not be able to take off without incinerating a few of the structures, both ahead and behind. He felt himself turning angry at the thought, but fought the anger down, lest it interfere with what he had to do.

"Let me in," he called, "I have something important to tell you." He knew, from his own ship, that the release code could be delivered only over the Command frequency, which he had no way of using, or through the on-board audio system. Exterior pickups for the audio system existed, but would not be active during the final preparations for launch.

"Negative," the computer said. "No civilian personnel are authorized for access to ship."

"It's urgent!"

"No civilian personnel are authorized for access to ship under any circumstances. Please clear the launch area."

"You can't take off yet!"

"Affirmative. Cyborg unit designated 'Flame' must be secure on acceleration couch before launch."

"That's not what I meant; listen, let me talk to Flame!"

After a second of silence, "What the hell do you want, traitor?" came over his communication circuit.

"Flame, I need to talk to you, orally. Turn on the exterior audio."

"Why? No, never mind. It's just another trick of some kind." He could feel her cut off the circuit.

A faint tremble ran through the ship. Turner's psychic senses detected a sudden surge of power, and he knew it was warming up for take-off. Desperate, he reached in his pocket and found the snark with the seventy percent charge.

He pulled it out, thumbed it to full power and its widest beam, and fired it point-blank at the airlock's outer door.

Metal dust glittered faintly in the last lingering daylight, and a moment later light poured out of a new hole and turned the particles into flecks of shadow in the beams from the brightly lit airlock.

The power dial had dropped to zero by the time he released the trigger button. He tossed the useless device aside and stooped, putting his mouth to the opening he had just made.

He called, "Valentina Mikhailovna Yessenina, Val..." He coughed, as some of the metallic dust got in his mouth, and he wished that Flame's real name was shorter. He swallowed, then tried again. "Valentina Mikhailovna Yessenina, Valentina Mikhailovna Yessenina, Valentina Mikhailovna Yessenina!" He choked again on the final syllable.

"Affirmative," a pleasant contralto voice replied from within the airlock, "Release code accepted. Awaiting orders."

Flame's scream came clearly over the airlock speaker.

TWENTY-FOUR

"Open the airlock," Turner yelled. "And abort the launch!"

"Affirmative," the computer's contralto monotone replied. The airlock door slid open, the dust from the snarkhole scraping audibly against the retraction sheath.

Flame was still screaming as Turner stepped inside.

He had forgotten what it was like. After eleven years, or ten if one figured it that way, he had completely forgotten how it felt to have the broken pieces of one's mind forcibly rammed back together into a single personality. He was fairly sure that he had not screamed — at least, not until later, when the pain-suppression mechanism had shut down and he had been able to feel the injuries he had sustained — but he had never been quite as dissociated as Flame.

He desperately wanted to know what she was thinking, but he dared not read her mind again. He did not want to open his own mind up to the pain and confusion and mangled sense of identity that he knew she was suffering.

He had never forgotten any detail of his ship's interior, and the airlock of Flame's ship was horribly familiar, despite subtle differences in the visible wear. Less subtly, a long streak of something black was smeared across one bulkhead, and several service panels had been removed and never replaced.

"Open the inner door," he ordered. He could have opened it himself, but the computer would be faster. Working the manual latch on his own ship had always taken him several seconds. While he waited for the hatch to open he pulled his hand laser from an inner pocket.

When the gap between the hatch and its frame was wide enough, he squeezed through quickly. He did not know what was happening, but he was sure he had no time to spare.

It occurred to him to wonder, as he ran down the narrow corridor to the control cabin, why the computer was obeying him without question. He knew that, once aboard, anyone could give certain emergency orders, but why had it let him aboard in the first place, when it had refused him once before? Was it simply because he had known the release code?

It must have been that, he decided, or perhaps something to do with its damaged status. In any case it didn't really matter why. The computer was obeying him, and that was enough.

If it would obey anyone who happened to speak to it, though, that could be dangerous. "Computer," he said as he neared the door to the control cabin. "Until further notice, you are only to obey orders given over cyborg communication circuits; you will ignore commands or instructions given by voice alone. Except for emergencies, that is. I know you're programmed to take emergency orders from anyone, and I'm not trying to override that. Do you understand?"

"Affirmative."

The screaming stopped.

Turner burst into the cabin, laser ready.

Flame was lying on the acceleration couch, eyes wide, staring fixedly at one of the extruded lightbars on the ceiling. Her spacesuit, smeared with mud and blood, was in hideous contrast to the sleek cleanliness of the ovoid chamber, and Turner involuntarily saw her, for a moment, as a sick beast, too far gone to clean itself, in a veterinarian's surgery.

Her weapons were gone. She would naturally have deposited them in an equipment locker, or back in the armory, before returning to the control cabin.

She turned her head as he entered, and stared just as fixedly at him as she had at the lightbar.

He thought, however, that she did not really see him. He began to reach out telepathically, but then drew back again. The reintegration of her personality was surely complete by now, but if she had gone completely around the bend into full-blown psychosis, he did not want to risk his own sanity by reading her mind.

"Ms. Yessenina?" he called gently. "Are you all right?"

She said nothing, but simply stared.

He thought she might be catatonic, or close to it. There were wizards who knew how to cope with that, using telepathy and psionic neurosurgery. He was still reluctant to try reading her mind himself. Repairing a damaged mind was a job for experts.

If he could get her out of the ship he could find an expert. As long as she stayed where she was, she was still dangerous, and he did not really want to bring any wizards aboard the starship. Not yet.

He pocketed the laser, then crossed to the couch slowly and cautiously, hands empty and held out for her to see. "Ms. Yessenina? Could you come with me, please? I'll find someone who can help you."

"No one can help me!" she screamed, suddenly.

Turner jumped back, startled.

He did not try to argue directly with what she had said. He had no real assurance that anyone could help her, even with wizardry. "What's the matter?" he asked. "I know the reintegration was a shock, but it's over —"

"I know it's over!" she screamed. "My mission is gone. You've taken my mission away from me." Her eyes were wild now, but she continued to stare at him.

"I know your mission is over," he said, reaching out toward her. "You're free now; you can stay —"

"No!" she said, pushing his hand away. "My mission was all I had, can't you see that?"

"Please, come with me —"

"No! I won't leave my ship, I tell you. I can't." Tears welled up in her eyes. "It's all I have left." Her voice broke. "You took my mission away from me."

"I'm sorry," he said desperately. "Please, Ms. Yessenina, listen to me..."

"I'm staying, I tell you!"

Pleading was not going to work, he could see. "But what can you do here?" he asked, trying to sound calmly reasonable.

She stared at him intently but silently for a moment before bursting out, "I can die, damn you! That's all you've left me; I can't kill anymore, but I can still die, and take my ship with me. You can't take that away. I can still die. You can't have my ship! Computer, I hereby disavow Old Earth! I surrender to the rebels! Kill me, damn you!"

The computer's calm voice replied, "This unit no longer possesses authority to terminate cyborg unit."

Yessenina/Flame screamed again, this time something in Russian that Turner could not follow. She flung herself off the couch onto him, knocking him back against the carpeted curve of the wall.

He tried to grab her. They were both cyborgs, but he was bigger and presumably somewhat stronger. He threw up quick telekinetic protection for his face and other especially vulnerable points, to guard against her attack.

He remembered that he had, only a short time before, thought of himself as the most powerful creature on the planet, yet here he was fighting for his life.

She was not attacking, though. Instead of striking him, or finding holds, her hands were sliding across his coat. She was searching for the pockets, and even as he realized that, she found one and reached quickly into it.

She smiled, the expression hideous. She had found what she was after. She pulled away from him, a snark in her hand.

Suddenly terrified, well aware that a snark was not affected at all by magical shields, Turner devoted all his energies to pushing her away and dodging, while calling silently for the computer's aid.

He cursed himself for allowing her to get the weapon. He should never have entered the cabin, he told himself. He had defeated Flame. He had no reason to try to help her. Dying now, letting her kill him after she had lost, would be stupid, unforgivably stupid.

He knew he might well die. He did not know which snark she had gotten. One held a five percent charge, which might not be enough to kill him, but the other still had a thirty percent charge, which would be enough to kill anything.

Once she had the snark, however, Yessenina ignored Turner completely. She put up no resistance when, terror-stricken, he flung her away. Even as she tumbled back across the floor, propelled by both his augmented muscles and his psionic wizardry, she flicked the control, turned the weapon toward her own face, and pushed the button.

Blood splashed across the carpet and the acceleration couch, and her body arched backward, then collapsed and lay still. She had had the thirty percent charge. Turner took one look at what remained of her head and vomited, emptying his stomach onto the beige carpet in a single choking heave.

"Excuse me, sir," the computer said in its smooth contralto, "Query: Confirm death of cyborg unit designated 'Flame'."

Startled, Turner swallowed, got to his feet again, and returned to be absolutely certain that she was dead.

There could be no doubt at all of that.

The worst part, he thought later when remembering the incident, was the sputtering wires and circuit boards that projected from the wetly gleaming bone and tissue.

"She's dead," he said, and closed his eyes.

"Query: Right thumb of cyborg unit designated 'Flame' substantially intact."

Turner did not want to take another look; instead he demanded, "Why?"

"An enemy sabotage device is in the computer core. Access panel has been coded for thumbprint access by cyborg unit designated 'Flame' only."

Turner wiped his mouth, opened his eyes, and looked up at the glossy poster of the ancient video star. "What?"

"Cyborg unit designated 'Flame' placed an enemy sabotage device in the computer core. Unless it is removed or reset, it will activate in eighty-two hours, ten minutes, and forty-four seconds."

Puzzled, still shocked by Flame's death, Turner asked, "Then why haven't you removed it?"

"Access panel has been coded for thumbprint access by cyborg unit designated 'Flame' only."

Turner did not want to think about sabotage devices or access panels, but he forced himself to stop and consider the situation.

"Was that . . . was that causing programming conflicts?"

"Affirmative."

That explained a lot. By placing such a device Flame had been insubordinate, almost treasonous — but taking the appropriate action and blowing her head off would have resulted in the destruction of the ship and computer, as well.

No wonder the computer had been confused! It was forced to accept Flame as its cyborg unit, and to obey her orders to some extent, when it *knew* she had booby-trapped her own ship, thereby aiding the enemy. It would have been in a constant state of internal conflict.

The computer, he knew from his own experiences, relied on the advice of humans to resolve programming conflicts. That was why CCC-IRU 247 had been so willing to do as it was told, so long as doing so did not create new conflicts; the perpetual tension the device created had made the machine highly suggestible as it searched for an external resolution to its dilemma.

Removing the device might make the computer less tractable, but if left alone, the thing, whatever it was, would destroy the ship. To let it be destroyed now seemed terribly wasteful. Besides, the Council wanted the ship intact, and he had not yet decided definitely that they shouldn't get it.

He looked at the access panel, just to the right of the old poster of the video star he didn't recognize.

He was a wizard; he needed no thumbprint. He could open the panel and remove the device.

Or he could leave it right where it was.

The wizards of Praunce wanted this ship; he could give it to them, or he could destroy it.

Or perhaps he could keep it for himself. He turned that idea over slowly in his mind as he stared at the access panel.

TWENTY-FIVE

Daylight poured in through the western windows, and where it passed through the faceted stained-glass "jewels" that had been set into every pane it spangled the fur carpets with colored sparks.

Seated on his cushion, Turner marveled at the simple beauty of the scene. It seemed somehow far more interesting and important than the earnest discussion going on around him. He had made his decisions before coming here, all of them, and he would not change them. He leaned over and slid an arm around his wife's waist.

The action did not go unobserved. "Sam," Ahnao said, visibly annoyed. "Can't you pay attention?"

"Yes," Shopaur agreed. "This is all your doing, after all."

"I know," Turner said, smiling calmly. "But it's done, isn't it?" He refused to give up his comfortable mood. After weeks of discomfort and danger he was safe at home again, his wife beside him. He had seen his children, and they, too, were safe. Zhrellia had cut another molar.

And he was, more than ever, indisputably the most powerful creature on Dest. He allowed himself a certain satisfaction at that thought as he studied the colored light.

"It's not exactly *all* done," Arzadel said. "There is still a working starship, with a demon still alive and active, sitting in the market square in Killalah."

"No," Turner said, "There isn't. It's in the air; I launched it this morning. I had the area evacuated, and I'll pay for the damages."

There was a moment of shocked silence.

"You acted without proper authority," Shopaur said in rebuke.

Turner shrugged. He did not feel that he had needed any authority but his own.

"And what about the dead and injured?" Shopaur demanded, annoyed, like Ahnao, by Turner's casual attitude. "Will you pay for them?"

Turner sighed in resignation, and lifted his gaze from the carpets. "We've been over that," he said. "I can't pay for them. No one can. I didn't kill anyone, I didn't injure anyone, and it's not my fault. I know that Flame came here looking for me, but I didn't send the message she answered, an automatic machine did, one I didn't know existed. And I certainly did my best to stop her from killing or harming anyone. I tried, and no one else could have done as well."

"Please," Arzadel said, "we *have* been through that. Let us not go over the same things all over again. We will all do what we can about the damages, whether they were caused by the ship or by this Flame person or by the storm that we, all the rest of us and not Sam, let get out of hand. That's not important. Recriminations do no good. What has happened has happened, and we can't change it, we can only deal with the results. The important thing is the ship. Our world has a working starship; don't you people see what that means?"

"No, I don't," Parrah replied bluntly. "What does it mean? Why does it mean anything?" Her arm had found its way around her husband's waist.

"It means we can rejoin the mainstream of civilization," Arzadel explained enthusiastically. "We can visit the stars! We could send a party to Old Earth itself, to see what's left there — there may have been survivors, and by now they may have built an entire new society, much as we have."

There was a moment of silence as everyone present considered this. Turner reluctantly decided to bring in a touch of harsh reality — just a touch. His final statement could wait. "I think you're being optimistic," he said.

"Oh?" Arzadel's tone remained friendly, but his gaze was not. "You think so?"

"Yes," Turner said, "I think so." He looked around at the Council, annoyed that they could not see what was so obvious to him. "What makes you think that there *is* any mainstream to civilization anymore?" he demanded. "If an active interstellar civilization is out there somewhere, wouldn't they have contacted us by now? Dest's location is no secret. Furthermore, I doubt that there's anything left on Old Earth that's worth the trip. I doubt there's anything anywhere that's worth the trip. Interstellar travel simply isn't worth the trouble. You seem to have forgotten the distances involved. It took me *three hundred years*, one way, to get here from Mars. True, I made stops along the way, but I doubt that a round trip from Dest to Old Earth and back could possibly be made in less than two hundred years. It wouldn't be two hundred years for the people aboard ship, but it would be for us, here on Dest. Do you really think that our great-great-grandchildren will care what's on Old Earth?"

"They might," Dekert said quietly.

"All right, then," Turner said. "Suppose, for the sake of argument, that we all agree that it's worth sending the ship out there somewhere, to Old Earth or one of the colony planets. Who is going to make the trip? The computer can fly the ship, but who is going to go? That's a one-man military scout, not a colony ship or an exploratory vessel. Only two or three people can go, at most — the algae tanks won't produce enough air and food for more than that, even if you squeezed them aboard — and the flight will take years."

"You're the only experienced pilot we have," Dekert said.

Several people nodded agreement or looked at him expectantly.

"Me?" Turner looked around at his fellow councilors. They were all watching him expectantly.

He had expected this. "No," he said, calmly and definitely, "Absolutely not. I'm forty-four years old. I have a wife and a family, and I like it here on Dest. I spent fourteen years in one of those ships. That's more than enough for anyone. Do any of you have any idea how *boring* spaceflight is? And it takes *years* to reach another star. Boring! Boring beyond comprehension! I'd probably go completely mad, now that my personality is reintegrated. Flame *did* go mad. She went completely mad from the sheer boredom of space travel. That was why she killed herself."

"But — " Wirozhess began.

Turner cut him off. "Forget it. I'm sorry, but I'm not going."

"What if we insist?" Wirozhess asked, a bit more loudly than necessary.

Turner stared at him for a moment, then pulled his arm from around Parrah's waist and stood up.

The entire Council watched him intently.

"I don't think you understand," he said softly. "I don't think you understand at all. You can't insist on anything. You have no power over me. You all seem to have forgotten that I, and I alone, control the ship. None of you except Parrah can even speak its language, and none of you know anything about its capabilities. I am the only person on Dest whose authority it recognizes, because I am the only one who can give orders over a cyborg internal communication circuit, and it won't accept orders any other way right now. I am the one who knew its release code. I can destroy it any time I want. That ship is *mine*. It is not the property of this Council, or of the empire of Praunce, whatever you people may have thought. It is *mine*. Furthermore, that ship — *my* ship — still carries enough firepower to obliterate your entire civilization." He paused, and looked around at uncomprehending faces.

"I," he said, "am the most powerful creature on this planet. I didn't ask for it, but I am. I need never again do anything I do not choose to do. *Nobody* can insist that I do *anything*. I am stronger and faster than any of you. I am a competent wizard, though not the most powerful here. And I can order the destruction of this entire city, and be obeyed instantly. If I die by violence, that ship will retaliate by obliterating the city I die in, and quite possibly the rest of the planet as well. I will do as I damn well please." He looked around at his comrades, their expressions ranging from open horror to amused acceptance.

"Now," he went on, "I am willing to be reasonable about this. I am, in effect, the ruler of this planet now, but I'm willing to be reasonable about it. Let me explain just what your choices are." He paused to take a breath.

"Now just a minute — " Shopaur began, rising from his seat.

"Sit down!" Turner ordered.

Startled, Shopaur sat down. Others, however, rose in his stead. "Who do you think you are?" Wirozhess demanded.

Turner, listening with his ears and psychic senses and communications circuit, smiled. "I'll show you who I am. I have a little demonstration planned, if you would all look out this window."

Puzzled, the councilors turned to the window.

Light flared, and a yellow flash across the skies headed directly toward them.

The tower suddenly shook under the impact of an ear-splitting sonic boom; the roar of the starship's passage deafened them all for a moment, and the red glare of its blazing heatshields lit the room brightly for an instant, washing them all in its lurid glow.

Even when the ship had passed, fading turbulence whistled around the corners of the building and a lingering warmth seeped through the walls and windows into the room. Somewhere below them a pane of glass broke with a distant rattle.

"I," Turner said, "am the master of that ship. You had the presumption to think that you could take it from me; you can't. You don't know anything about the technology involved. That pass was just the ship itself, in flight; you have no idea of what the weapons it carries can do. I can't demonstrate them; they're too powerful. None of you know *anything* about it."

Parrah smiled, obviously proud of her man.

"We could learn," Arzadel said, calmly. "Don't you think you're being somewhat arrogant about this? Why do *you* want the ship? You said yourself that you aren't interested in visiting other stars; what else is it good for? Setting yourself up as a dictator? Do you really want to do that?"

"No," Turner admitted. "I don't, not really. However, right now, whether I like it or not, and whether you like it or not, I have the power to *be* a dictator here. Which brings me back to that choice I was about to offer you."

He paused, looking around.

"Go on," Arzadel said. "We won't interrupt this time."

Turner nodded. "All right, then. Your first choice is to accept me as the ruler of Dest. If you do that, I intend to be a benevolent despot, not merely a tyrant. That doesn't mean, though, that I'll let things go on unguided. Firstly, I'll see that Dest is united, by force if necessary. The ship's nukes, the Bad Times city-destroying bombs, shouldn't be needed; I have other weapons, kept hidden these past eleven years, and another arsenal aboard the ship as well — enough in all to equip an impressive little army. I don't think we'll have any trouble uniting the planet. Hligosh, just flying the ship over most towns should be enough to coax a surrender!"

A murmur of agreement greeted this.

"Furthermore," Turner continued, "under my rule social justice will be established as far as possible; this elitist system of wizards and commoners will be cut back. It's time the people of Dest returned to the democratic principles of their ancestors. Anyone who is interested will be actively invited to apprentice to a wizard. Government officials other than myself will be elected — though I suppose at first we'll have to be selective about who can vote, to allow for the social adjustments. People aren't used to elections yet."

This time the murmuring was much less positive. Turner had expected that. "The commoners can't — " Shopaur began.

"Shut up!" Turner snapped.

Shopaur subsided uneasily.

Turner continued, "Education will be encouraged. Schools will be established. I'll do everything I can to stamp out ignorance. Anyone who wants to learn will be allowed to learn. And if anyone wants to learn science, or technology, right up to and including the technology to build starships, that's fine; I'll do my best to see that that education is available. If the people of Dest want the technology that built my ship, they can have it — but they'll have to build it up for themselves. The computer and I will provide whatever information is necessary, but the people will need to build their own industrial base."

That drew no murmur, only puzzlement.

"There's an old saying from Old Earth," Turner explained. "Give a man a fish, and he eats for a day; teach him to fish, and he eats every day. If I give you that ship, if you just use the one starship, that's all you'll ever have, just one starship, and no way to maintain it. You can't repair anything if it goes wrong — and the computer is already damaged. If you choose to accept me as dictator, and if you build up the necessary industries to build starships, then you can have, and maintain, all the ships you want. It will take years, maybe decades, maybe even centuries, but the technology will be *yours*, it won't be stolen from a dead world. I don't think Dest is ready for starships, but if you learn how to build your own, you will be."

His audience grew restless. He saw Wirozhess and Shopaur exchanging ominous glances.

"I expect opposition," Turner said. "I'm ready for it. If I set up as ruler and die by violence, the ship will nuke whatever city I died in. If I die from what appear to be natural causes, the ship will destroy itself." He had the timed termite for that.

The other wizards were watching him closely, but he could not read their expressions anymore.

"I would point out," he said, "that I have as much right to rule as anyone. The people of Praunce have never had any say in their government; they won't care whether they serve one master, or the few dozen they have now."

Shopaur grimaced.

"You do, of course, have a second choice," Turner said. "You can reject me, tell me that you won't have me as dictator. I don't want to bother fighting you. I'll accept your decision; I won't argue about it. If you refuse to accept my terms, I'll accept that — and I'll destroy the ship right now. You can go on as you always have, but without me and without the ship. Which would you prefer?"

Wirozhess snorted.

"Actually," Turner said, "I shouldn't even be asking you people. I should be polling the commoners. I don't have the means to do that, though, and besides, they've all been trained since childhood to leave matters of state to the councils and advisers. We wizards are the rulers of Praunce, of all Dest, really. We have no right to be, but we are. So I'm asking you to make the decision on behalf of the people of this planet, and I'll abide by that decision."

There was a moment of silence, then a babble of voices. Turner held up his hands.

"You talk it over," he said. "You decide, and then send someone to fetch me." He marched from the room.

Parrah leapt up and followed him.

"They won't do it," she said as she stepped out the window behind him.

"I know," he answered. "But it will take them some time to decide that. Let's go home."

Two hours later, as he sprawled comfortably on cushions in his apartments while Parrah fetched another bottle of wine, he felt the touch of a telepathic message.

"Stand ready," he told the computer. The ship was waiting in orbit overhead; it had used the two hours to resume its preferred synchronous position.

"Acknowledged," the computer replied.

"*Yes?*" he asked.

The mental voice he heard was Shopaur's, and he knew immediately what the answer would be.

"We can never accept an arbitrary dictator," Shopaur began. "But we are eager to discuss possibilities for compromise..."

Turner wondered briefly why an arbitrary dictator was so much worse than an arbitrary council or an arbitrary nobility.

It didn't really matter. The decisions were all made. He cut Shopaur off. "*No,*" he replied.

"Sam!" Parrah said from the doorway, the bottle in her hand. She had heard.

"Parrah, I'm sure," he said before she could say anything more. "I almost did this even before they answered." He switched languages and transmitted, "As Old Earth's representative on this planet, I hereby order the immediate destruction of all war-surplus spacecraft."

"Acknowledged," the computer replied.

That was the last transmission.

Even from orbit, the silent flash of the explosion was far brighter than Dest's primary. It blazed up instantly, whiting out the heavens overhead with its glare, turning the windows of the towers to sheets of white fire, washing all color out of the world and leaving only stark white light and black shadow.

The light beat upon them for an interminable half second and then died slowly away, white to yellow to gold to orange to red, down from a bright crimson to a dull rust, and then to nothingness, leaving only blue sky above. The blinding whiteness faded into the darkness of mere daylight, letting all the colors of the world seep back into shocked, blinking eyes.

Flame's ship was gone.

The brilliance of the flash had caught Turner by surprise; he hoped that no one had been blinded. He had not thought of the possibility before. He had not been sure just how big the explosion would be, whether the computer would use the fusion drive or a warhead, or something less devastating.

He still did not know, and never would, just what the computer had done. He could only hope that no one had been looking up at the time, and that the explosion had been clean.

At least it had been powerful enough that there would be no debris big enough to reach ground, and had occurred well above the atmosphere, so that there would be no sound, no shockwave.

There was just the flash, and then nothing. No united planet, no improved education, no forced democracy, no guided industry. Dest would go on as if he had never come.

Or, just possibly, he mused, the knowledge of the missed opportunity might drive people on a little bit faster.

"They aren't going to like this at all," Parrah said as she settled onto the cushions by his side, "They wanted that ship."

"I know," Turner replied. "We'll have to leave Praunce. We won't be welcome here anymore. I'm sorry about that."

"It's all right," she said. "It's better than trying to run the world. You're only human, Sam." She leaned over and kissed him.

He kissed her back. "I know," he whispered. "But it's too bad Dest lost its chance at all that knowledge."

Parrah waved that away. "We don't need it," she said. "When we do, we'll find it for ourselves, we won't have to pick Old Earth's corpse." She kissed him again, then rose. "I'll go tell the children we're leaving."

THE END

ABOUT THE AUTHOR

Lawrence Watt-Evans was born and raised in eastern Massachusetts, the fourth of six children. Both parents were long-time science-fiction readers, so from an early age he read and enjoyed a variety of speculative fiction. He also tried writing it, starting at age seven, but with very little success.

After finishing twelve years of public schooling in Bedford, Massachusetts, he tried to maintain family tradition by attending Princeton University, as had his father and grandfather. He was less successful than his ancestors, and after two attempts left college without a degree.

During the break in his academic career, he lived in Pittsburgh, a city he considers one of the most underrated in the country. At this time he began seriously trying to write for money, as that seemed easier than finding a real job. He sold one page of fiction in a year and a half.

In 1977, after leaving Princeton for the second and final time, he married his long-time girl friend and settled in Lexington, Kentucky, where his wife had a job that would support them both while he again tried to write. He was more successful this time, producing a fantasy novel that sold readily, beginning his full-time career as a writer.